Regal Academy™

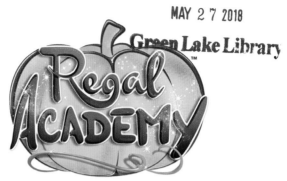

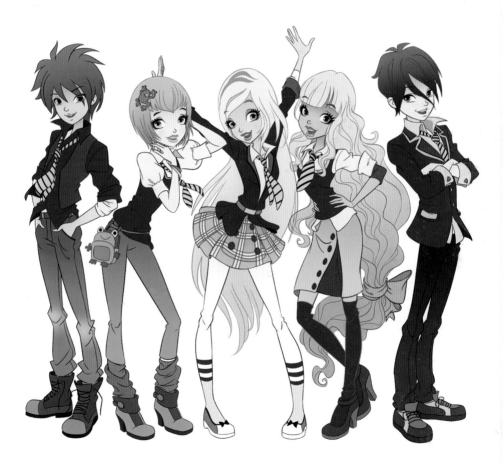

PAPERCUTZ™

Magical Surprise Download Here!

Use either the QR code or this link:

http://www.regalacademy.com/en/download/pap774

to download your exclusive REGAL ACADEMY content. Enjoy!

#1 "A School for Fairy Tales"

Series created and directed by Iginio Straffi. www.regalacademy.com

"A School for Fairy Tales"
Script: Rainbow Srl/Luana Vergari
Comics: Rainbow Srl/Red Whale

"A Perfect Smile"
Script: Rainbow Srl/Luana Vergari
Comics: Rainbow Srl/Red Whale

"The Seven Baby Goats Realm"
Script: Rainbow Srl/Luana Vergari
Comics: Rainbow Srl/Red Whale

"One Thousand and One Stories"
Script: Rainbow Srl/Luana Vergari
Comics: Rainbow Srl/Red Whale

Papercutz books may be purchased for business or promotional use.
For information on bulk purchases please contact Macmillan Corporate and Premium Sales Department at (800) 221-7945 x5442

Lettering and Production – Manosaur Martin
Editorial Intern – Spenser Nellis
Editor – Jeff Whitman
Jim Salicrup
Editor-in-Chief

PB ISBN: 978-1-62991-883-9
HC ISBN: 978-1-62991-884-6

Printed in China
January 2018

Distributed by Macmillan
First Papercutz Printing

#1 "A School for Fairy Tales"

Table of Contents

PAPERCUTZ

New York

Get to know Regal Academy!

ROSE CINDERELLA

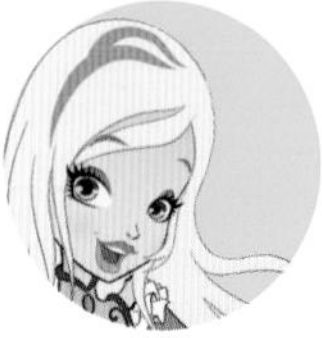

Rose is a modern teenager who never lost her love of fairy tales. Having grown up on Earth, she constantly experiences a "culture shock" between her modern, shoe-filled life on Earth and the magical Fairy Tale Land. She is a very positive girl who thinks everything is great all the time. She is happy even if she gets the worst grades in her class! She is never sad or disappointed but always full of sunshine, acting as a ray of hope for the team.

TRAVIS BEAST

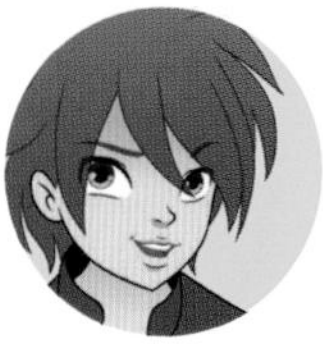

Travis is a frail, artsy sort of boy, but when he gets angry he becomes a real Beast! When it comes to getting physical though, he would much rather focus on his artistic skills. He is a true artist thanks to the talent inherited from Beauty, his grandmother, but he is totally underrated. Since he comes from Earth, Travis manages to recreate very beautiful paintings and sculptures inspired by earthly masterpieces. He aims to control his beastly strength and become a true artist.

ASTORIA RAPUNZEL

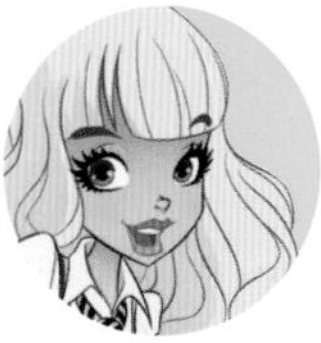

Regal Academy's resident bookworm and perfect, poised, princess... just as long as everything goes her way. Her perfectionist streak has her snapping from being absorbed in a book to up in arms, to back to studying quietly in an instant! She aims to be the best student, always the first to reply to the teachers' questions, always asking for more hours at school, more homework, or for more complicated exams.

JOY LEFROG

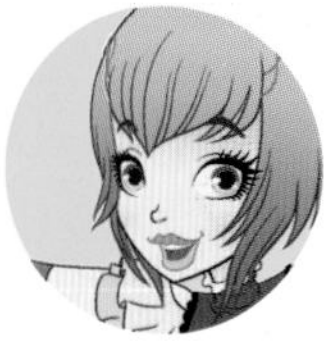

Joy loves creepy-crawlies and sometimes forgets that not everyone else does! She loves to cheer on her friends, but she's as likely to encourage their BAD ideas as well as their good ones! Because of her curse, she accidentally turns into a frog – and can't turn back unless someone is available to kiss her. Most of the times, Hawk or Travis have to save her... even if they'd rather do anything else than kiss a frog.

HAWK SNOWWHITE

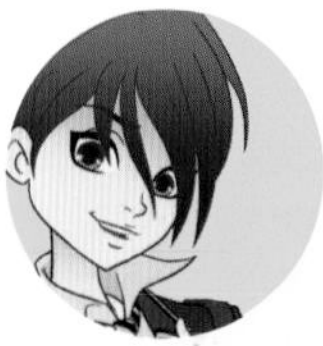

Hawk thinks he's the perfect fairy tale hero, but to his level-headed friends and the teachers, his habit of leaping head-first into trouble makes him a regal pain, because he puts himself and his team in danger! His love of apples and the ladies of Regal Academy is second only to his love of proving himself. He wants to be the best fairy tale in all of history but he's got a long way to go if he's ever going to make it.

PROFESSOR SNOWWHITE

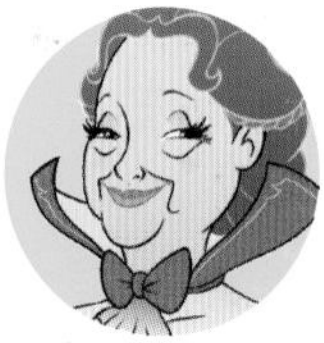

Professor SnowWhite is a stickler for the school rules and often ends up butting heads with our heroes on their adventures. This puts her at odds with her rebellious grandson Hawk, wanting him to become the most proper prince he can be. Despite her strictness, her mind is still "pure as snow" so she is very trusting. Our heroes (and the villains as well) can often get by her with a bit of cleverness.

HEADMISTRESS CINDERELLA

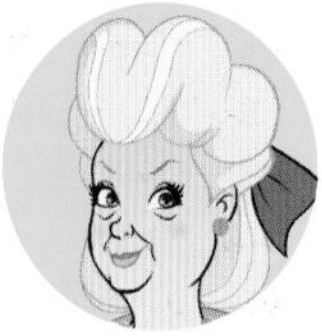

Headmistress Cinderella was able to hold her own against her mean stepmother and stepsisters when she was a teenager, so she sure isn't afraid to speak her mind now that she's a grandmother. She often sticks up for the heroes against the strict Professor Snow White. She's a kindly mentor who has watched over Rose her entire life.

COACH BEAST

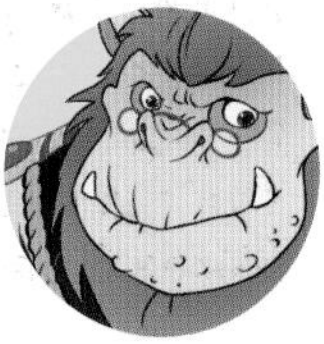

The Beast is a brash teacher, always yelling at the students to run a thousand laps or do a thousand pushups. When the Headmistress has a problem with someone breaking the rules, he scoops them up and carries them off to detention. He's always pushing his grandson Travis to give up art and become a real warrior with his beastly strength. Underneath it all, he has a heart of gold that occasionally pops up and compels him to help our heroes out of a jam.

MAGISTER RAPUNZEL

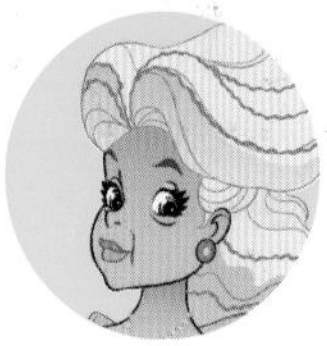

Magister Rapunzel has spent way too much time locked in her tower and has a carefree attitude on life. She excitedly wants to chat or show off her books to anyone who will listen, but often accidentally forgets herself and starts talking to statues or paintings instead of real people. She tries to get her perfectionist granddaughter, Astoria, to relax and let loose at times.

DOCTOR LEFROG

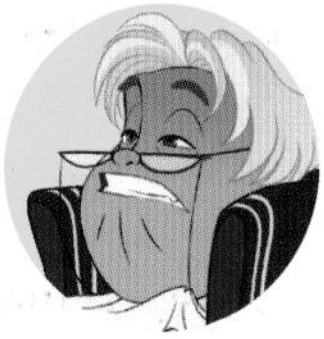

Doctor LeFrog is an old-fashioned professor at Regal Academy. He tends to be absent-minded at times, even if his classroom was exploding he would keep on teaching. He is also very blind without his glasses. He always embarrasses his number-one granddaughter, Joy, by introducing frogs to her as possible dates but wants only the best for her.

VICKY BROOMSTICK

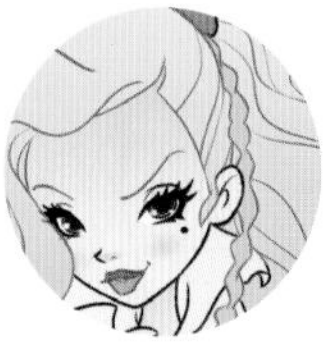

Vicky is Regal Academy's resident Mean Girl, leading her pack of villainous grandkids to accomplish her goals by any means necessary! Vicky is the intelligent and powerful granddaughter of the Broomstick Witch, but every time she tries to carry out her evil plans something goes wrong and she's thwarted by Rose and her friends. Rose and her friends are all that's preventing Vicky from opening up the Gate and releasing the old Fairytale Villains on Earth!

RUBY STEPSISTER

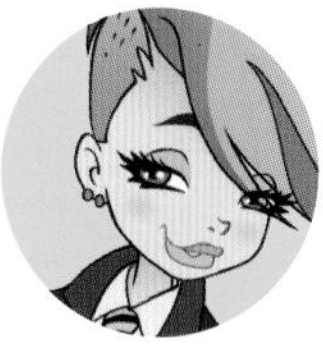

Ruby is one of Vicky's loyal henchmen in the Mean Team and not the sharpest tool in the shed. Utterly in love with Hawk SnowWhite, she helps Vicky in all of her evil plans just so she can get a chance to see her beloved. She's more than happy to do whatever dirty work Vicky couldn't be bothered with if it means being near Hawk.

CYRUS BROOMSTICK

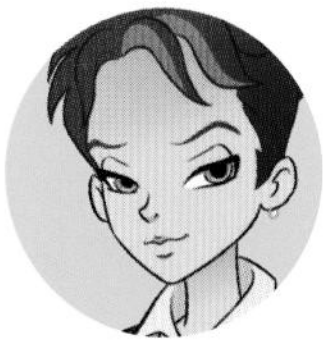

Cyrus is the lazy and cowardly grandson of the Broomstick Witch, as well as Vicky's cousin and reluctant member of the Mean Team. He is so lazy that he must be bribed by Vicky to help with her evil plans. He'd much rather be sleeping than plotting world domination.

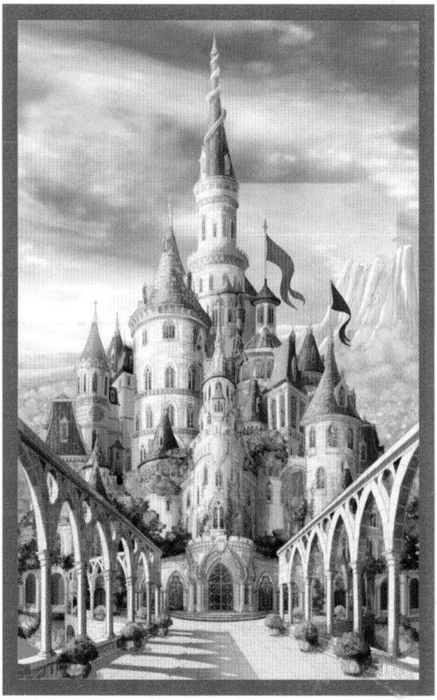

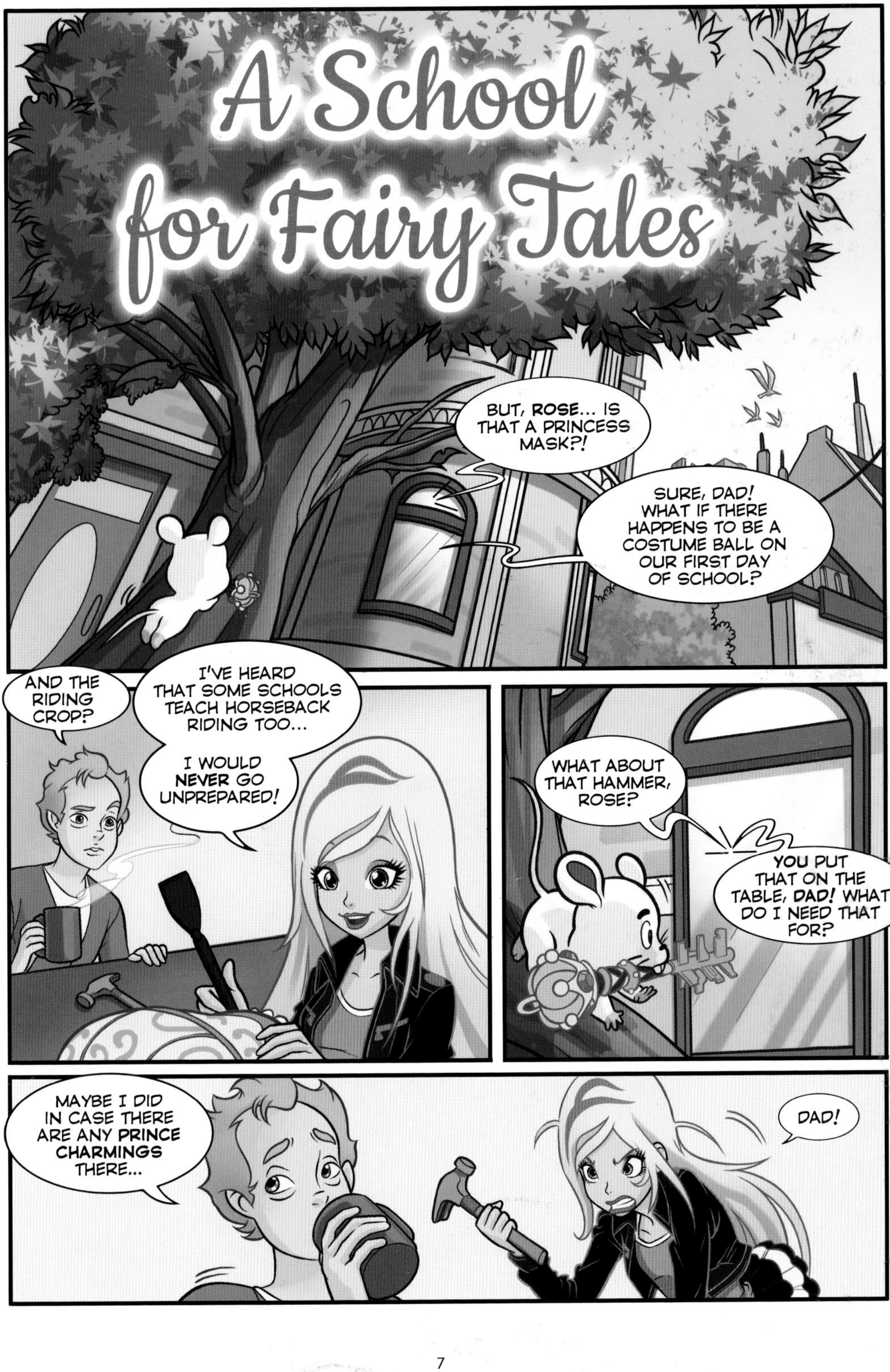
A School for Fairy Tales
BUT, ROSE... IS THAT A PRINCESS MASK?!
SURE, DAD! WHAT IF THERE HAPPENS TO BE A COSTUME BALL ON OUR FIRST DAY OF SCHOOL?
AND THE RIDING CROP?
I'VE HEARD THAT SOME SCHOOLS TEACH HORSEBACK RIDING TOO...
I WOULD NEVER GO UNPREPARED!
WHAT ABOUT THAT HAMMER, ROSE?
YOU PUT THAT ON THE TABLE, DAD! WHAT DO I NEED THAT FOR?
MAYBE I DID IN CASE THERE ARE ANY PRINCE CHARMINGS THERE...
DAD!

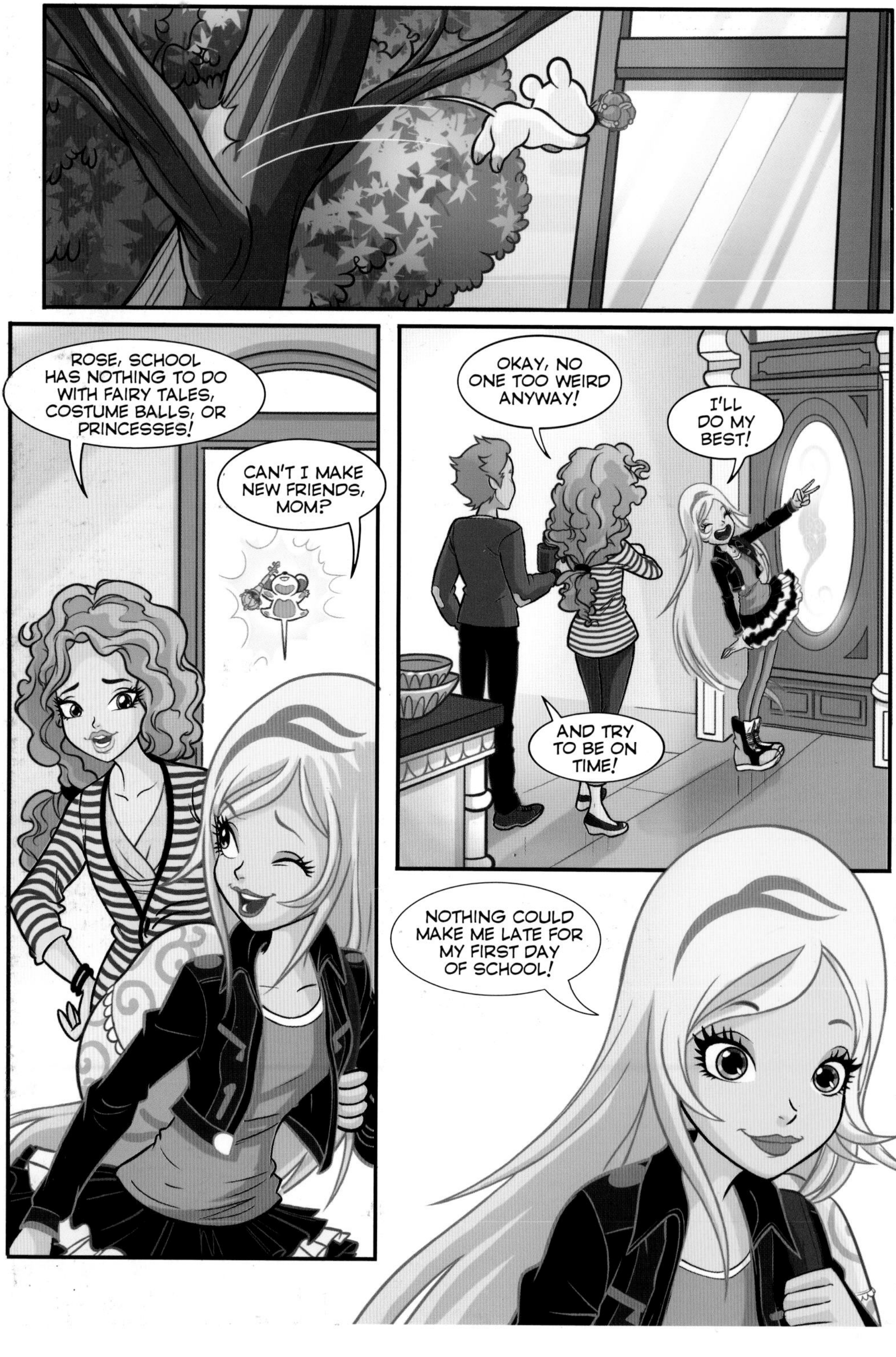
ROSE, SCHOOL HAS NOTHING TO DO WITH FAIRY TALES, COSTUME BALLS, OR PRINCESSES!
CAN'T I MAKE NEW FRIENDS, MOM?
OKAY, NO ONE TOO WEIRD ANYWAY!
I'LL DO MY BEST!
AND TRY TO BE ON TIME!
NOTHING COULD MAKE ME LATE FOR MY FIRST DAY OF SCHOOL!

ONE MINUTE AND 42 SECONDS LATER...

EXCEPT... SHOE SALES!

I'LL JUST HAVE A QUICK LOOK!

THERE'S NOTHING BETTER THAN A PAIR OF NEW SHOES TO MAKE A GOOD FIRST IMPRESSION!

HOW MAY I HELP YOU, MISS?

I'D LIKE TO TRY THOSE RED BOOTS ON, THEN...

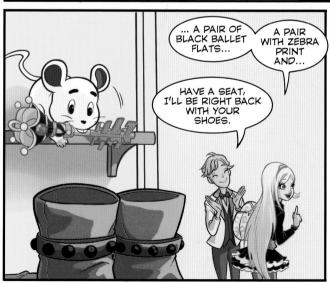

... A PAIR OF BLACK BALLET FLATS...

A PAIR WITH ZEBRA PRINT AND...

HAVE A SEAT, I'LL BE RIGHT BACK WITH YOUR SHOES.

AND SHINY SANDALS, BUT NOT IN BLUE, I ALREADY HAVE THEM... I'D SAY... IN LILAC!

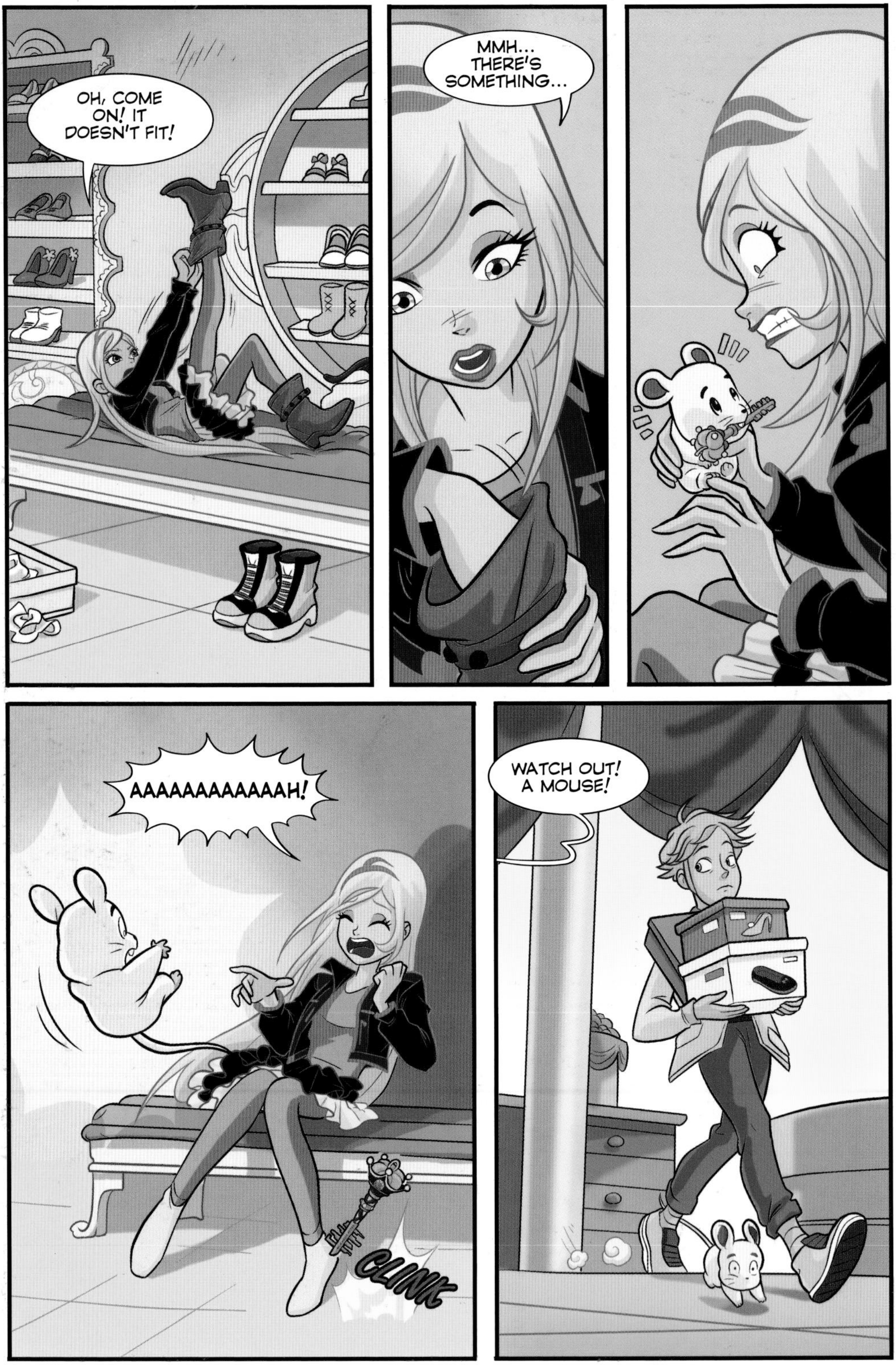
OH, COME ON! IT DOESN'T FIT!
MMH... THERE'S SOMETHING...
AAAAAAAAAAAAH!
CLINK
WATCH OUT! A MOUSE!

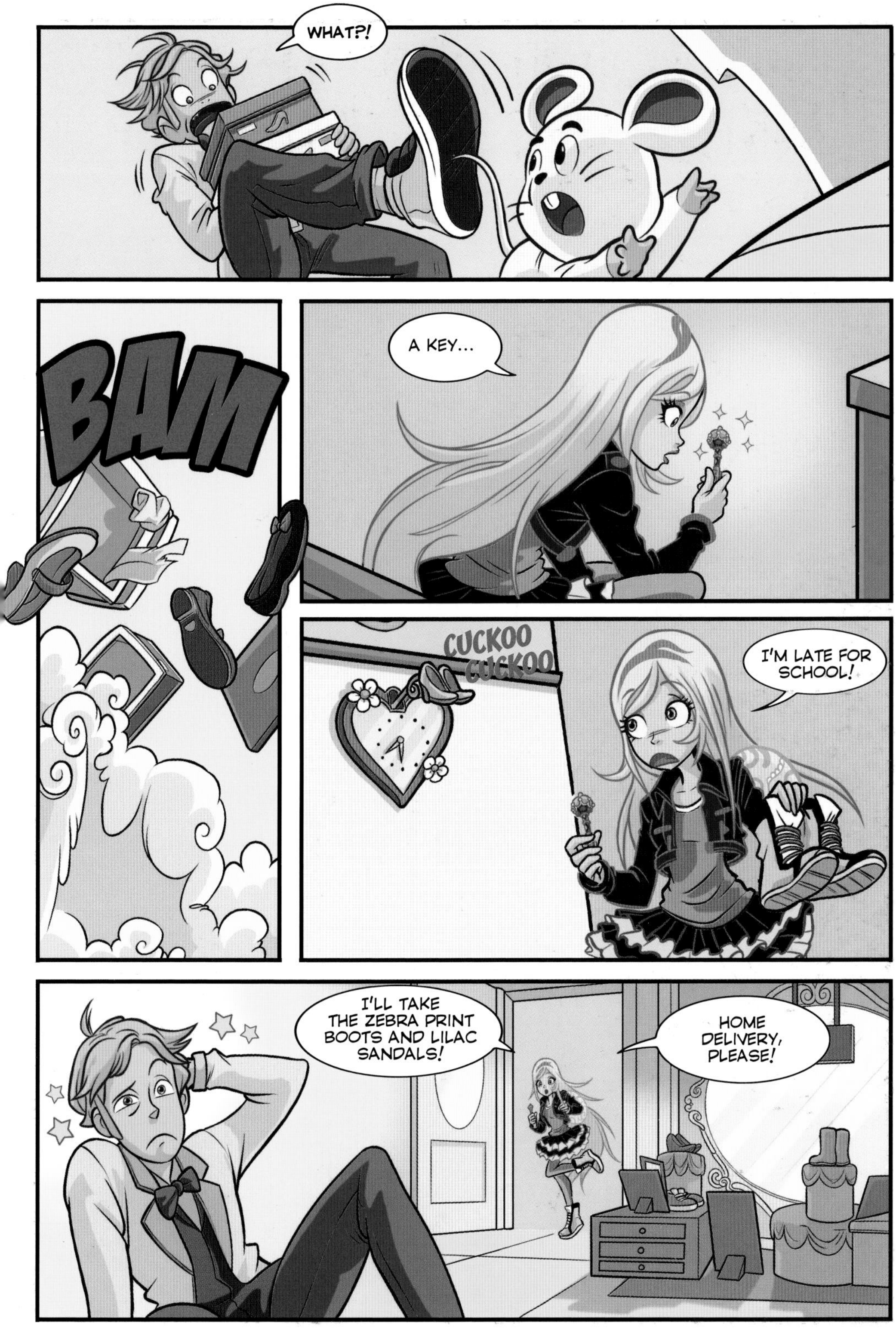
WHAT?!
BAM
A KEY...
CUCKOO
CUCKOO
I'M LATE FOR SCHOOL!
I'LL TAKE THE ZEBRA PRINT BOOTS AND LILAC SANDALS!
HOME DELIVERY, PLEASE!

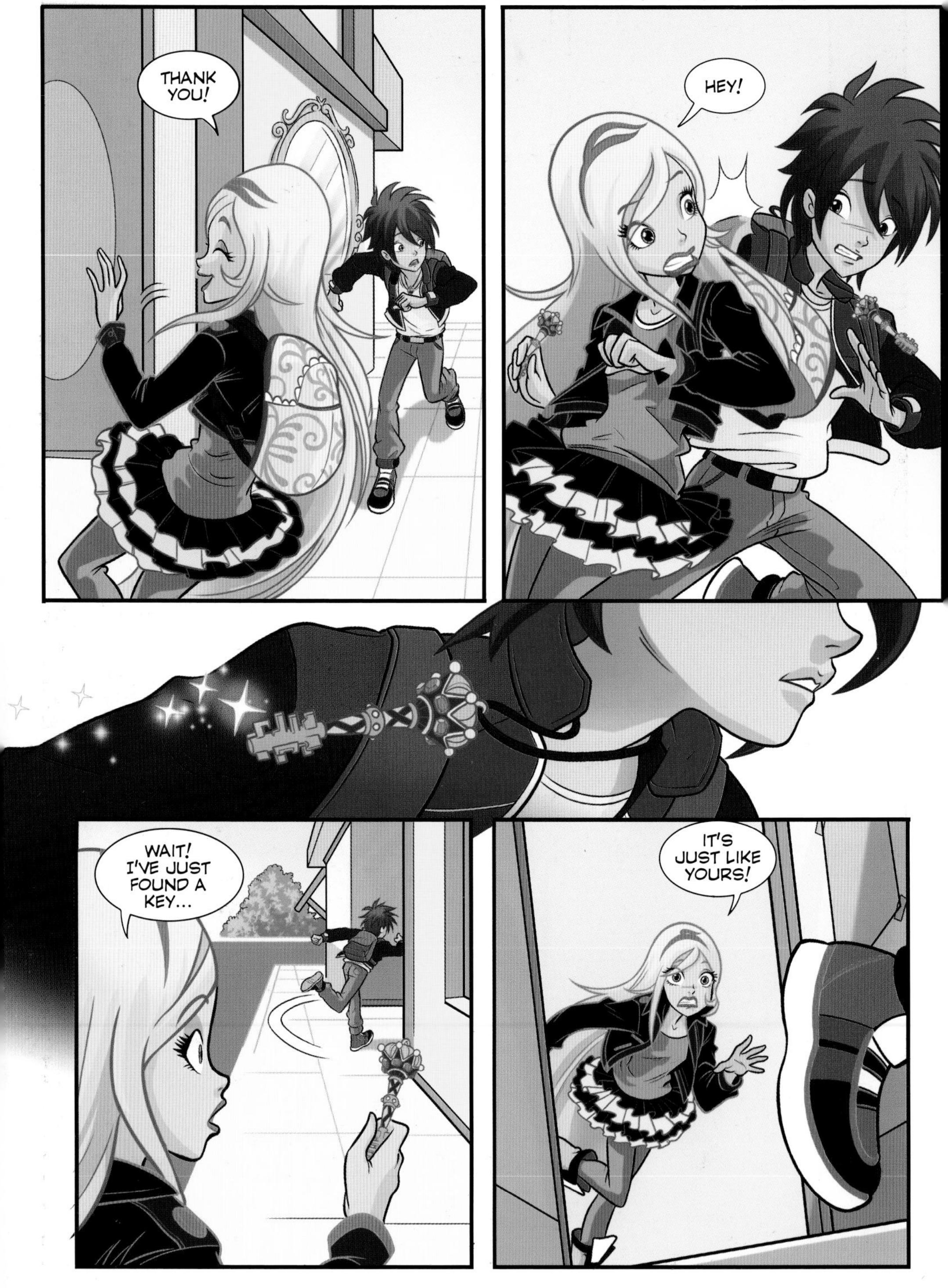
THANK YOU!
HEY!
WAIT! I'VE JUST FOUND A KEY...
IT'S JUST LIKE YOURS!

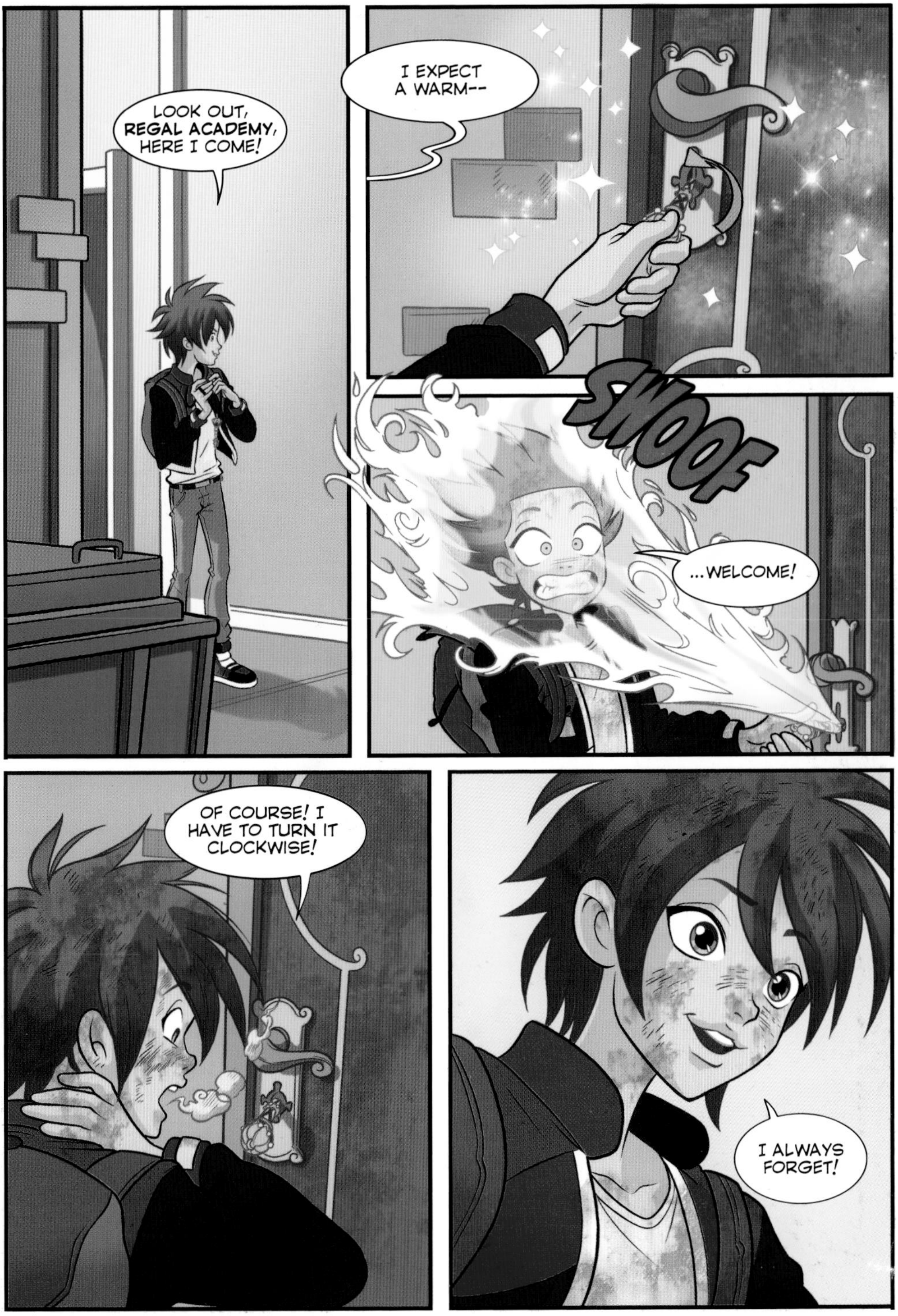
LOOK OUT, REGAL ACADEMY, HERE I COME!
I EXPECT A WARM--
SWOOF
...WELCOME!
OF COURSE! I HAVE TO TURN IT CLOCKWISE!
I ALWAYS FORGET!

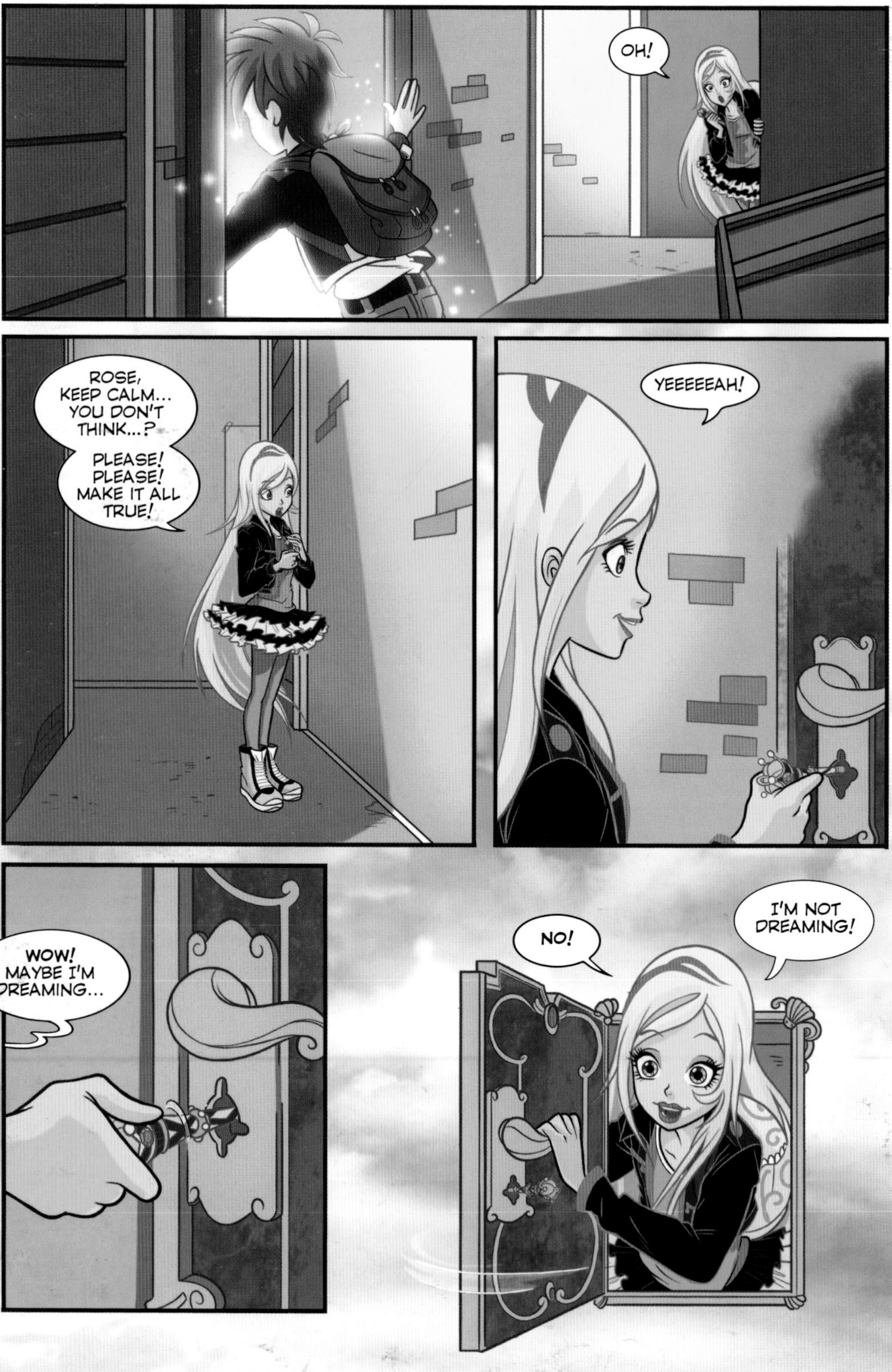
OH!
ROSE, KEEP CALM... YOU DON'T THINK...?
PLEASE! PLEASE! MAKE IT ALL TRUE!
YEEEEEAH!
WOW! MAYBE I'M DREAMING...
NO!
I'M NOT DREAMING!

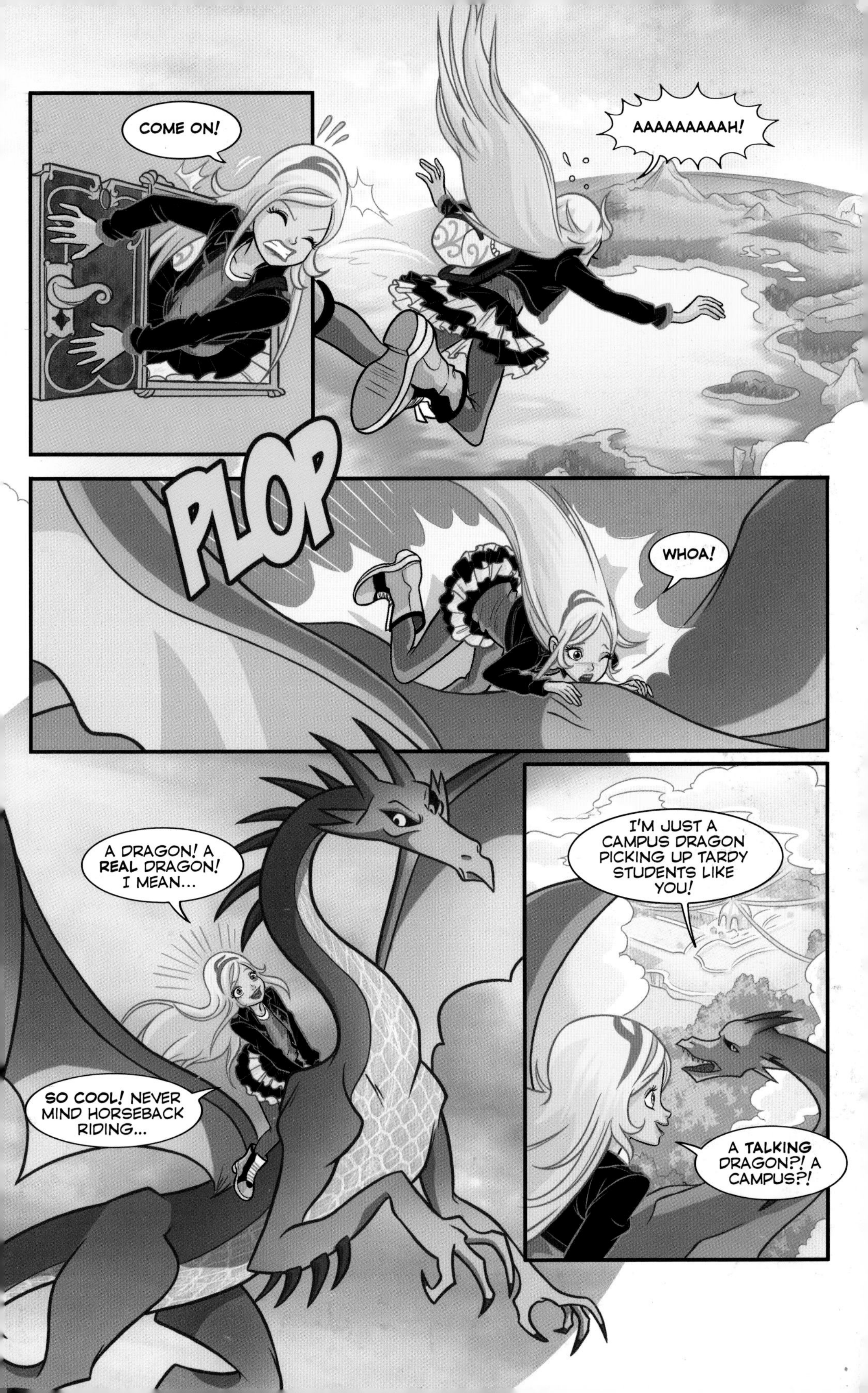
COME ON!
AAAAAAAAAH!
PLOP
WHOA!
A DRAGON! A REAL DRAGON! I MEAN...
SO COOL! NEVER MIND HORSEBACK RIDING...
I'M JUST A CAMPUS DRAGON PICKING UP TARDY STUDENTS LIKE YOU!
A TALKING DRAGON?! A CAMPUS?!

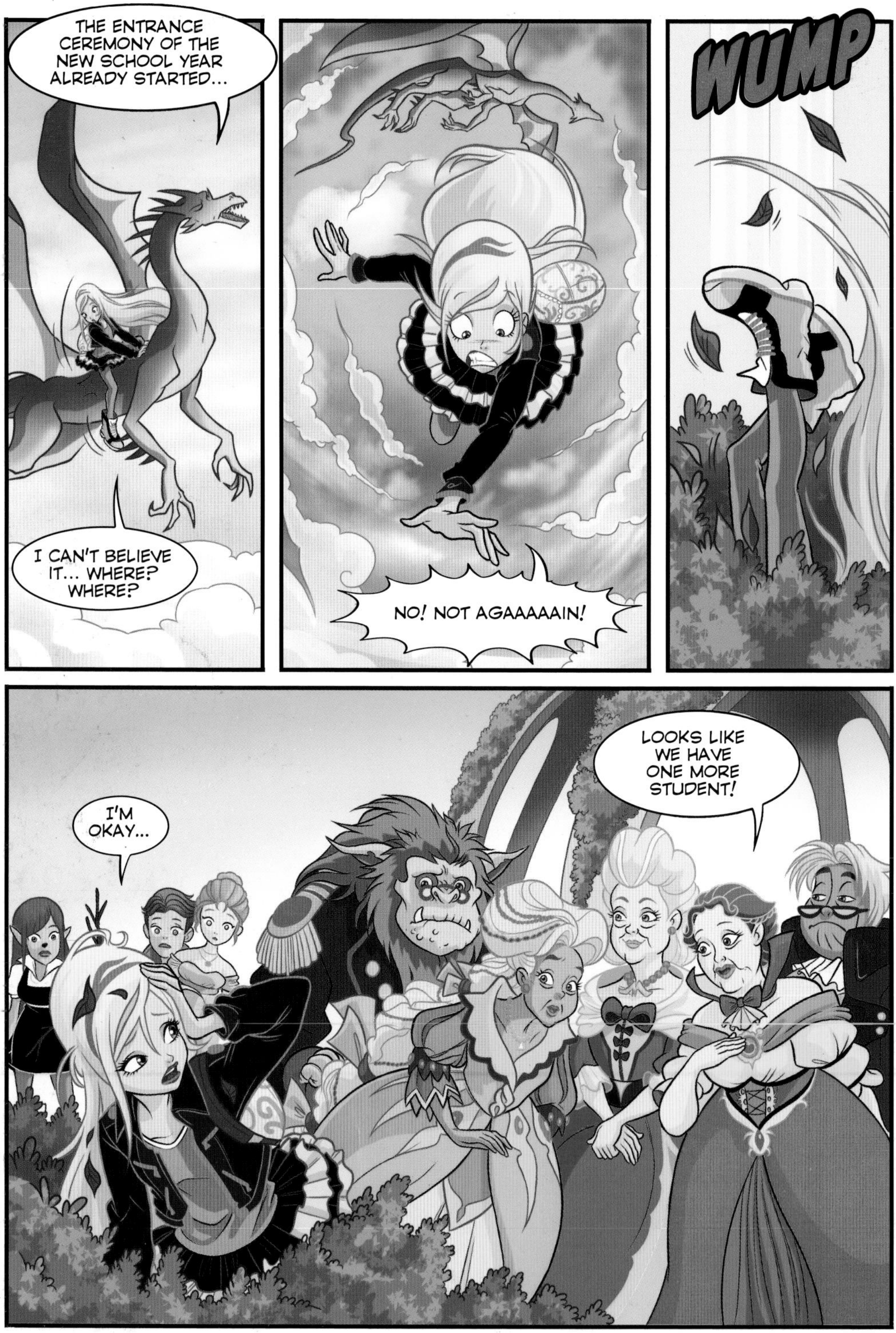
THE ENTRANCE CEREMONY OF THE NEW SCHOOL YEAR ALREADY STARTED...
I CAN'T BELIEVE IT... WHERE? WHERE?
NO! NOT AGAAAAAIN!
WUMP
I'M OKAY...
LOOKS LIKE WE HAVE ONE MORE STUDENT!

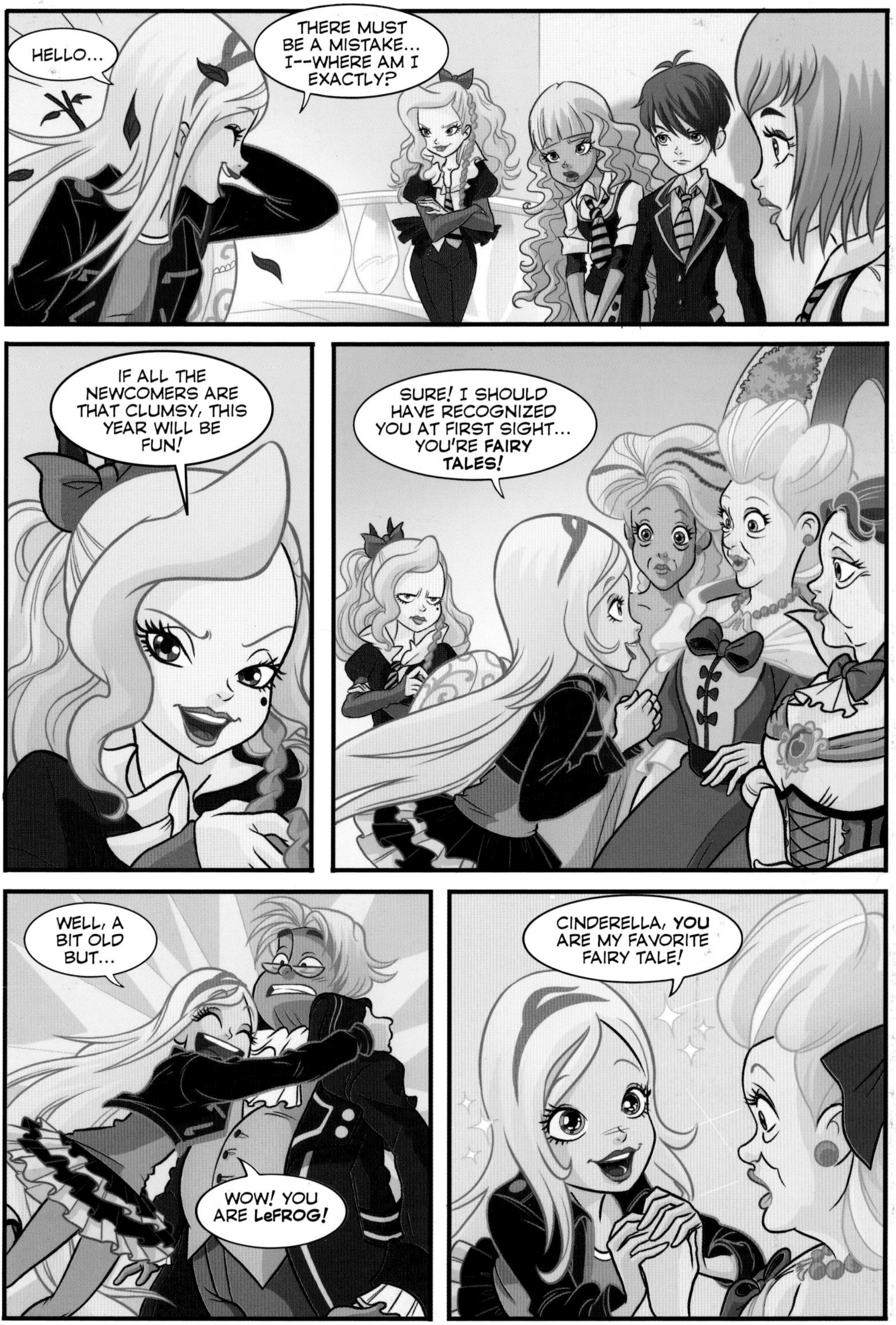
HELLO...
THERE MUST BE A MISTAKE... I--WHERE AM I EXACTLY?
IF ALL THE NEWCOMERS ARE THAT CLUMSY, THIS YEAR WILL BE FUN!
SURE! I SHOULD HAVE RECOGNIZED YOU AT FIRST SIGHT... YOU'RE FAIRY TALES!
WELL, A BIT OLD BUT...
WOW! YOU ARE LeFROG!
CINDERELLA, YOU ARE MY FAVORITE FAIRY TALE!

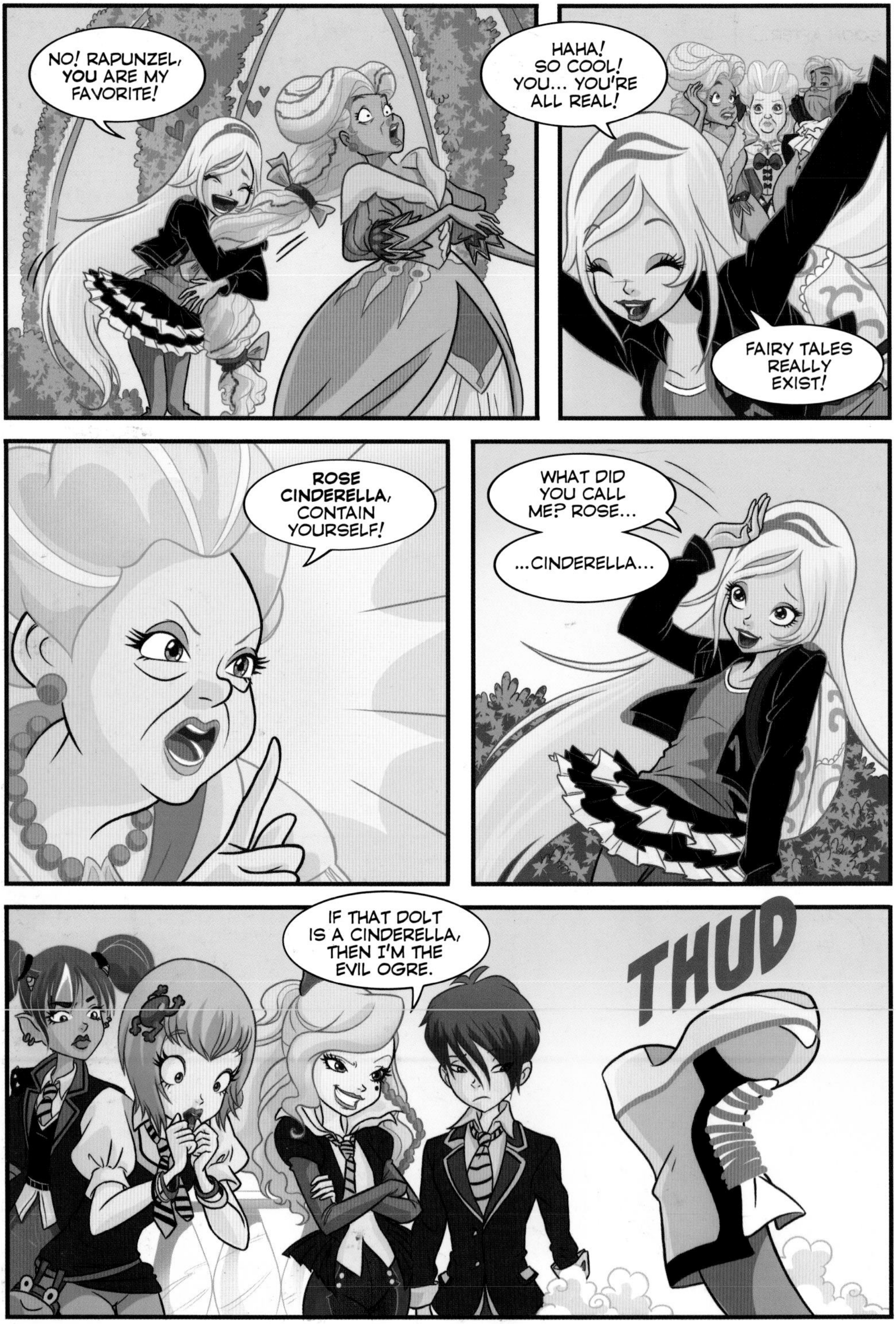
NO! RAPUNZEL, YOU ARE MY FAVORITE!
HAHA! SO COOL! YOU... YOU'RE ALL REAL!
FAIRY TALES REALLY EXIST!
ROSE CINDERELLA, CONTAIN YOURSELF!
WHAT DID YOU CALL ME? ROSE...
...CINDERELLA...
IF THAT DOLT IS A CINDERELLA, THEN I'M THE EVIL OGRE.
THUD

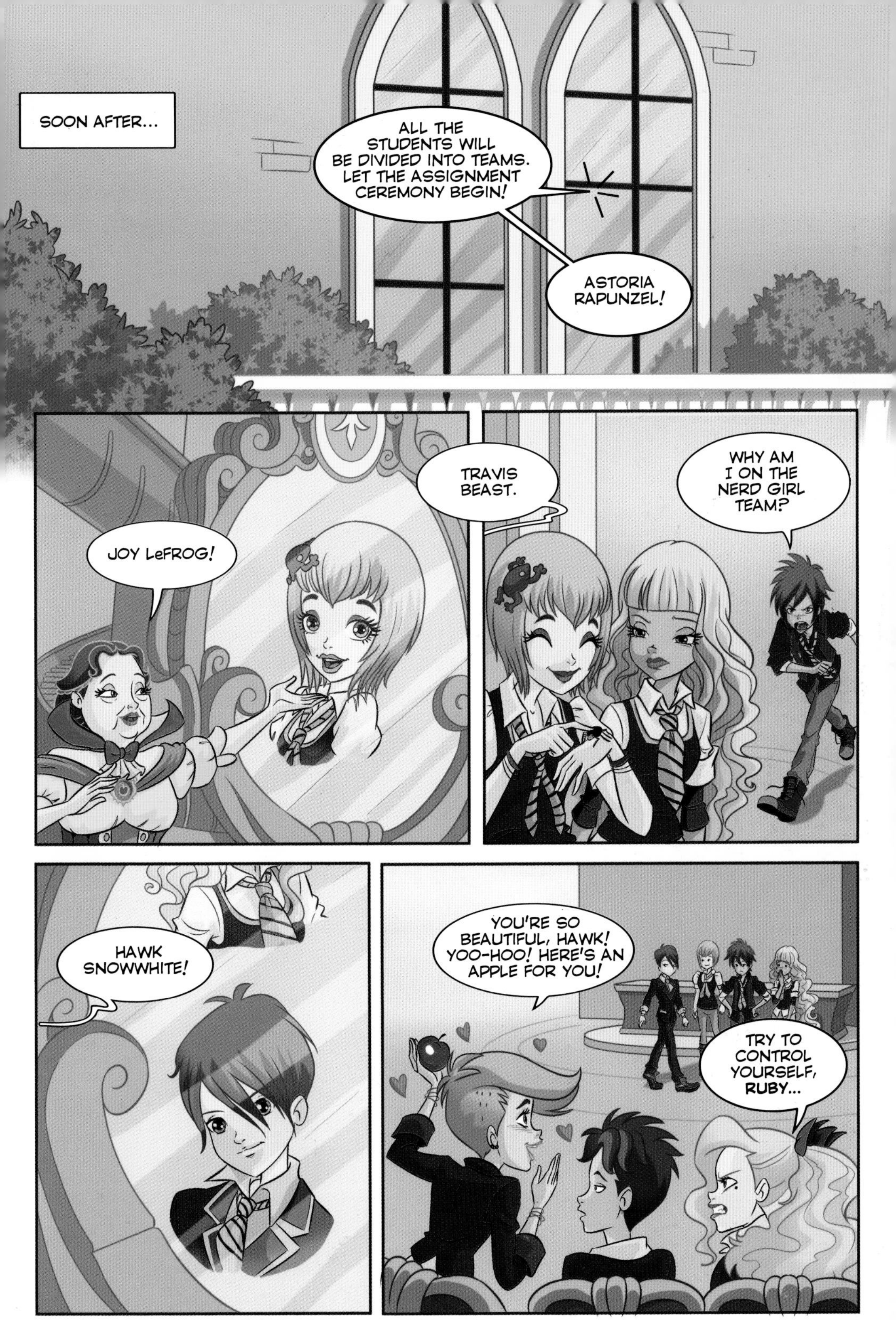
SOON AFTER...
ALL THE STUDENTS WILL BE DIVIDED INTO TEAMS. LET THE ASSIGNMENT CEREMONY BEGIN!
ASTORIA RAPUNZEL!
JOY LeFROG!
TRAVIS BEAST.
WHY AM I ON THE NERD GIRL TEAM?
HAWK SNOWWHITE!
YOU'RE SO BEAUTIFUL, HAWK! YOO-HOO! HERE'S AN APPLE FOR YOU!
TRY TO CONTROL YOURSELF, RUBY...

WATCH OUT!

AN APPLE IN DANGER!

CRUNCH

IT WOULD BE IMPOSSIBLE TO BE ON A WORSE TEAM...

ROSE CINDERELLA.

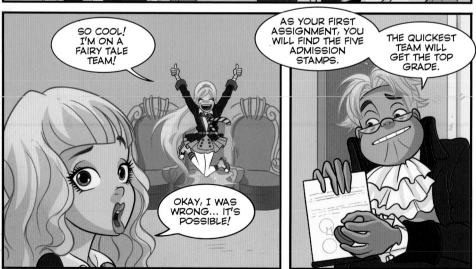

SO COOL! I'M ON A FAIRY TALE TEAM!

AS YOUR FIRST ASSIGNMENT, YOU WILL FIND THE FIVE ADMISSION STAMPS.

THE QUICKEST TEAM WILL GET THE TOP GRADE.

OKAY, I WAS WRONG... IT'S POSSIBLE!

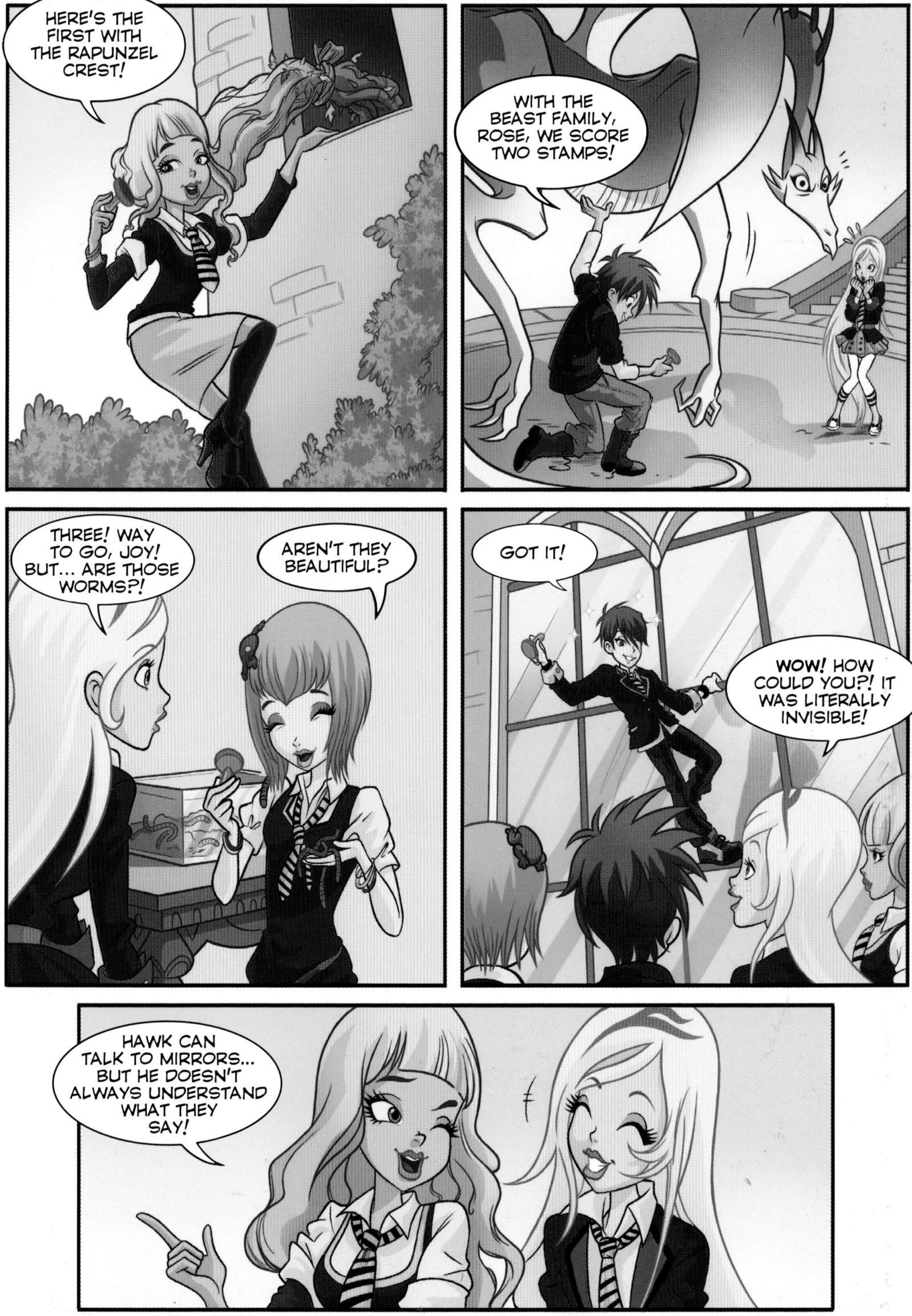
HERE'S THE FIRST WITH THE RAPUNZEL CREST!
WITH THE BEAST FAMILY, ROSE, WE SCORE TWO STAMPS!
THREE! WAY TO GO, JOY! BUT... ARE THOSE WORMS?!
AREN'T THEY BEAUTIFUL?
GOT IT!
WOW! HOW COULD YOU?! IT WAS LITERALLY INVISIBLE!
HAWK CAN TALK TO MIRRORS... BUT HE DOESN'T ALWAYS UNDERSTAND WHAT THEY SAY!

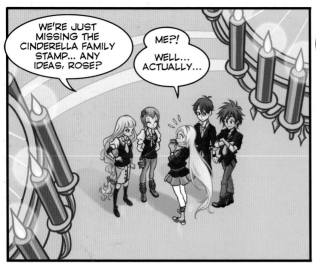

WE'RE JUST MISSING THE CINDERELLA FAMILY STAMP... ANY IDEAS, ROSE?

ME?! WELL... ACTUALLY...

OKAY, DON'T MISUNDERSTAND ME GUYS, EVERYTHING IS AWESOME, BUT I'M NOT CINDERELLA'S GRANDDAUGHTER!

BUT SINCE I'M HERE, I'LL DO MY BEST TO LIVE THIS FAIRY TALE!

GREAT!

LET'S GET IT STARTED THEN! THE MAGIC CHANDELIER LOOKS LIKE A GOOD PLACE TO START.

CAN YOU SEE IT, ROSE?

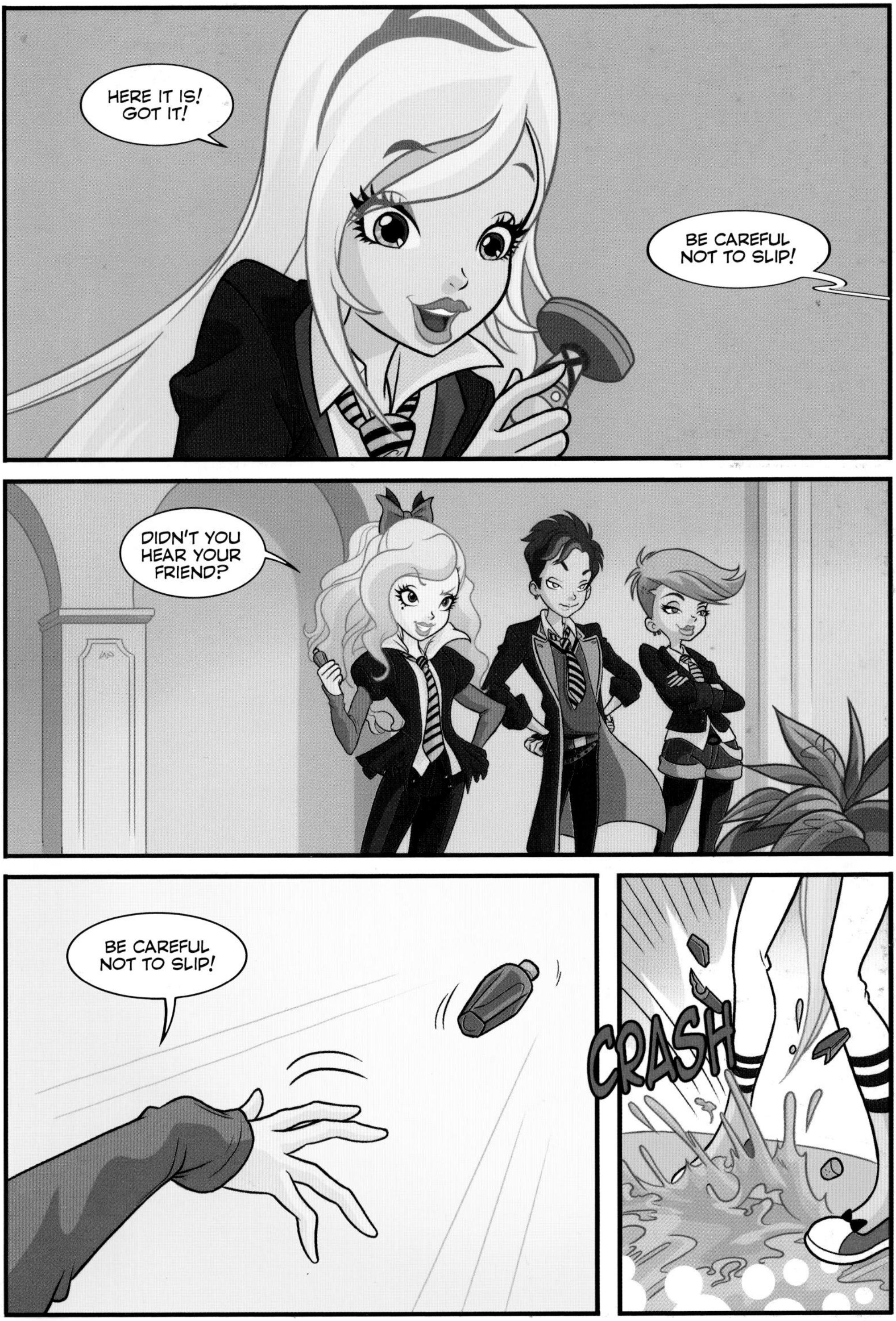
HERE IT IS! GOT IT!
BE CAREFUL NOT TO SLIP!
DIDN'T YOU HEAR YOUR FRIEND?
BE CAREFUL NOT TO SLIP!
CRASH

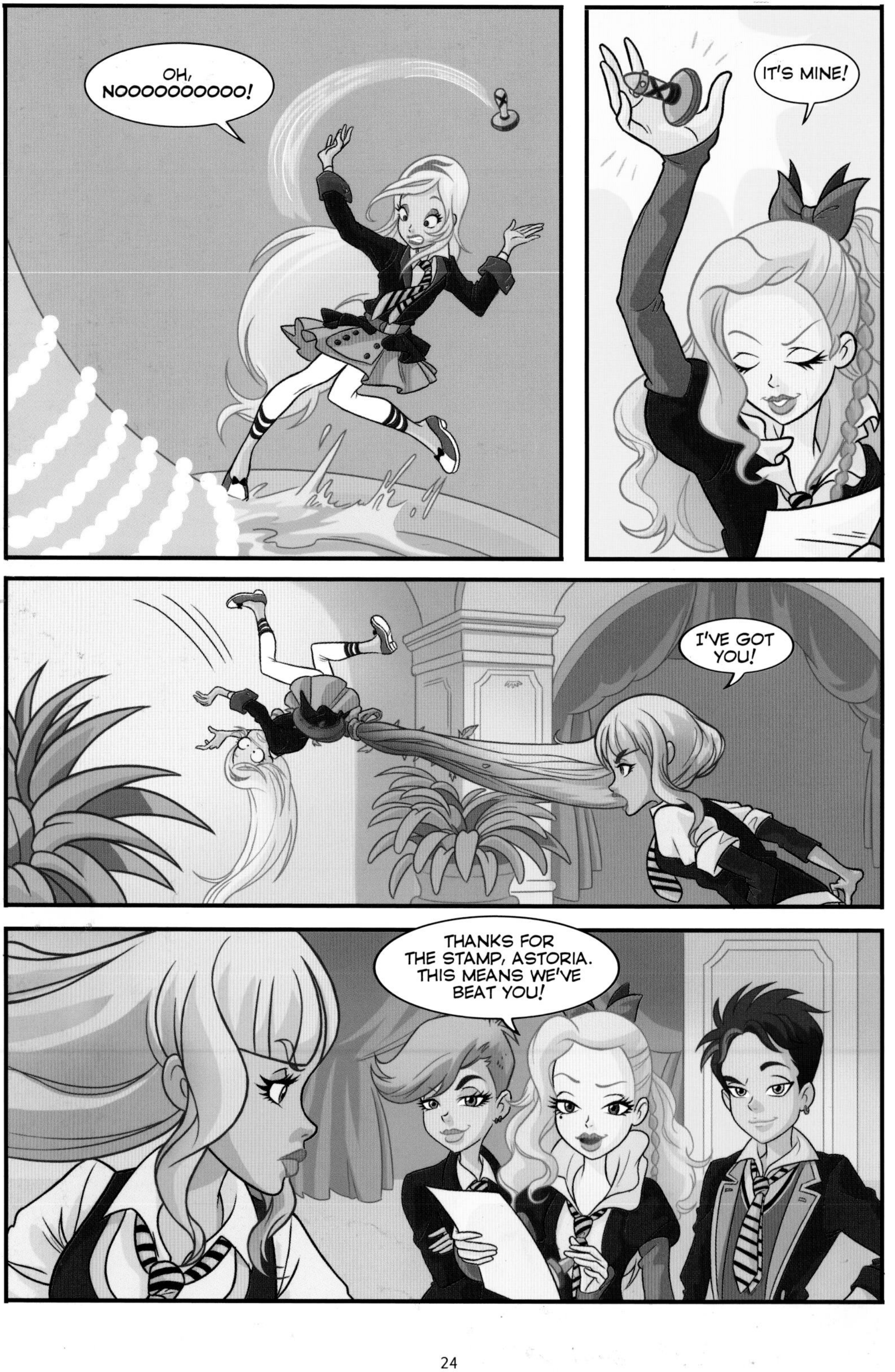
OH, NOOOOOOOOOO!
IT'S MINE!
I'VE GOT YOU!
THANKS FOR THE STAMP, ASTORIA. THIS MEANS WE'VE BEAT YOU!

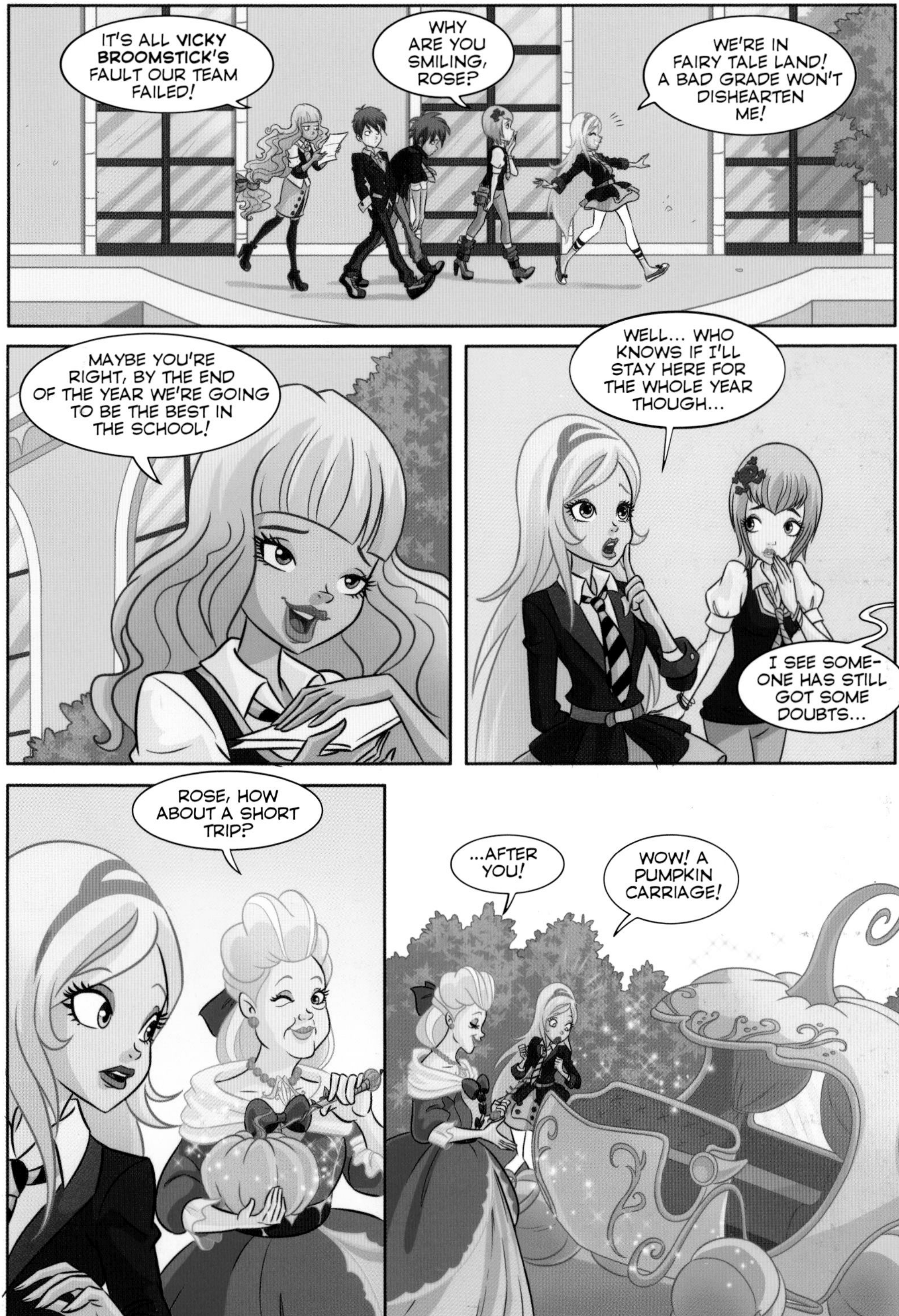
IT'S ALL VICKY BROOMSTICK'S FAULT OUR TEAM FAILED!
WHY ARE YOU SMILING, ROSE?
WE'RE IN FAIRY TALE LAND! A BAD GRADE WON'T DISHEARTEN ME!
MAYBE YOU'RE RIGHT, BY THE END OF THE YEAR WE'RE GOING TO BE THE BEST IN THE SCHOOL!
WELL... WHO KNOWS IF I'LL STAY HERE FOR THE WHOLE YEAR THOUGH...
I SEE SOME-ONE HAS STILL GOT SOME DOUBTS...
ROSE, HOW ABOUT A SHORT TRIP?
...AFTER YOU!
WOW! A PUMPKIN CARRIAGE!

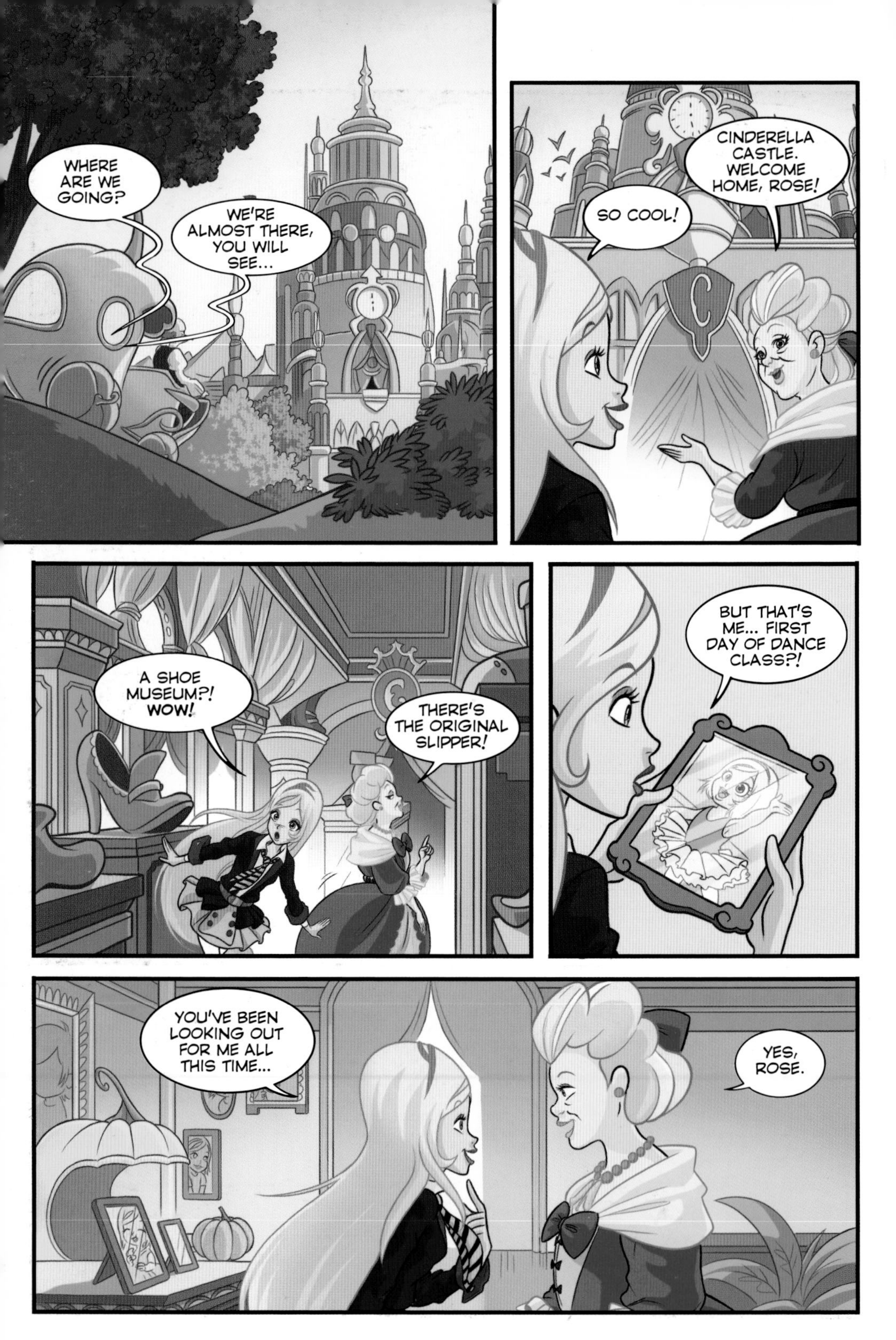
WHERE ARE WE GOING?
WE'RE ALMOST THERE, YOU WILL SEE...
SO COOL!
CINDERELLA CASTLE. WELCOME HOME, ROSE!
A SHOE MUSEUM?! WOW!
THERE'S THE ORIGINAL SLIPPER!
BUT THAT'S ME... FIRST DAY OF DANCE CLASS?!
YOU'VE BEEN LOOKING OUT FOR ME ALL THIS TIME...
YES, ROSE.

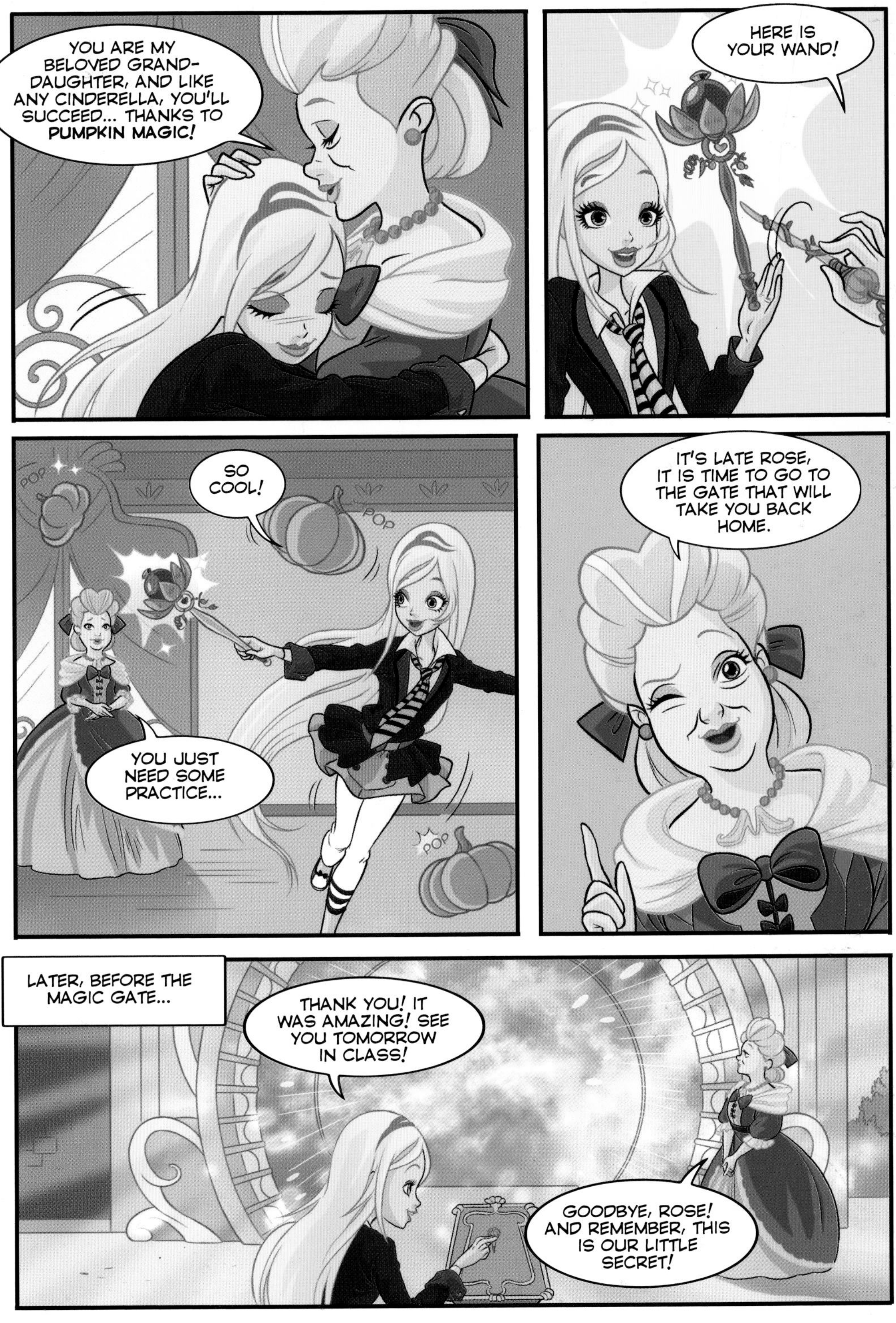

YOU ARE MY BELOVED GRAND-DAUGHTER, AND LIKE ANY CINDERELLA, YOU'LL SUCCEED... THANKS TO PUMPKIN MAGIC!
HERE IS YOUR WAND!
POP
SO COOL!
POP
YOU JUST NEED SOME PRACTICE...
POP
IT'S LATE ROSE, IT IS TIME TO GO TO THE GATE THAT WILL TAKE YOU BACK HOME.
LATER, BEFORE THE MAGIC GATE...
THANK YOU! IT WAS AMAZING! SEE YOU TOMORROW IN CLASS!
GOODBYE, ROSE! AND REMEMBER, THIS IS OUR LITTLE SECRET!

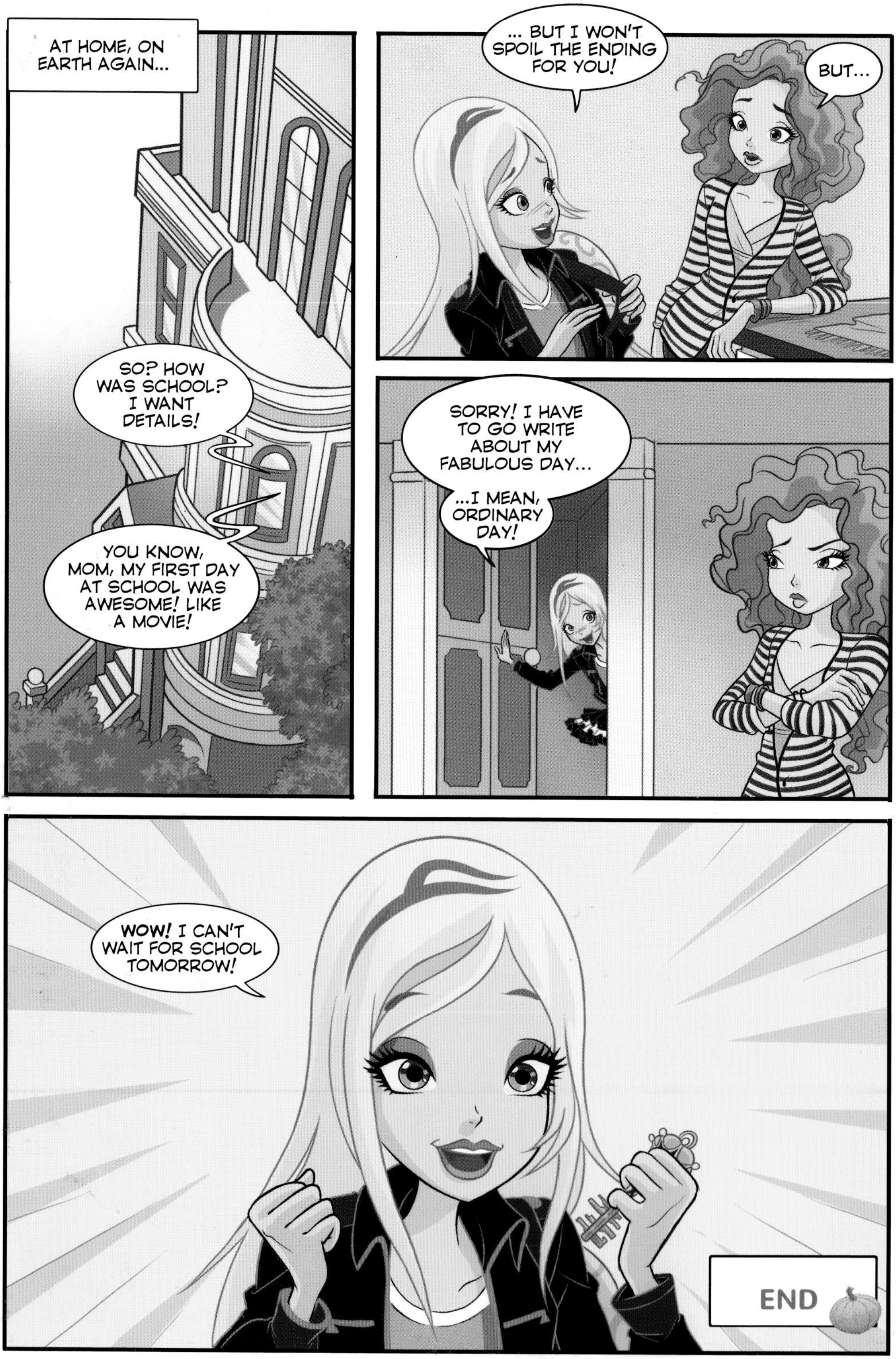
AT HOME, ON EARTH AGAIN...
SO? HOW WAS SCHOOL? I WANT DETAILS!
YOU KNOW, MOM, MY FIRST DAY AT SCHOOL WAS AWESOME! LIKE A MOVIE!
... BUT I WON'T SPOIL THE ENDING FOR YOU!
BUT...
SORRY! I HAVE TO GO WRITE ABOUT MY FABULOUS DAY...
...I MEAN, ORDINARY DAY!
WOW! I CAN'T WAIT FOR SCHOOL TOMORROW!
END

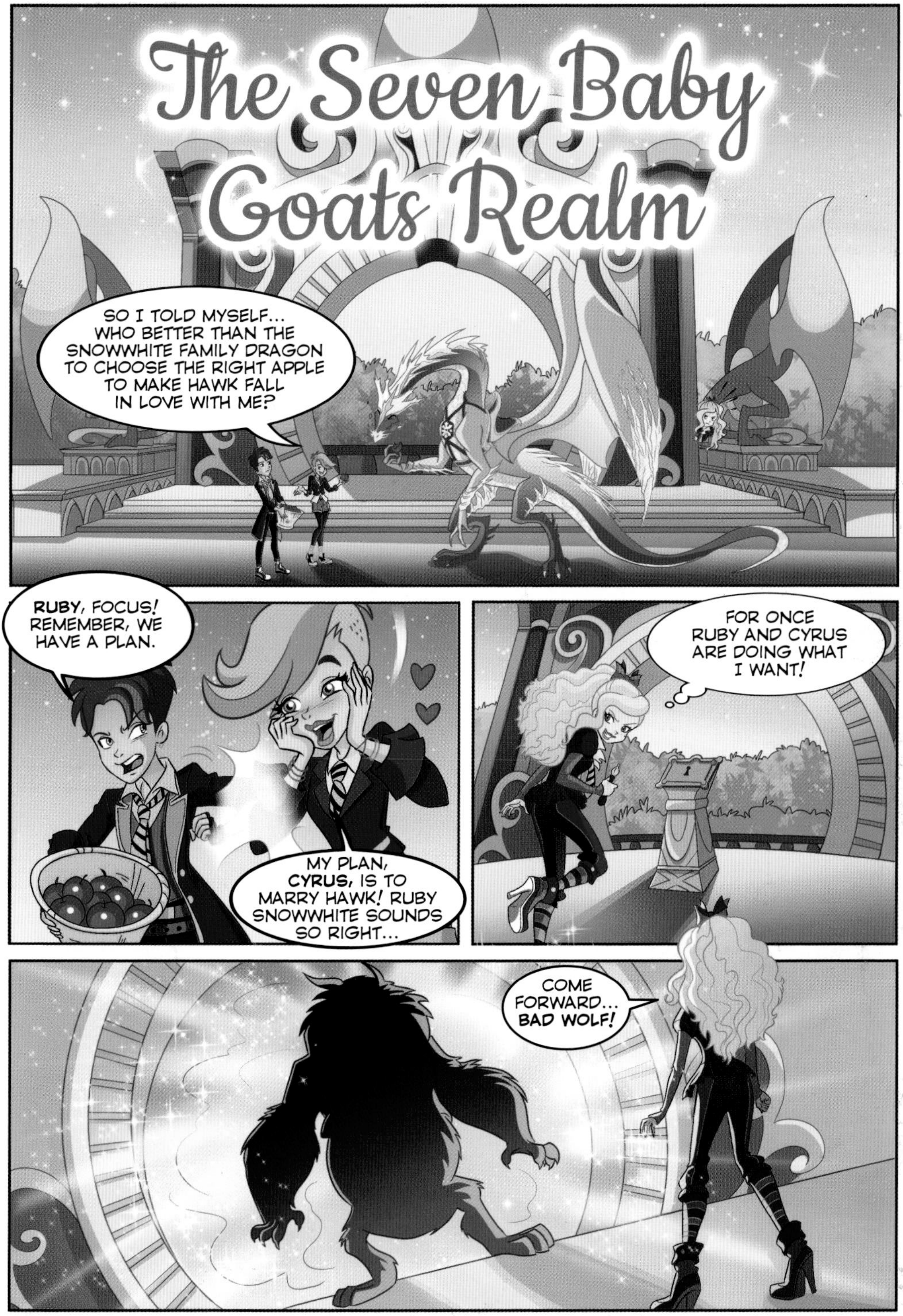
The Seven Baby Goats Realm
SO I TOLD MYSELF... WHO BETTER THAN THE SNOWWHITE FAMILY DRAGON TO CHOOSE THE RIGHT APPLE TO MAKE HAWK FALL IN LOVE WITH ME?
RUBY, FOCUS! REMEMBER, WE HAVE A PLAN.
MY PLAN, CYRUS, IS TO MARRY HAWK! RUBY SNOWWHITE SOUNDS SO RIGHT...
FOR ONCE RUBY AND CYRUS ARE DOING WHAT I WANT!
COME FORWARD... BAD WOLF!

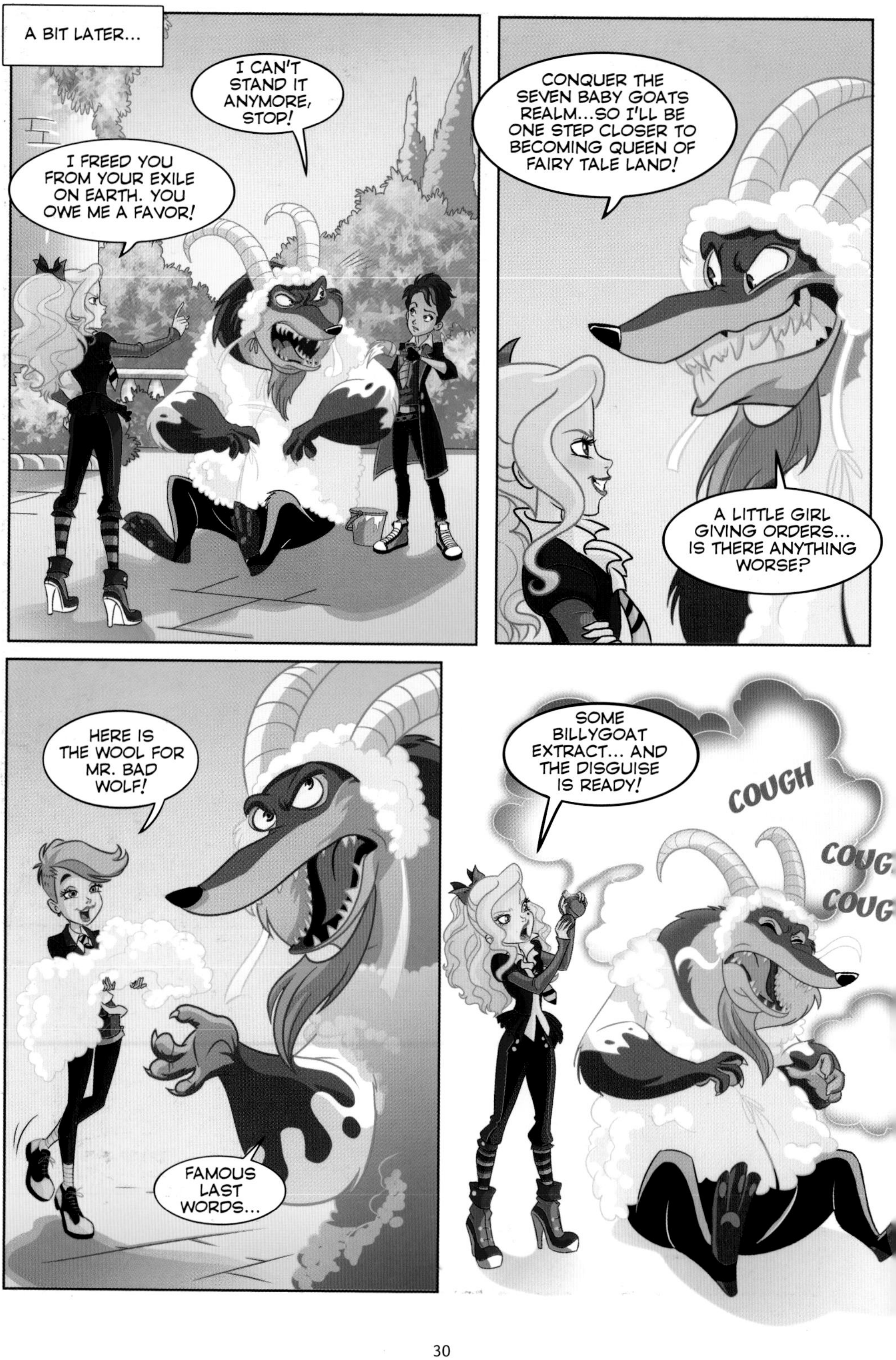
A BIT LATER...
I FREED YOU FROM YOUR EXILE ON EARTH. YOU OWE ME A FAVOR!
I CAN'T STAND IT ANYMORE, STOP!
CONQUER THE SEVEN BABY GOATS REALM...SO I'LL BE ONE STEP CLOSER TO BECOMING QUEEN OF FAIRY TALE LAND!
A LITTLE GIRL GIVING ORDERS... IS THERE ANYTHING WORSE?
HERE IS THE WOOL FOR MR. BAD WOLF!
FAMOUS LAST WORDS...
SOME BILLYGOAT EXTRACT... AND THE DISGUISE IS READY!
COUGH

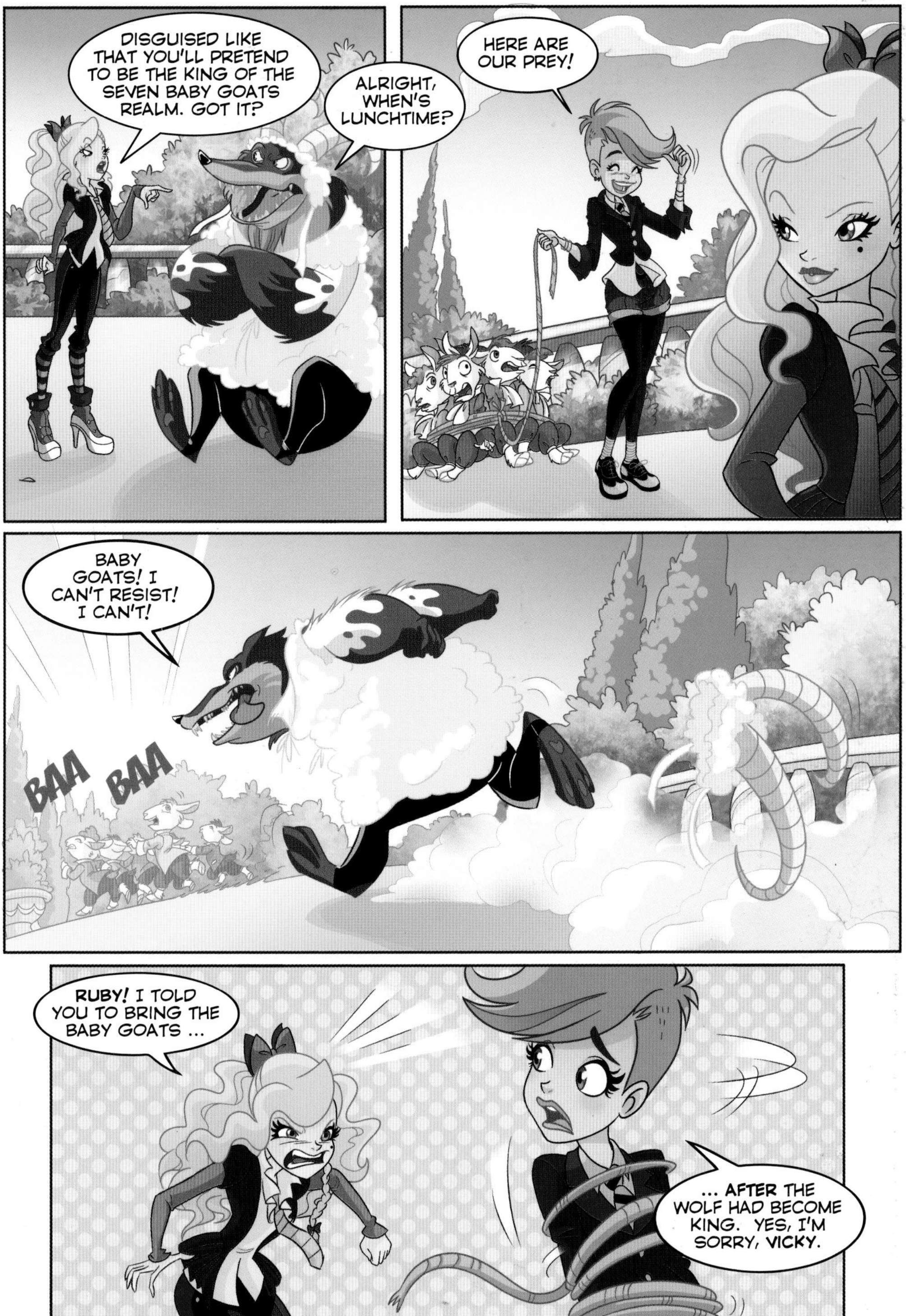
DISGUISED LIKE THAT YOU'LL PRETEND TO BE THE KING OF THE SEVEN BABY GOATS REALM. GOT IT?
ALRIGHT, WHEN'S LUNCHTIME?
HERE ARE OUR PREY!
BABY GOATS! I CAN'T RESIST! I CAN'T!
BAA
BAA
RUBY! I TOLD YOU TO BRING THE BABY GOATS ...
... **AFTER** THE WOLF HAD BECOME KING. YES, I'M SORRY, **VICKY**.

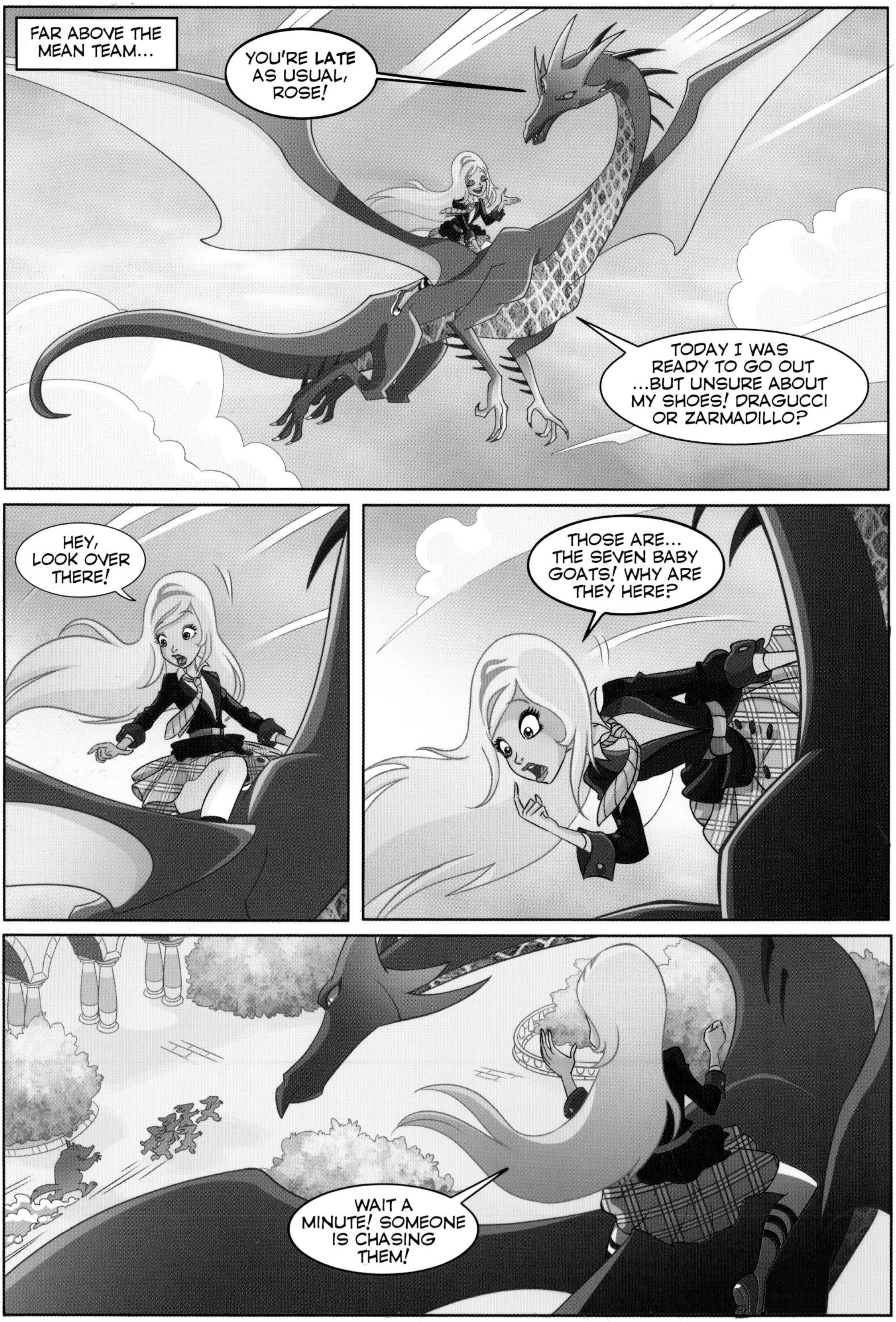
FAR ABOVE THE MEAN TEAM...
YOU'RE LATE AS USUAL, ROSE!
TODAY I WAS READY TO GO OUT ...BUT UNSURE ABOUT MY SHOES! DRAGUCCI OR ZARMADILLO?
HEY, LOOK OVER THERE!
THOSE ARE... THE SEVEN BABY GOATS! WHY ARE THEY HERE?
WAIT A MINUTE! SOMEONE IS CHASING THEM!

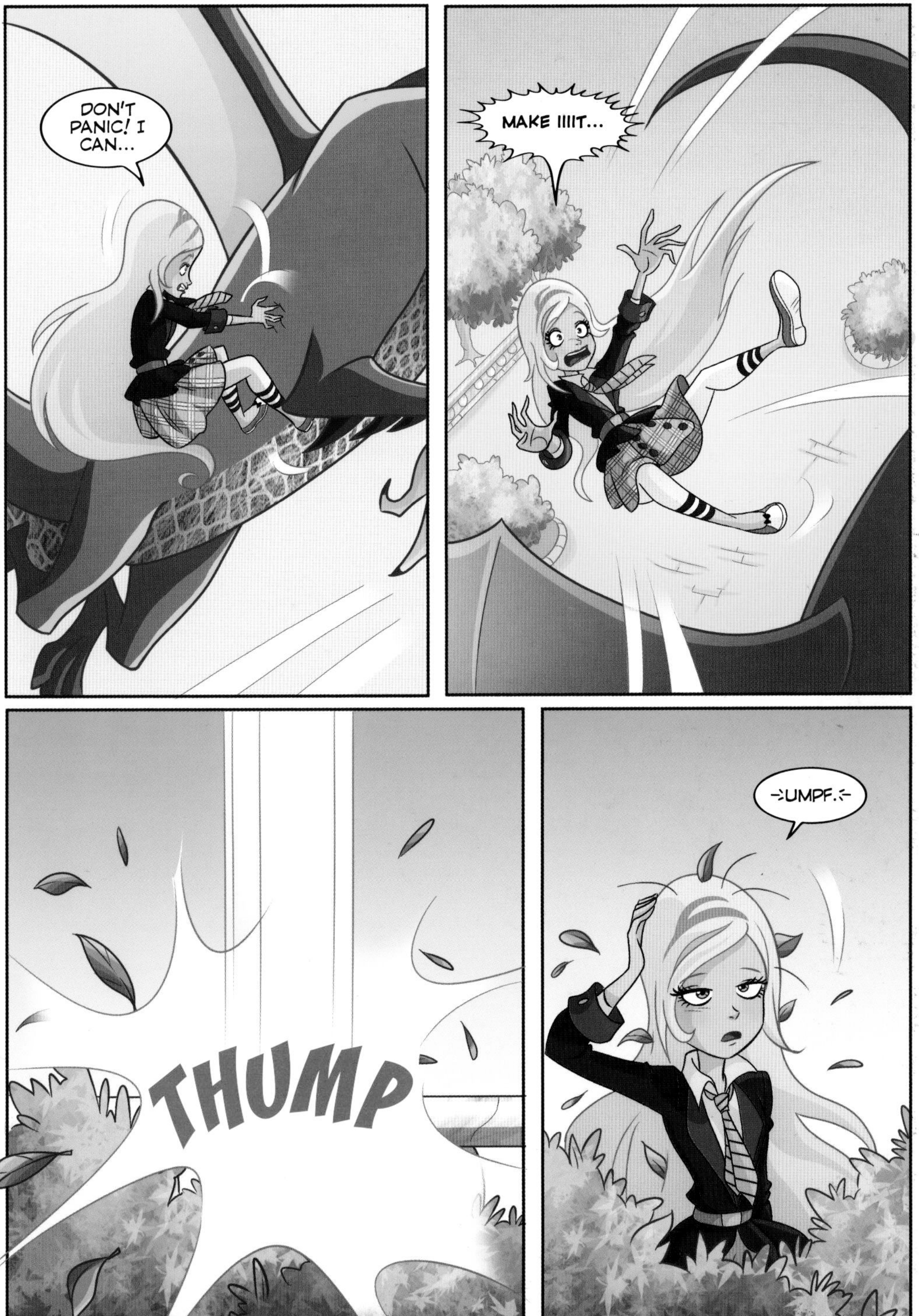
DON'T PANIC! I CAN...
MAKE IIIIT...
THUMP
UMPF.

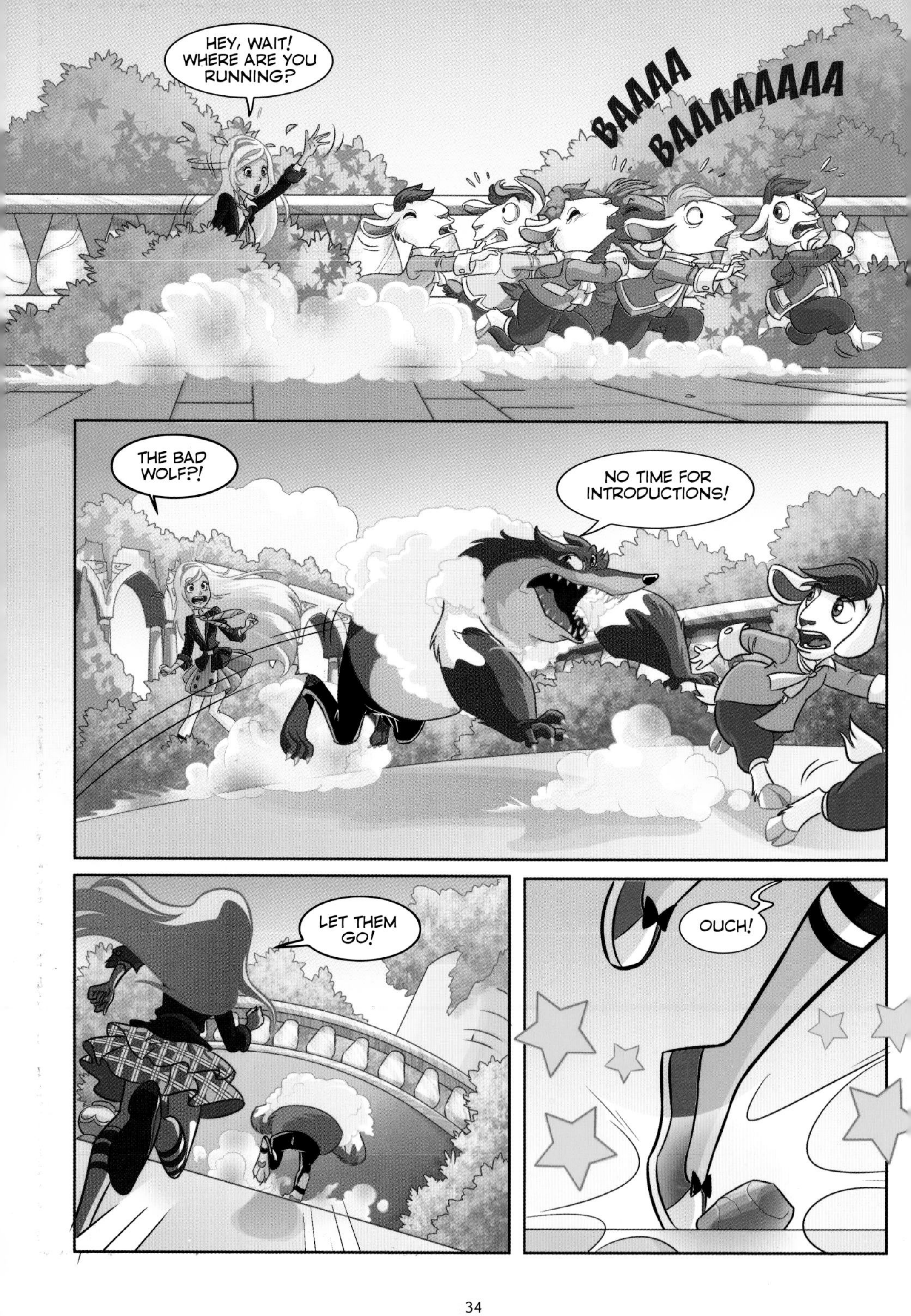
HEY, WAIT! WHERE ARE YOU RUNNING?
BAAAA
BAAAAAAAA
THE BAD WOLF?!
NO TIME FOR INTRODUCTIONS!
LET THEM GO!
OUCH!

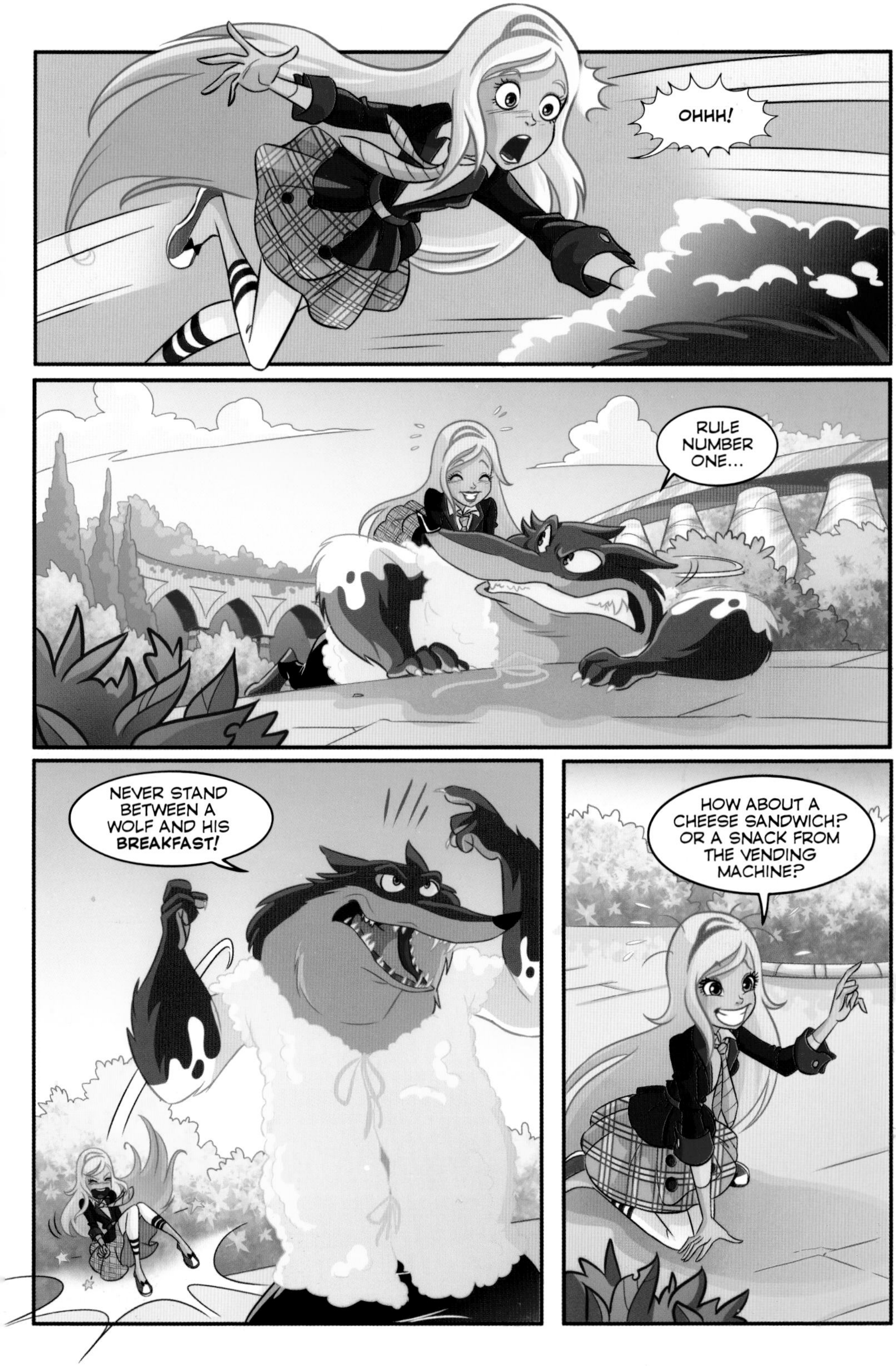
OHHH!
RULE NUMBER ONE...
NEVER STAND BETWEEN A WOLF AND HIS BREAKFAST!
HOW ABOUT A CHEESE SANDWICH? OR A SNACK FROM THE VENDING MACHINE?

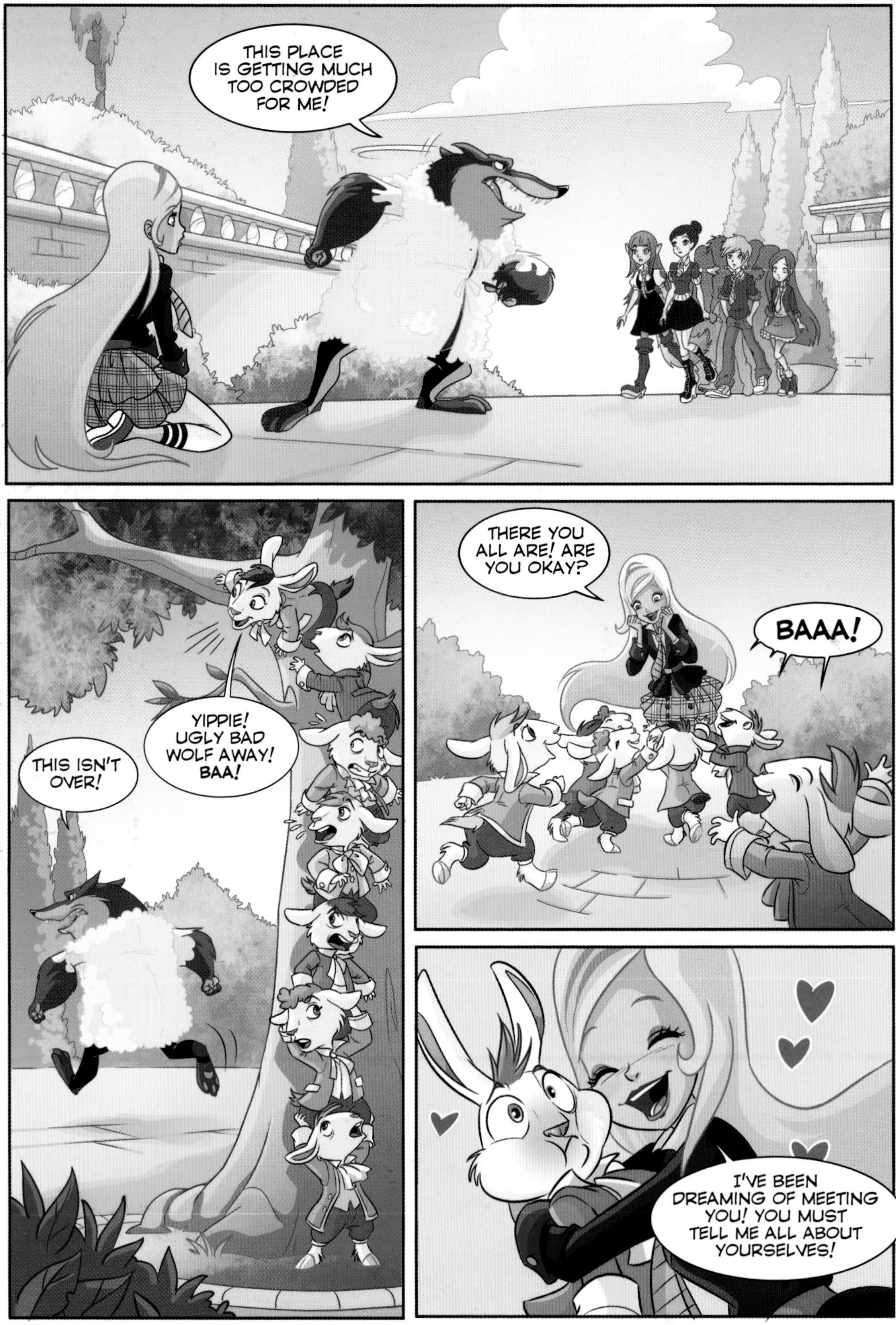
THIS PLACE IS GETTING MUCH TOO CROWDED FOR ME!
YIPPIE! UGLY BAD WOLF AWAY! BAA!
THIS ISN'T OVER!
THERE YOU ALL ARE! ARE YOU OKAY?
BAAA!
I'VE BEEN DREAMING OF MEETING YOU! YOU MUST TELL ME ALL ABOUT YOURSELVES!

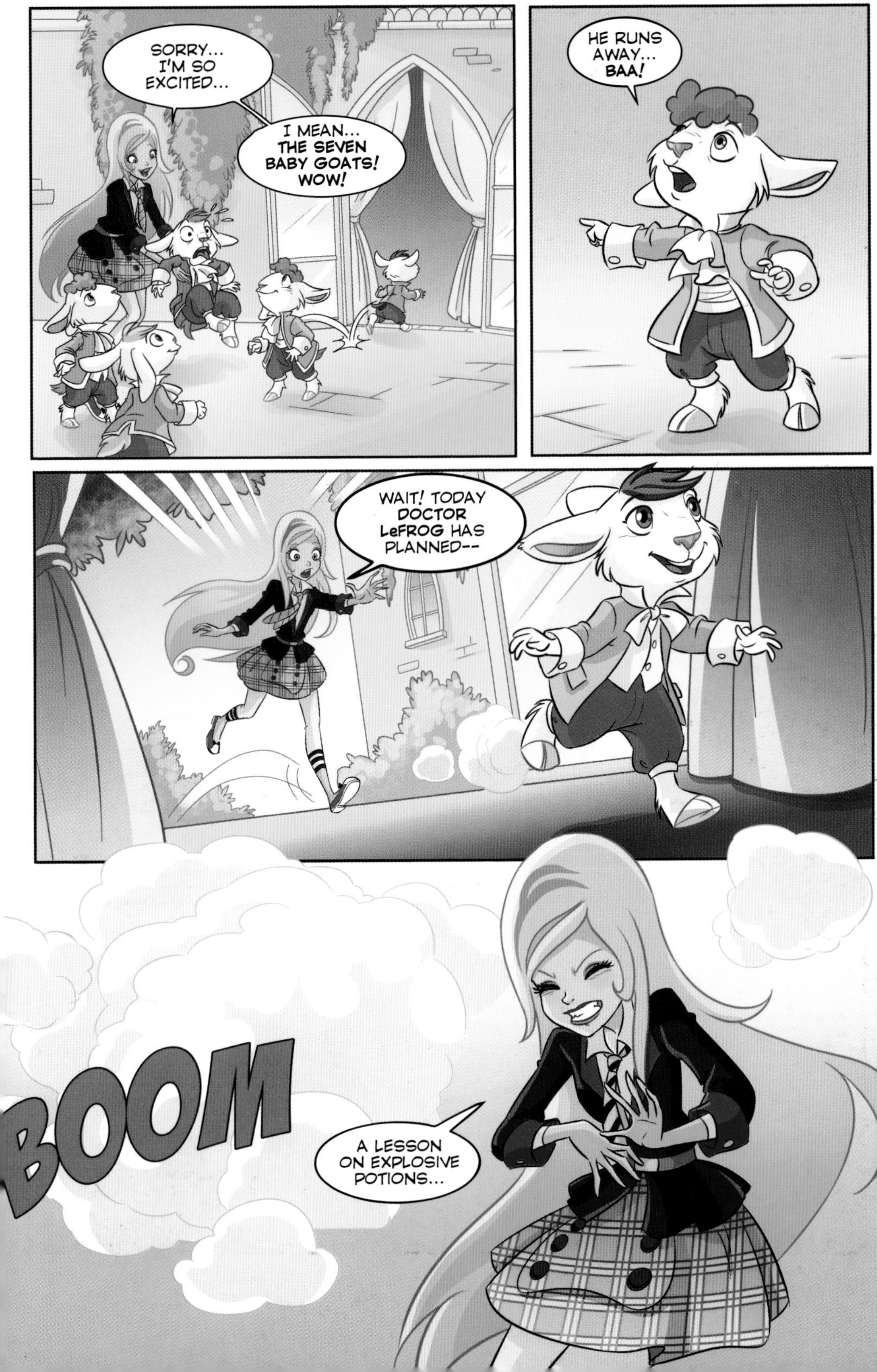
SORRY... I'M SO EXCITED...
I MEAN... THE SEVEN BABY GOATS! WOW!
HE RUNS AWAY... BAA!
WAIT! TODAY DOCTOR LeFROG HAS PLANNED--
BOOM
A LESSON ON EXPLOSIVE POTIONS...

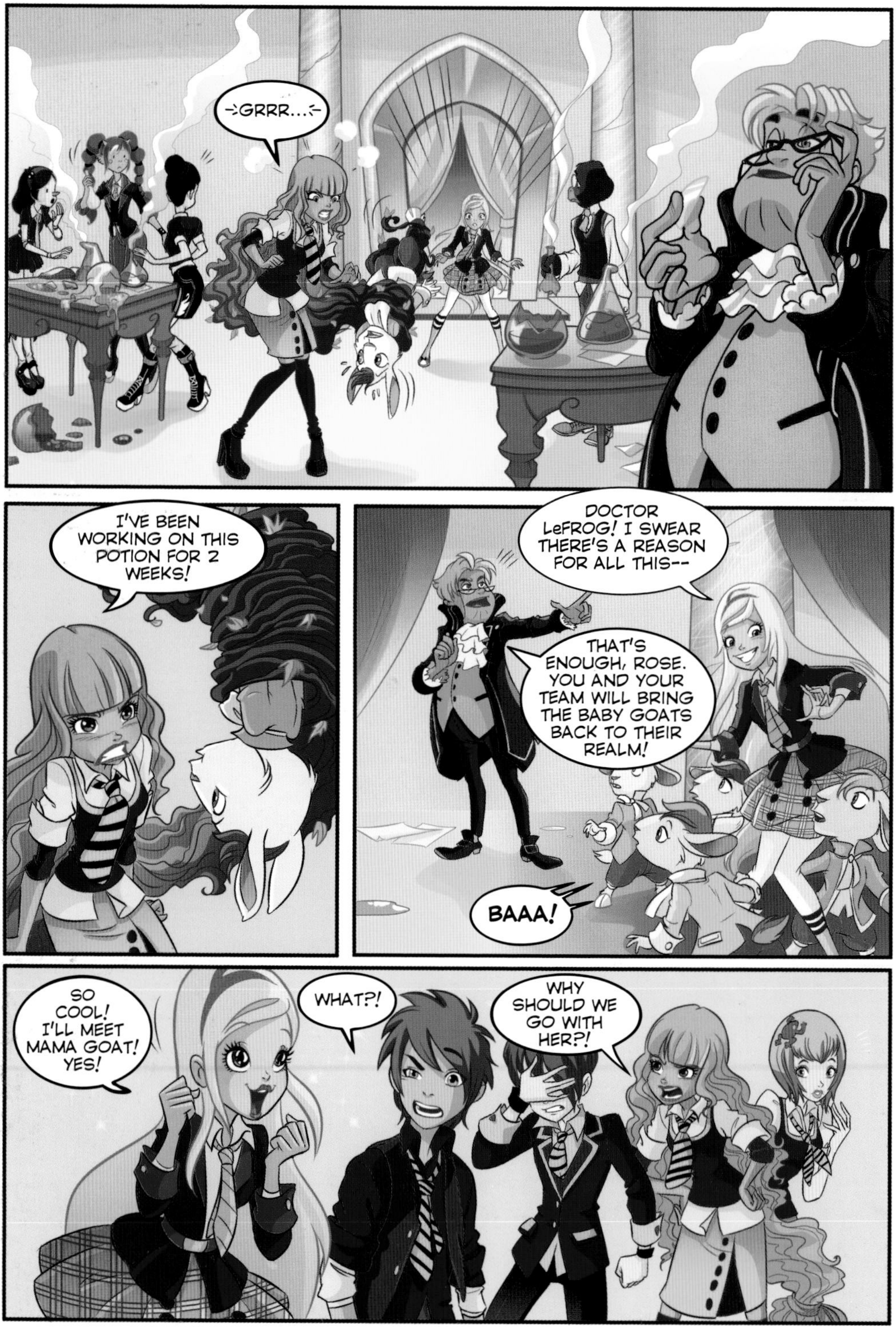
-GRRR...-
I'VE BEEN WORKING ON THIS POTION FOR 2 WEEKS!
DOCTOR LeFROG! I SWEAR THERE'S A REASON FOR ALL THIS--
THAT'S ENOUGH, ROSE. YOU AND YOUR TEAM WILL BRING THE BABY GOATS BACK TO THEIR REALM!
BAAA!
SO COOL! I'LL MEET MAMA GOAT! YES!
WHAT?!
WHY SHOULD WE GO WITH HER?!

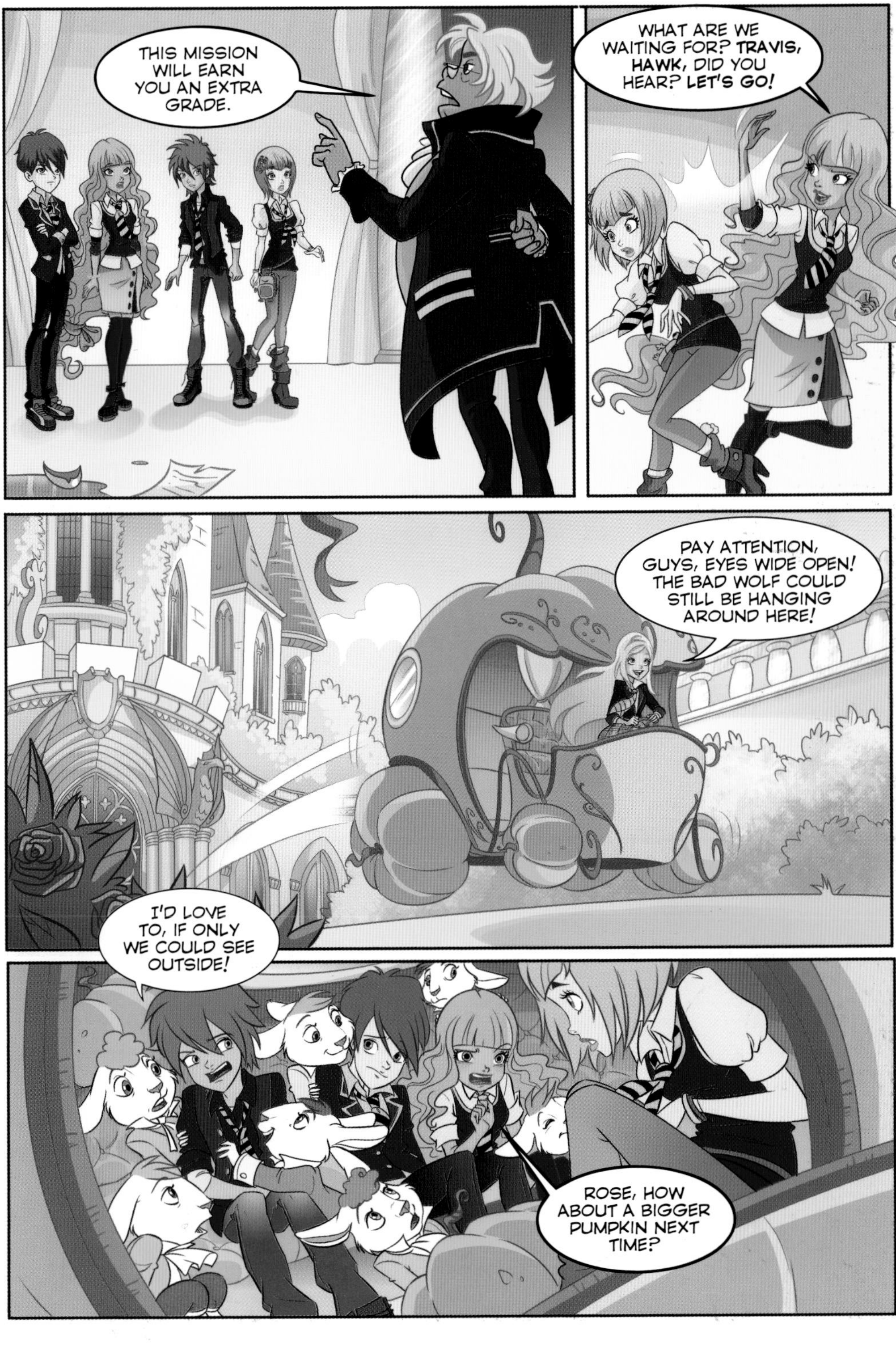
THIS MISSION WILL EARN YOU AN EXTRA GRADE.
WHAT ARE WE WAITING FOR? **TRAVIS, HAWK**, DID YOU HEAR? **LET'S GO!**
PAY ATTENTION, GUYS, EYES WIDE OPEN! THE BAD WOLF COULD STILL BE HANGING AROUND HERE!
I'D LOVE TO, IF ONLY WE COULD SEE OUTSIDE!
ROSE, HOW ABOUT A BIGGER PUMPKIN NEXT TIME?

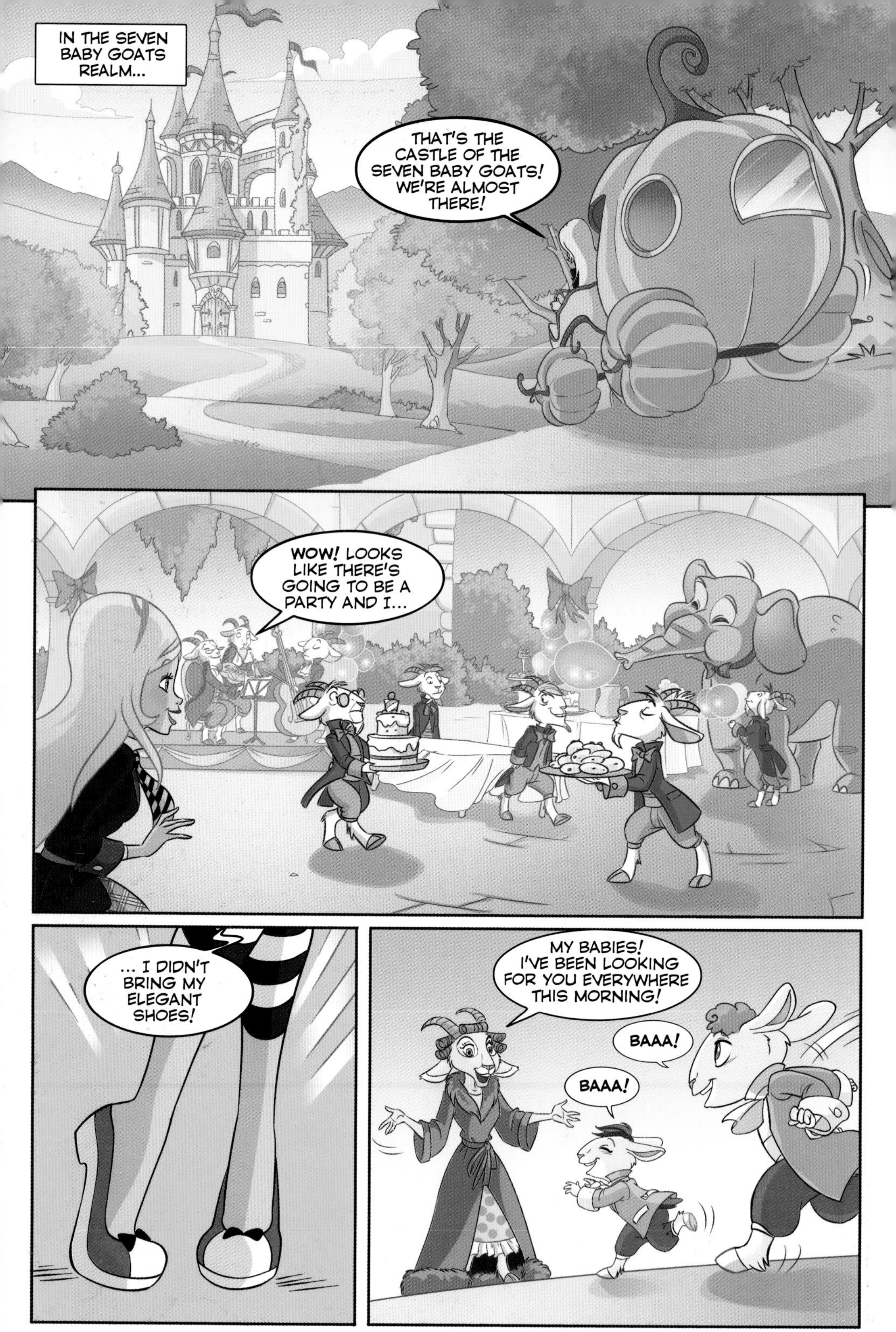
IN THE SEVEN BABY GOATS REALM...
THAT'S THE CASTLE OF THE SEVEN BABY GOATS! WE'RE ALMOST THERE!
WOW! LOOKS LIKE THERE'S GOING TO BE A PARTY AND I...
... I DIDN'T BRING MY ELEGANT SHOES!
MY BABIES! I'VE BEEN LOOKING FOR YOU EVERYWHERE THIS MORNING!
BAAA!
BAAA!

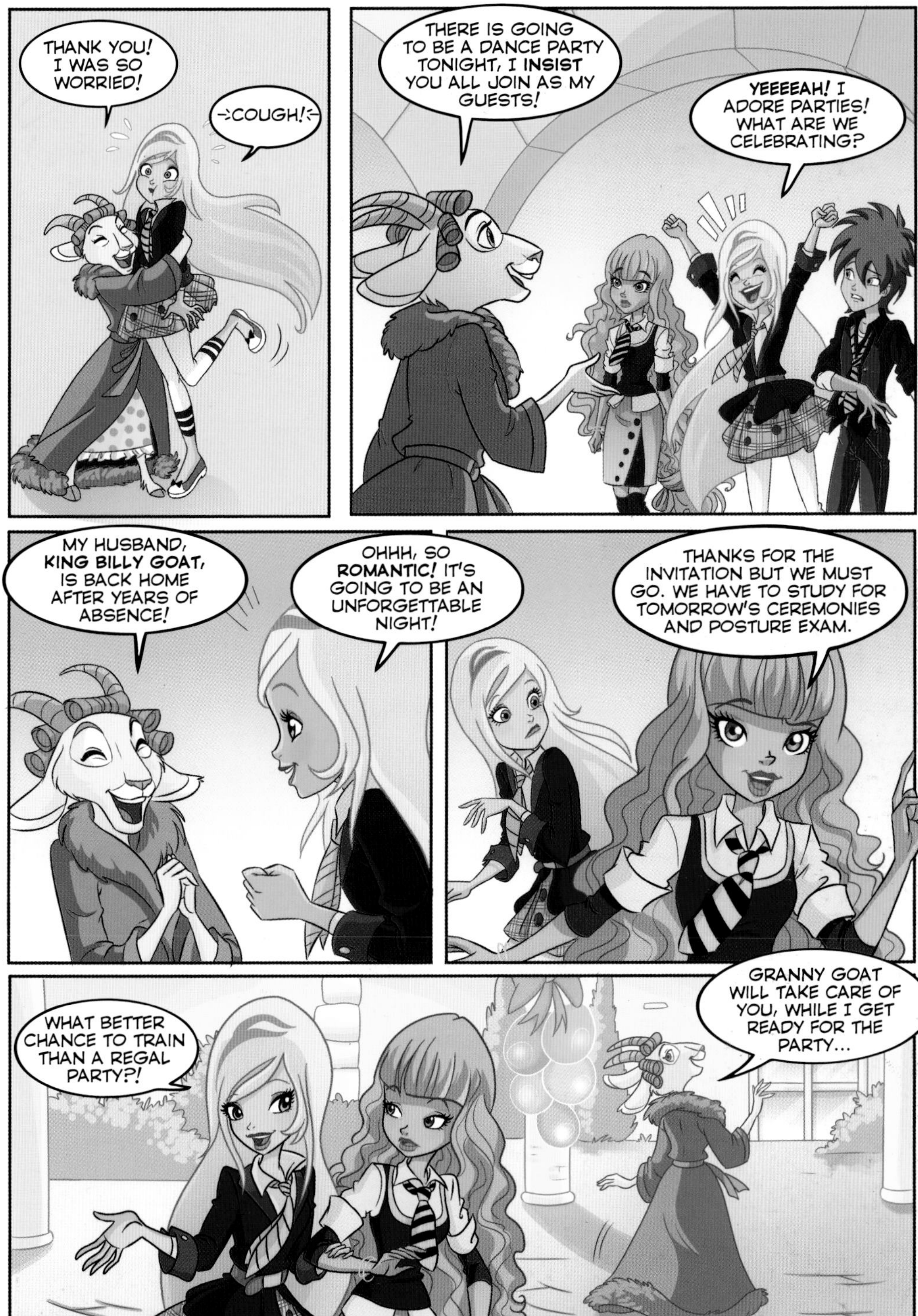
THANK YOU! I WAS SO WORRIED!
COUGH!
THERE IS GOING TO BE A DANCE PARTY TONIGHT, I **INSIST** YOU ALL JOIN AS MY GUESTS!
YEEEEAH! I ADORE PARTIES! WHAT ARE WE CELEBRATING?
MY HUSBAND, **KING BILLY GOAT**, IS BACK HOME AFTER YEARS OF ABSENCE!
OHHH, SO **ROMANTIC!** IT'S GOING TO BE AN UNFORGETTABLE NIGHT!
THANKS FOR THE INVITATION BUT WE MUST GO. WE HAVE TO STUDY FOR TOMORROW'S CEREMONIES AND POSTURE EXAM.
WHAT BETTER CHANCE TO TRAIN THAN A REGAL PARTY?!
GRANNY GOAT WILL TAKE CARE OF YOU, WHILE I GET READY FOR THE PARTY...

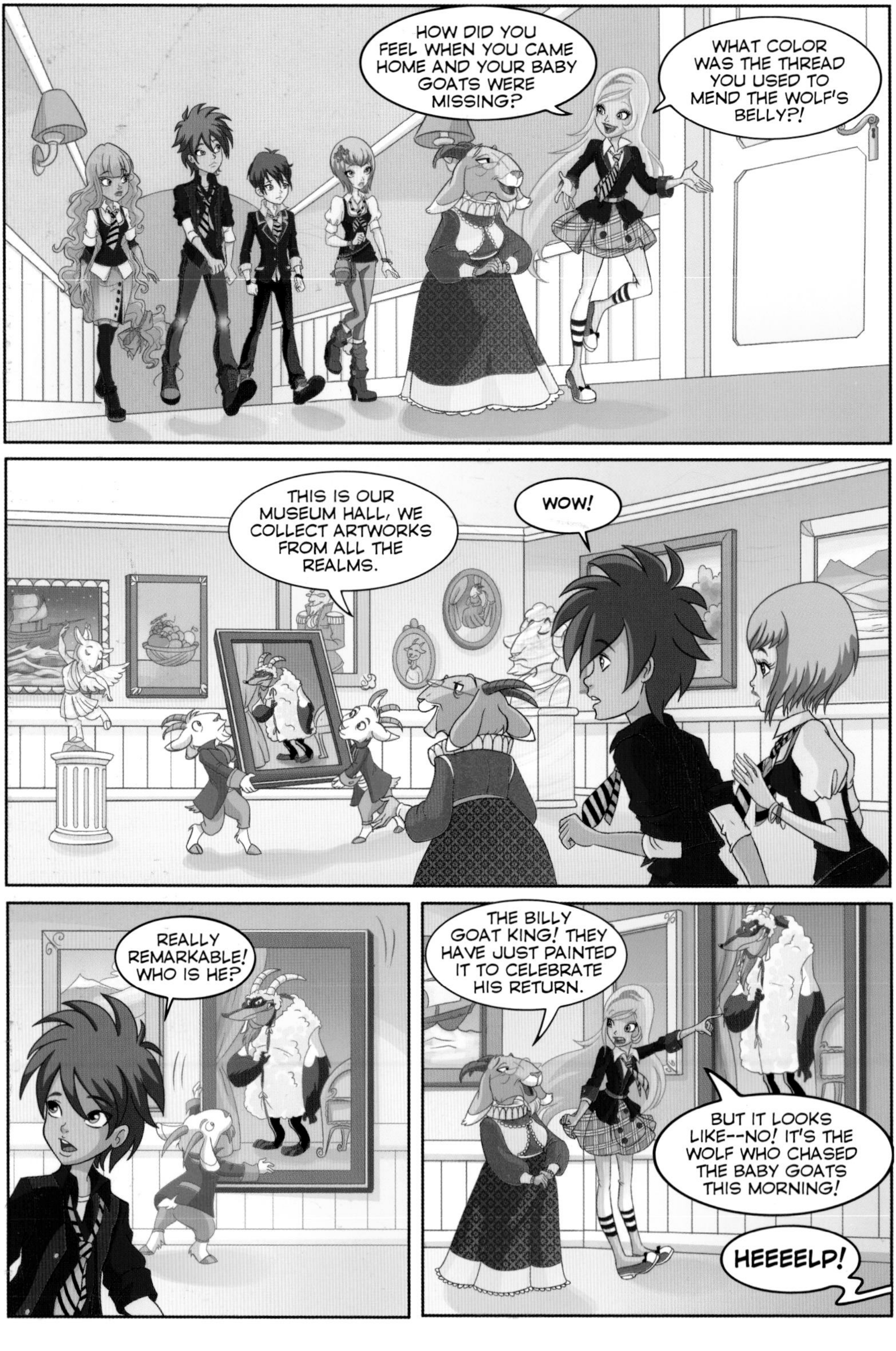
HOW DID YOU FEEL WHEN YOU CAME HOME AND YOUR BABY GOATS WERE MISSING?
WHAT COLOR WAS THE THREAD YOU USED TO MEND THE WOLF'S BELLY?!
THIS IS OUR MUSEUM HALL, WE COLLECT ARTWORKS FROM ALL THE REALMS.
WOW!
REALLY REMARKABLE! WHO IS HE?
THE BILLY GOAT KING! THEY HAVE JUST PAINTED IT TO CELEBRATE HIS RETURN.
BUT IT LOOKS LIKE--NO! IT'S THE WOLF WHO CHASED THE BABY GOATS THIS MORNING!
HEEEELP!

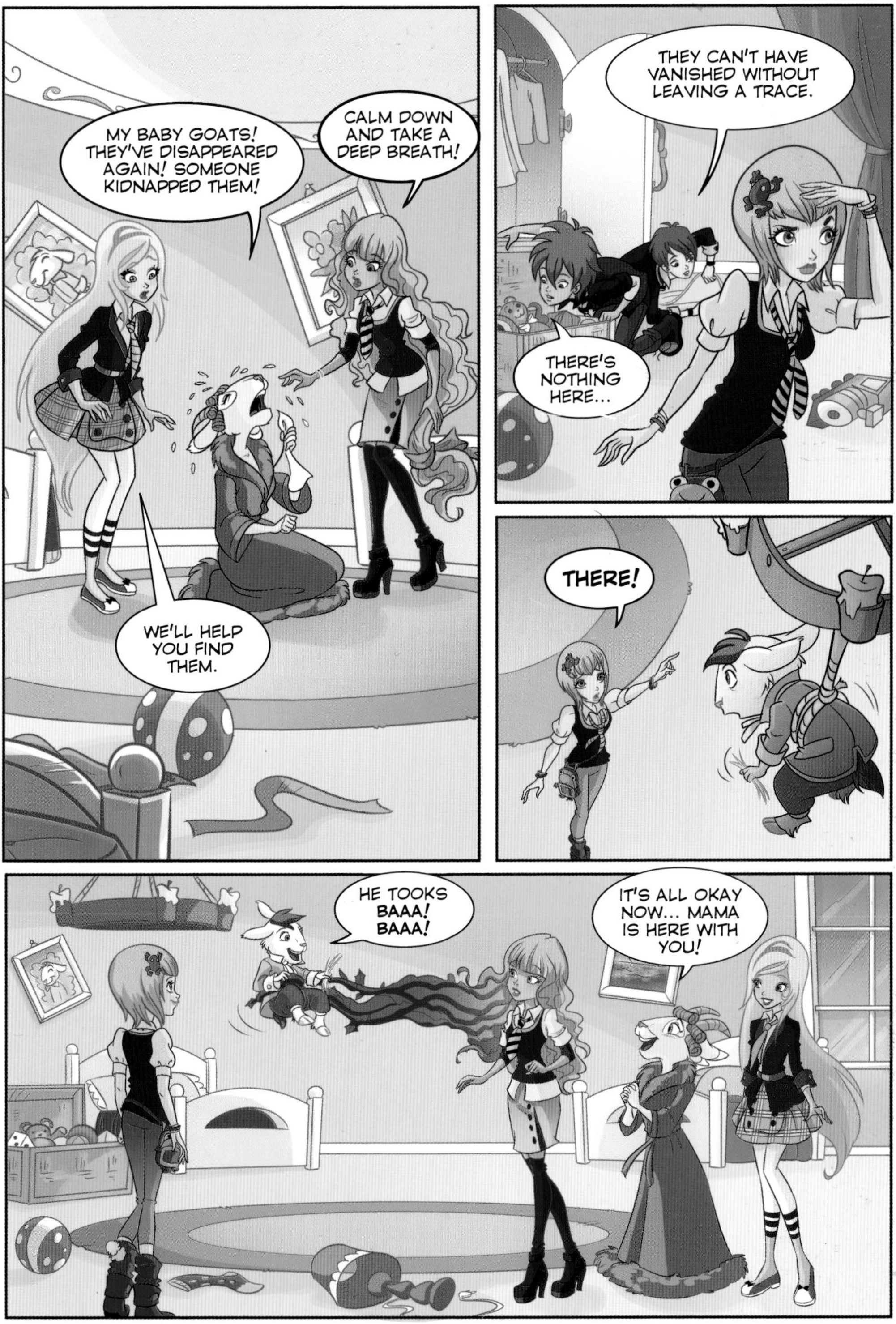
MY BABY GOATS! THEY'VE DISAPPEARED AGAIN! SOMEONE KIDNAPPED THEM!
CALM DOWN AND TAKE A DEEP BREATH!
WE'LL HELP YOU FIND THEM.
THEY CAN'T HAVE VANISHED WITHOUT LEAVING A TRACE.
THERE'S NOTHING HERE...
THERE!
HE TOOKS BAAA! BAAA!
IT'S ALL OKAY NOW... MAMA IS HERE WITH YOU!

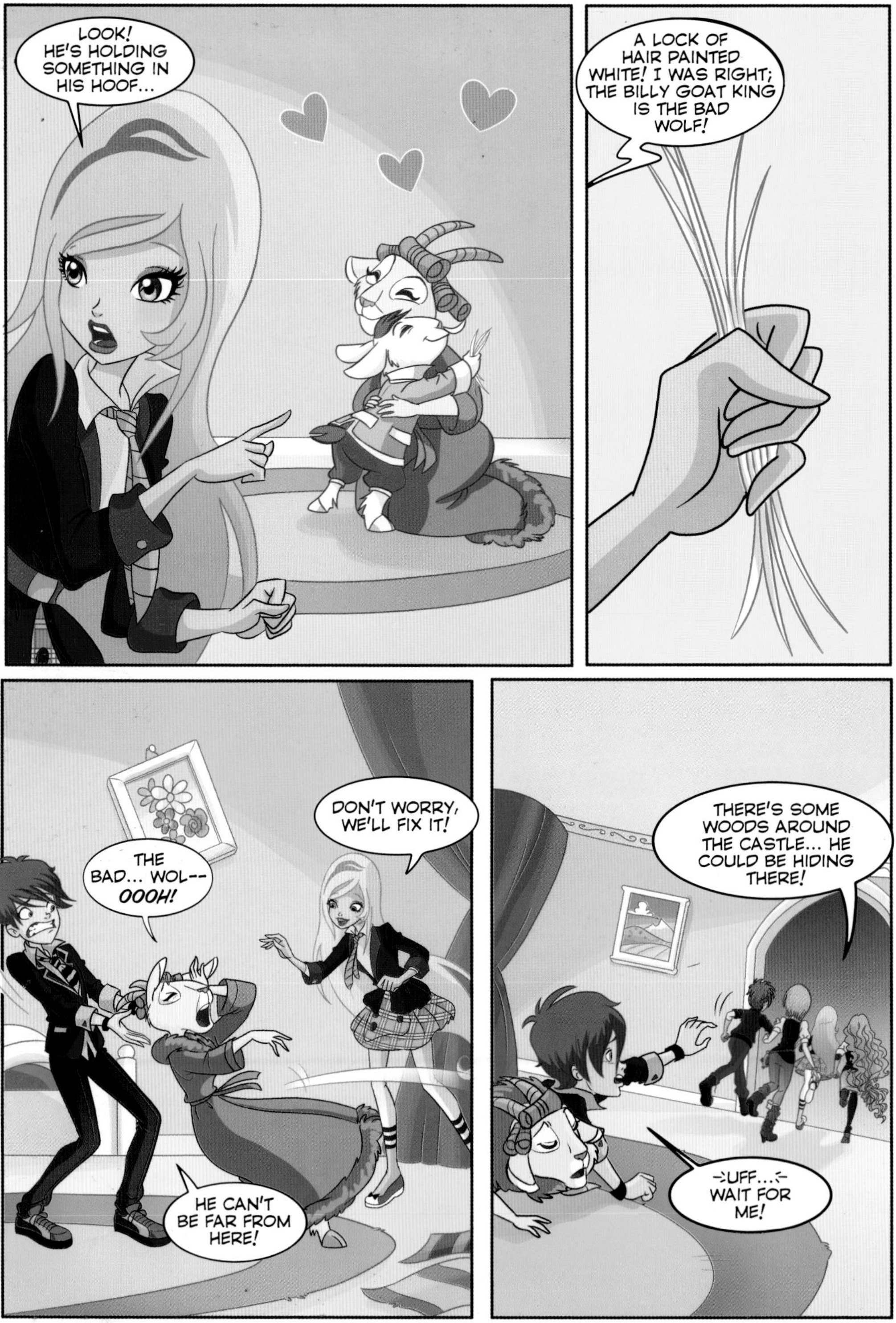
LOOK! HE'S HOLDING SOMETHING IN HIS HOOF...
A LOCK OF HAIR PAINTED WHITE! I WAS RIGHT; THE BILLY GOAT KING IS THE BAD WOLF!
DON'T WORRY, WE'LL FIX IT!
THE BAD... WOL-- OOOH!
HE CAN'T BE FAR FROM HERE!
THERE'S SOME WOODS AROUND THE CASTLE... HE COULD BE HIDING THERE!
UFF... WAIT FOR ME!

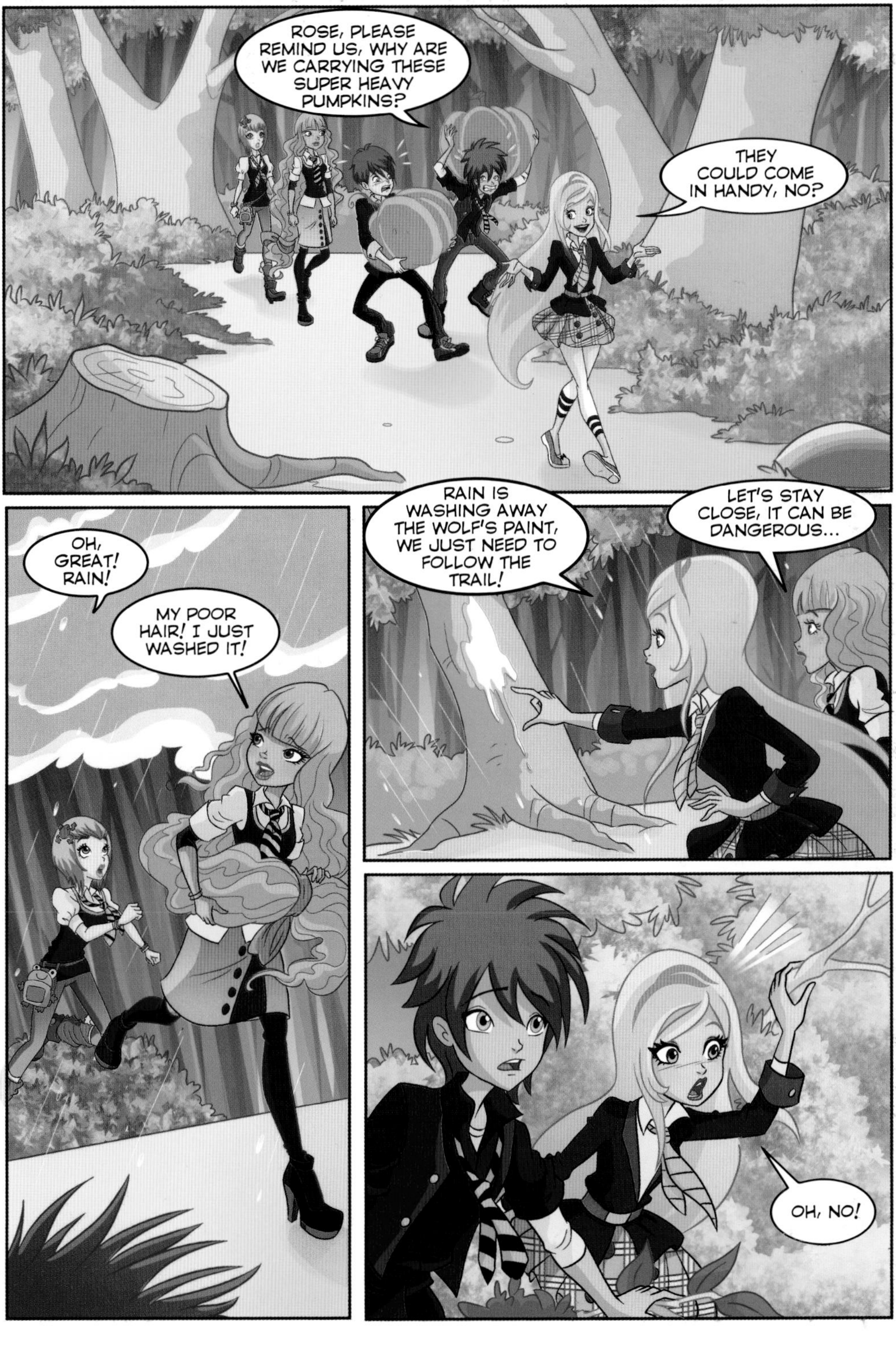
ROSE, PLEASE REMIND US, WHY ARE WE CARRYING THESE SUPER HEAVY PUMPKINS?
THEY COULD COME IN HANDY, NO?
OH, GREAT! RAIN!
MY POOR HAIR! I JUST WASHED IT!
RAIN IS WASHING AWAY THE WOLF'S PAINT, WE JUST NEED TO FOLLOW THE TRAIL!
LET'S STAY CLOSE, IT CAN BE DANGEROUS...
OH, NO!

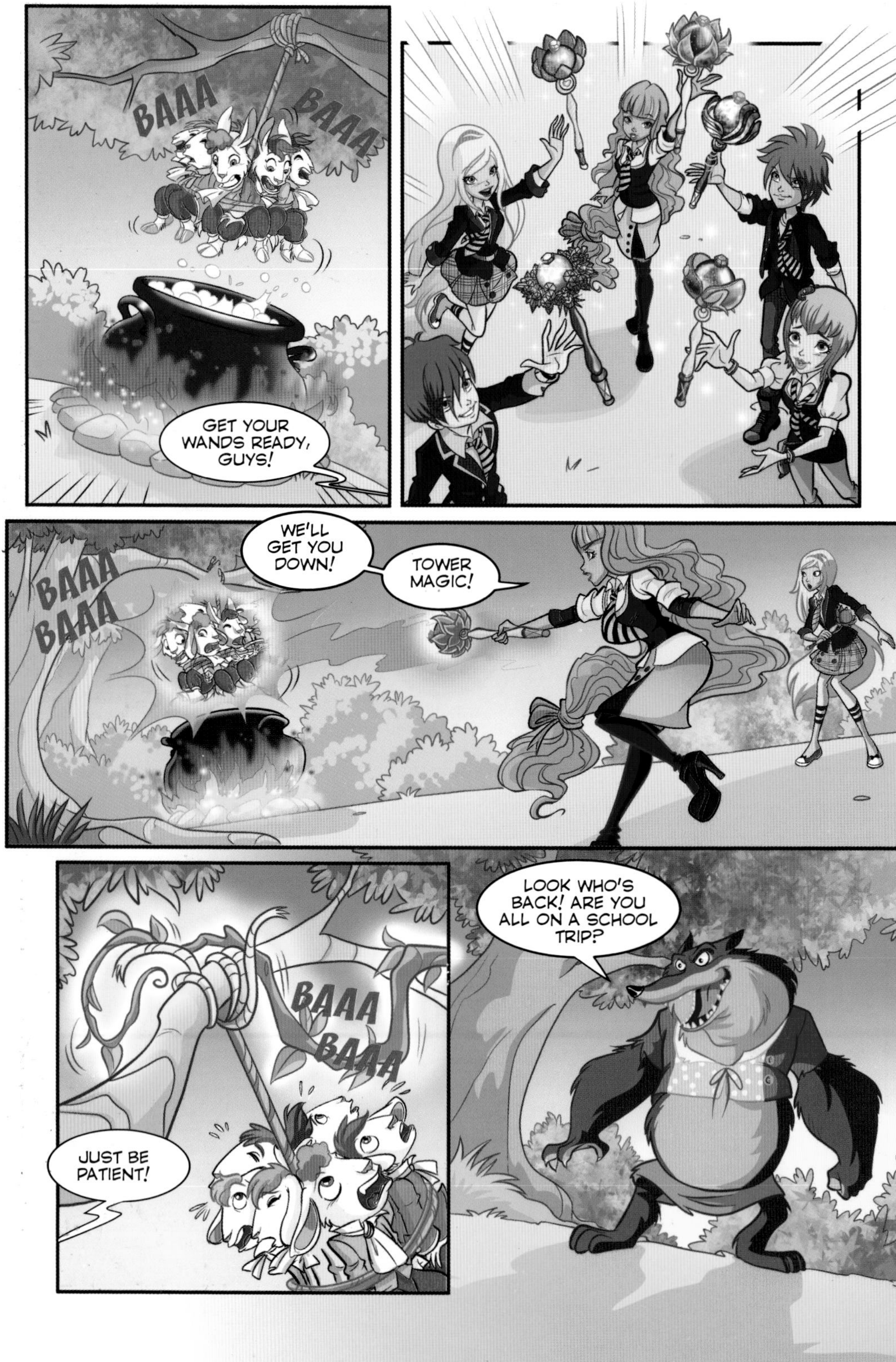
BAAA
BAAA
GET YOUR WANDS READY, GUYS!
WE'LL GET YOU DOWN!
TOWER MAGIC!
BAAA
BAAA
BAAA
BAAA
JUST BE PATIENT!
LOOK WHO'S BACK! ARE YOU ALL ON A SCHOOL TRIP?

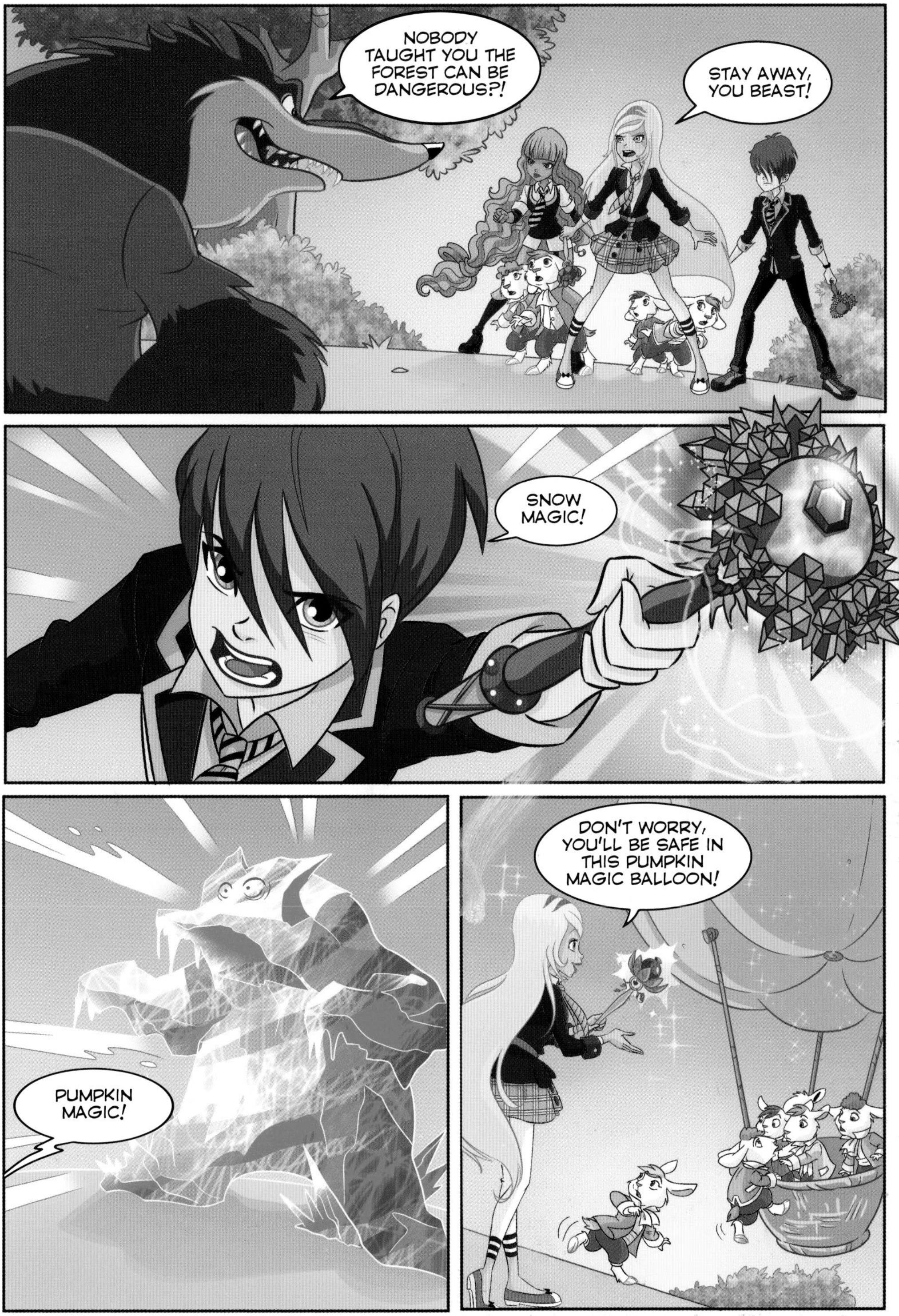
NOBODY TAUGHT YOU THE FOREST CAN BE DANGEROUS?!
STAY AWAY, YOU BEAST!
SNOW MAGIC!
PUMPKIN MAGIC!
DON'T WORRY, YOU'LL BE SAFE IN THIS PUMPKIN MAGIC BALLOON!

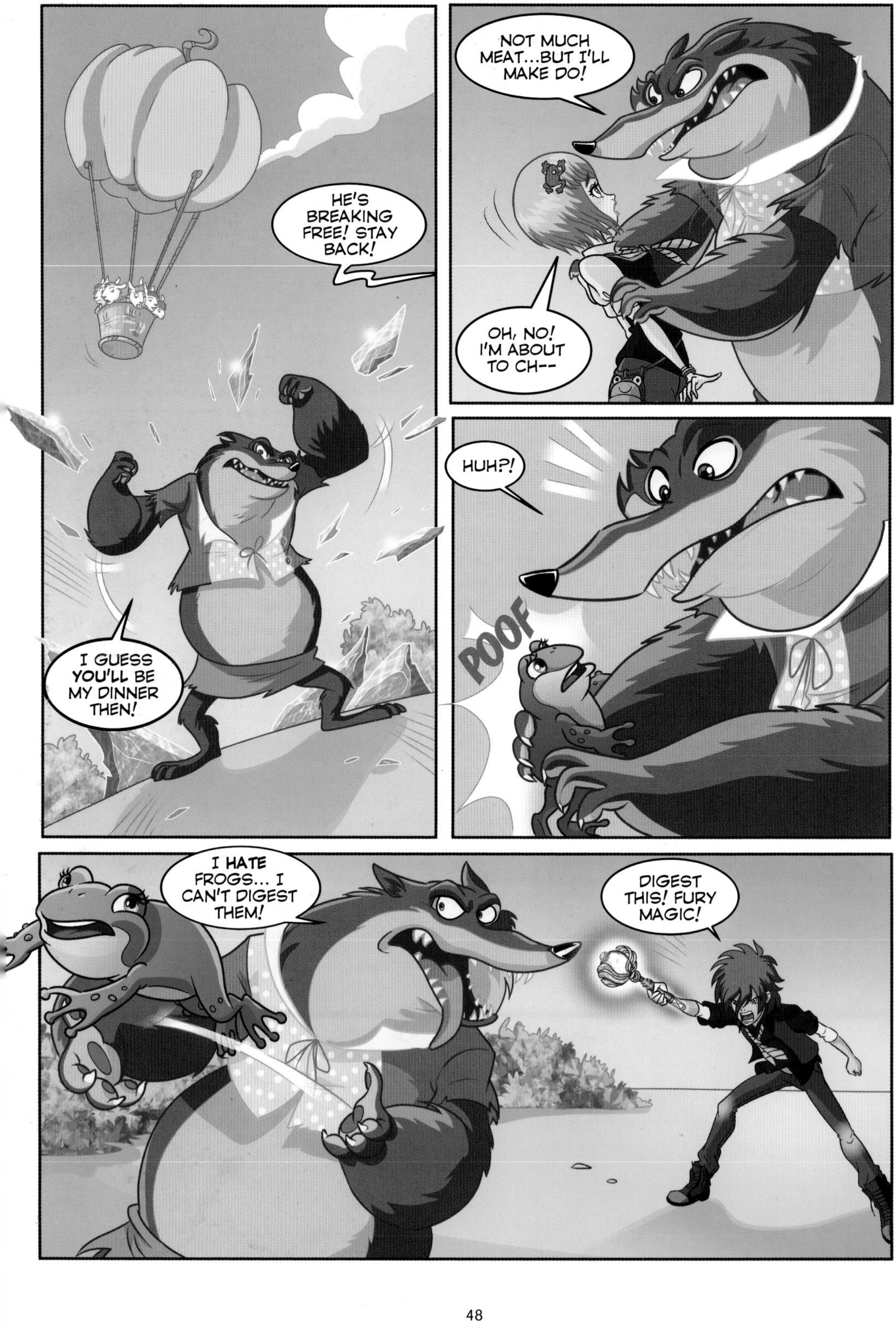
HE'S BREAKING FREE! STAY BACK!
I GUESS YOU'LL BE MY DINNER THEN!
NOT MUCH MEAT...BUT I'LL MAKE DO!
OH, NO! I'M ABOUT TO CH--
HUH?!
POOF
I HATE FROGS... I CAN'T DIGEST THEM!
DIGEST THIS! FURY MAGIC!

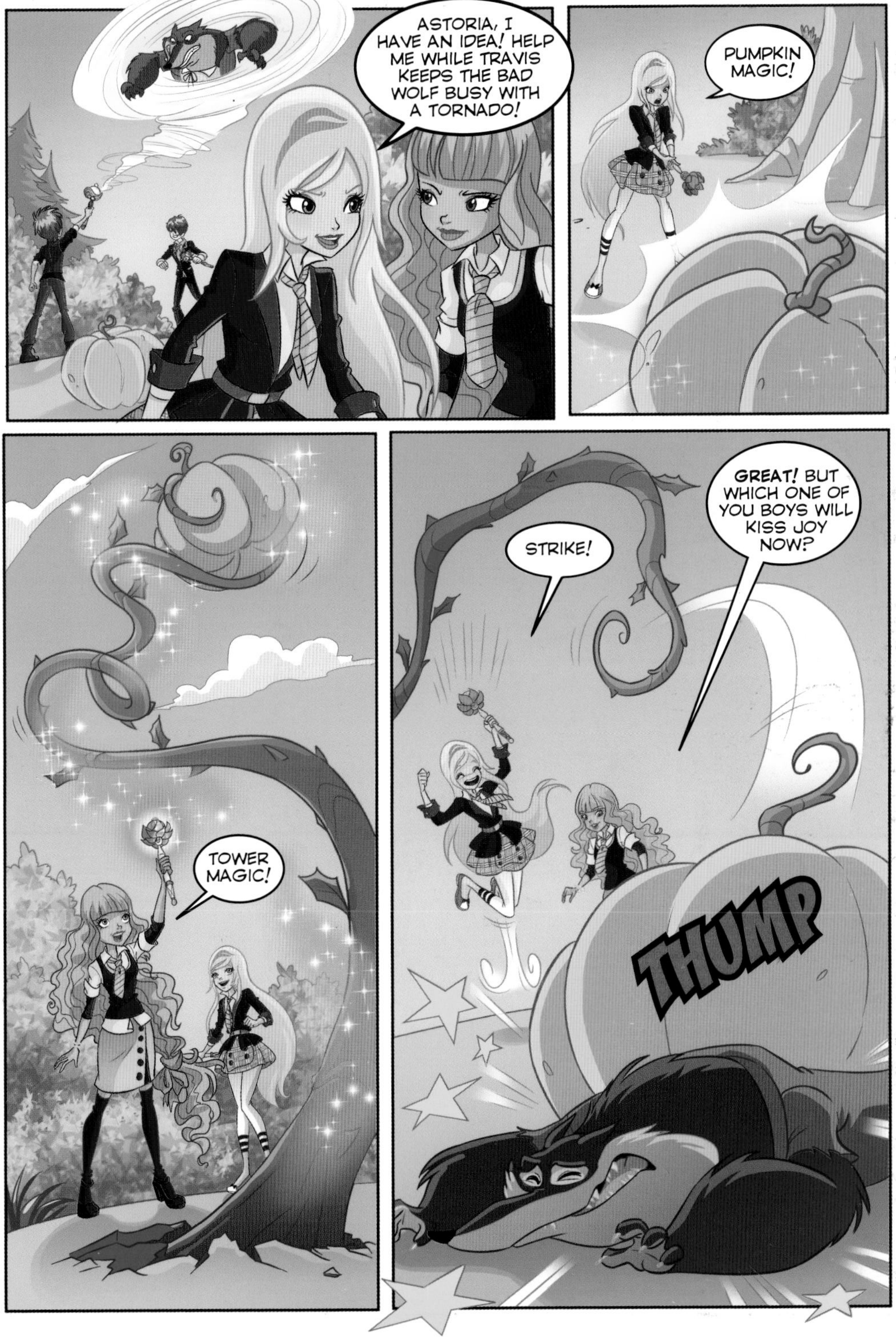
ASTORIA, I HAVE AN IDEA! HELP ME WHILE TRAVIS KEEPS THE BAD WOLF BUSY WITH A TORNADO!
PUMPKIN MAGIC!
TOWER MAGIC!
STRIKE!
GREAT! BUT WHICH ONE OF YOU BOYS WILL KISS JOY NOW?
THUMP

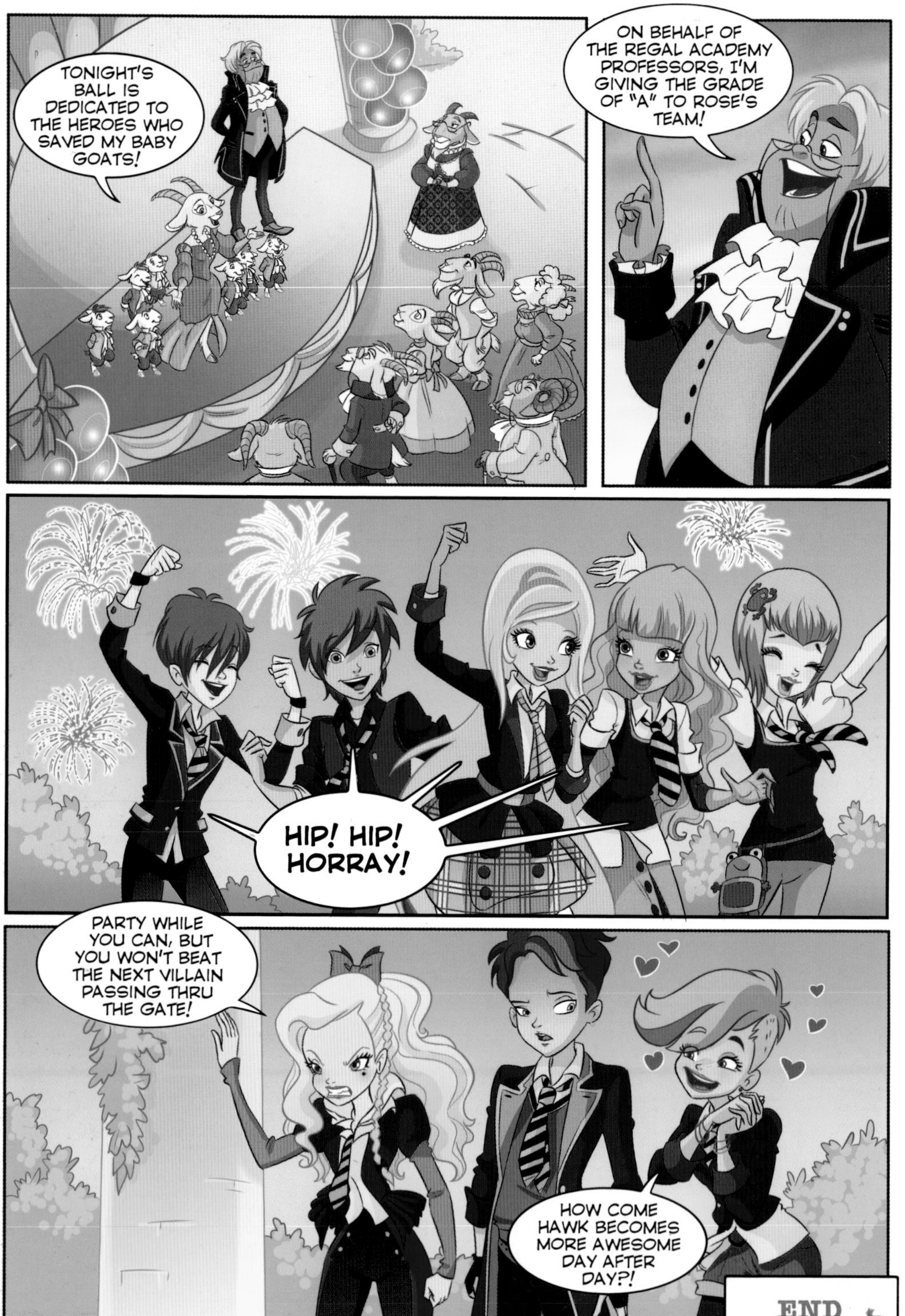
TONIGHT'S BALL IS DEDICATED TO THE HEROES WHO SAVED MY BABY GOATS!
ON BEHALF OF THE REGAL ACADEMY PROFESSORS, I'M GIVING THE GRADE OF "A" TO ROSE'S TEAM!
HIP! HIP! HORRAY!
PARTY WHILE YOU CAN, BUT YOU WON'T BEAT THE NEXT VILLAIN PASSING THRU THE GATE!
HOW COME HAWK BECOMES MORE AWESOME DAY AFTER DAY?!
END

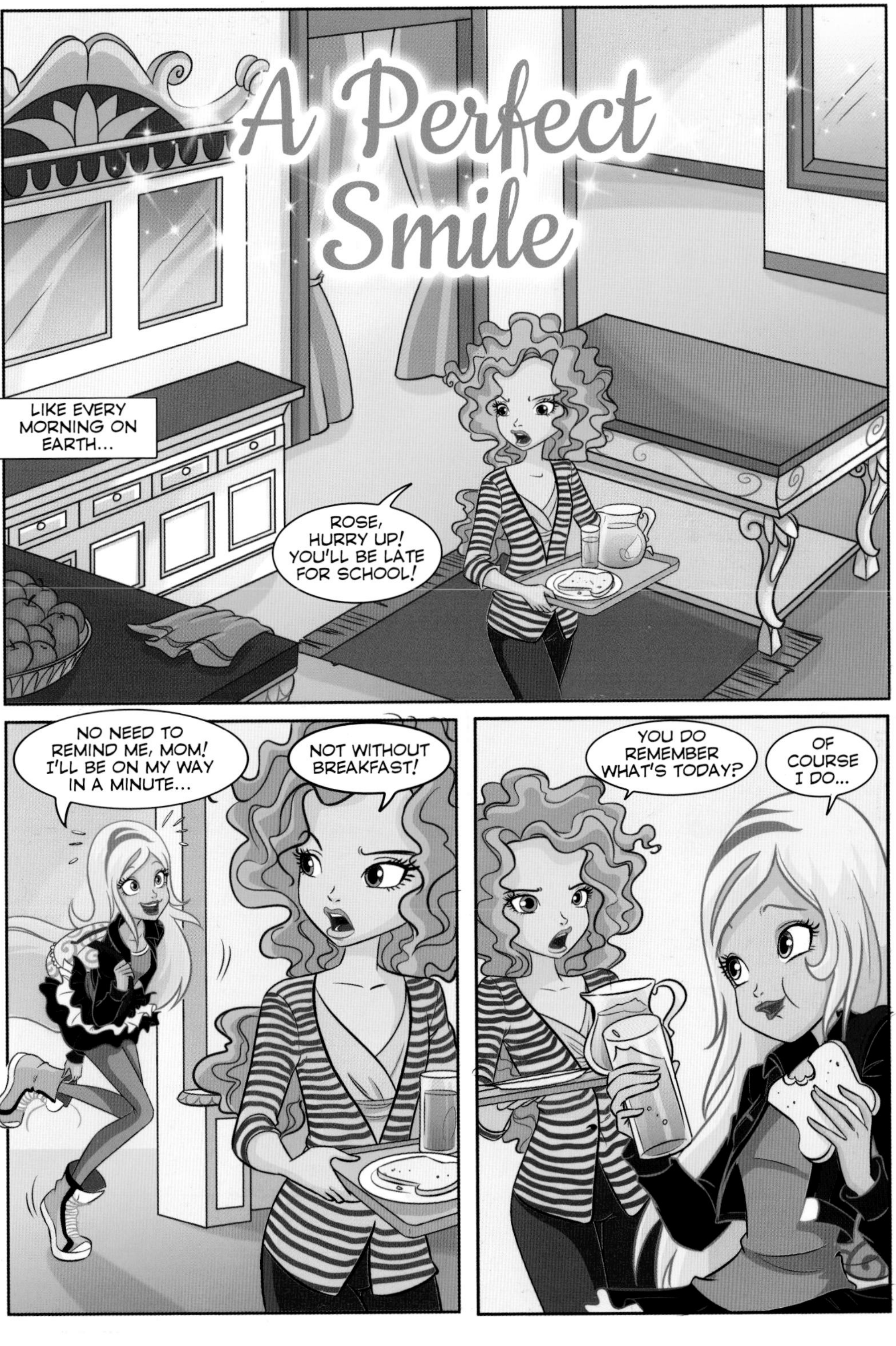
A Perfect Smile
LIKE EVERY MORNING ON EARTH...
ROSE, HURRY UP! YOU'LL BE LATE FOR SCHOOL!
NO NEED TO REMIND ME, MOM! I'LL BE ON MY WAY IN A MINUTE...
NOT WITHOUT BREAKFAST!
YOU DO REMEMBER WHAT'S TODAY?
OF COURSE I DO...

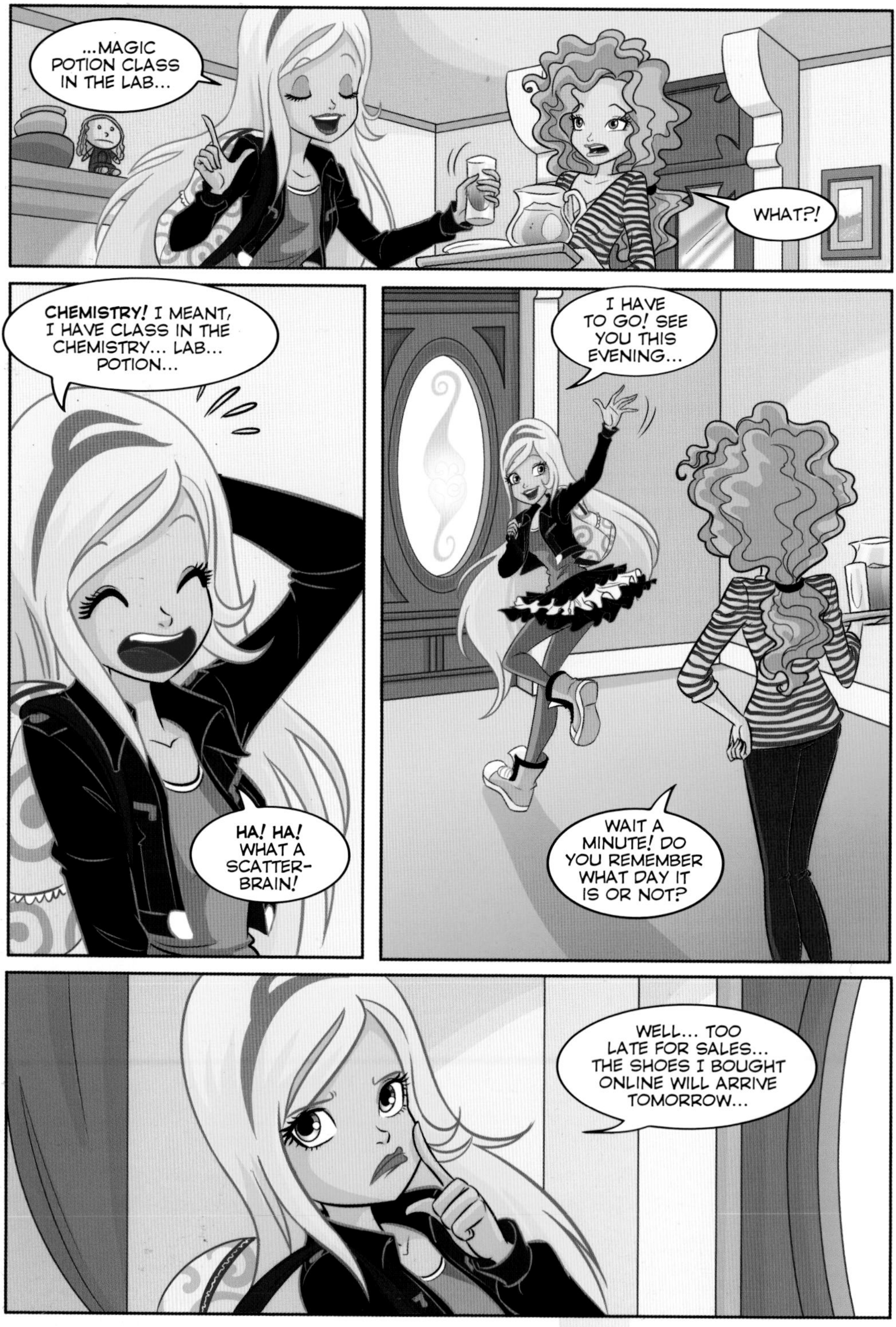
...MAGIC POTION CLASS IN THE LAB...
WHAT?!
CHEMISTRY! I MEANT, I HAVE CLASS IN THE CHEMISTRY... LAB... POTION...
HA! HA! WHAT A SCATTER-BRAIN!
I HAVE TO GO! SEE YOU THIS EVENING...
WAIT A MINUTE! DO YOU REMEMBER WHAT DAY IT IS OR NOT?
WELL... TOO LATE FOR SALES... THE SHOES I BOUGHT ONLINE WILL ARRIVE TOMORROW...

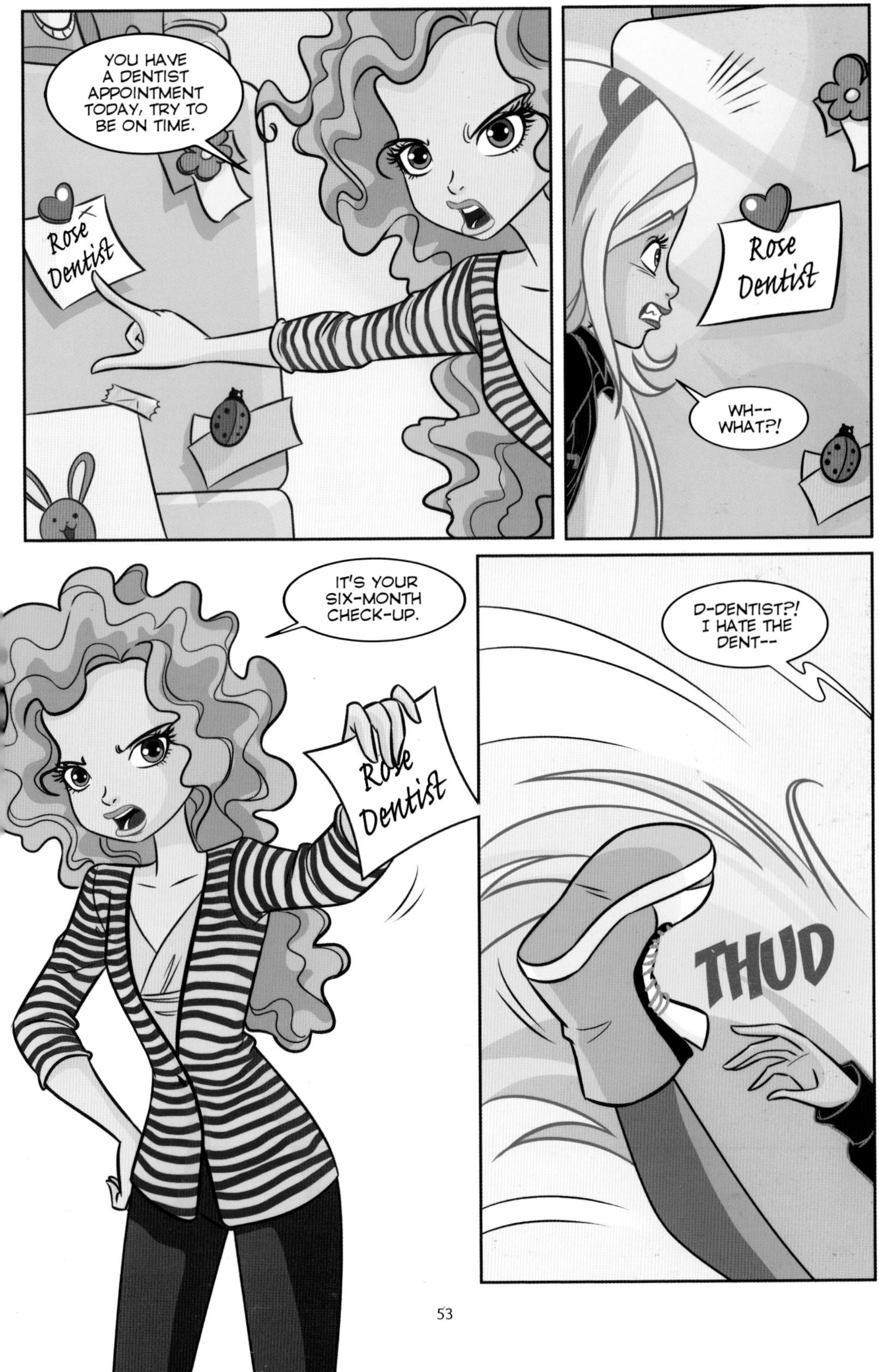
YOU HAVE A DENTIST APPOINTMENT TODAY, TRY TO BE ON TIME.
Rose Dentist
Rose Dentist
WH-- WHAT?!
IT'S YOUR SIX-MONTH CHECK-UP.
Rose Dentist
D-DENTIST?! I HATE THE DENT--
THUD

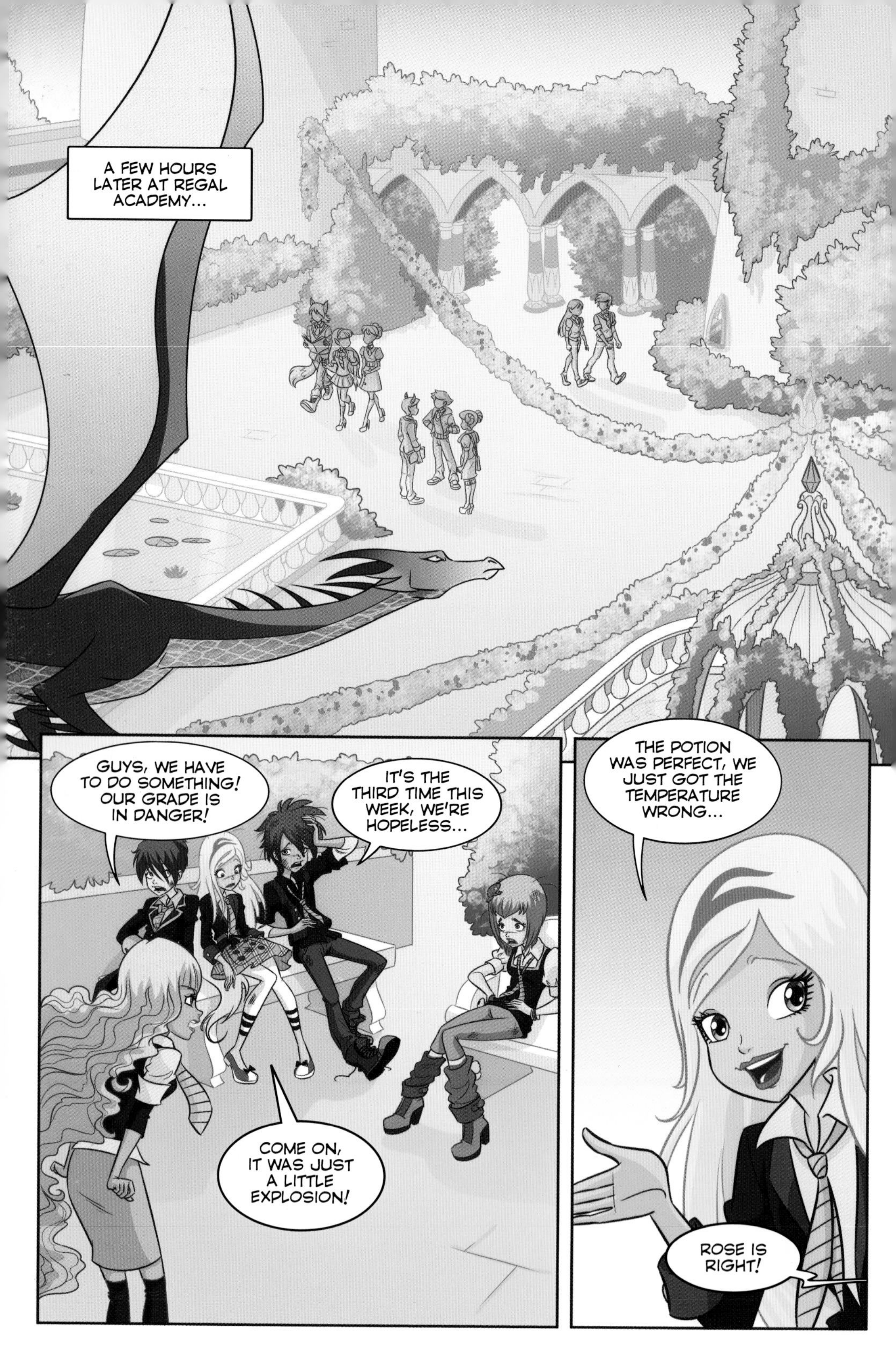
A FEW HOURS LATER AT REGAL ACADEMY...
GUYS, WE HAVE TO DO SOMETHING! OUR GRADE IS IN DANGER!
IT'S THE THIRD TIME THIS WEEK, WE'RE HOPELESS...
COME ON, IT WAS JUST A LITTLE EXPLOSION!
THE POTION WAS PERFECT, WE JUST GOT THE TEMPERATURE WRONG...
ROSE IS RIGHT!

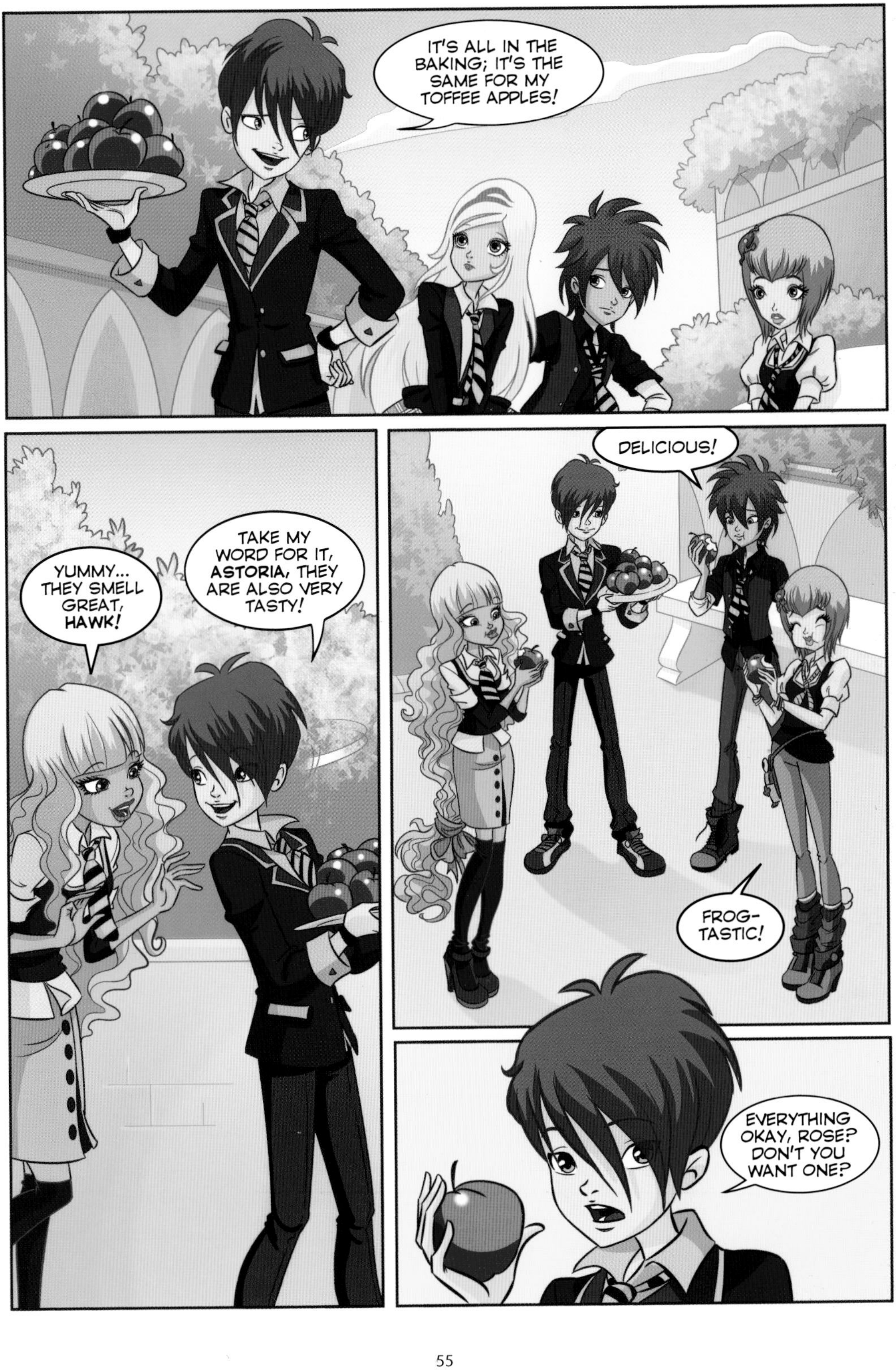
IT'S ALL IN THE BAKING; IT'S THE SAME FOR MY TOFFEE APPLES!
YUMMY... THEY SMELL GREAT, **HAWK**!
TAKE MY WORD FOR IT, **ASTORIA**, THEY ARE ALSO VERY TASTY!
DELICIOUS!
FROG-TASTIC!
EVERYTHING OKAY, ROSE? DON'T YOU WANT ONE?

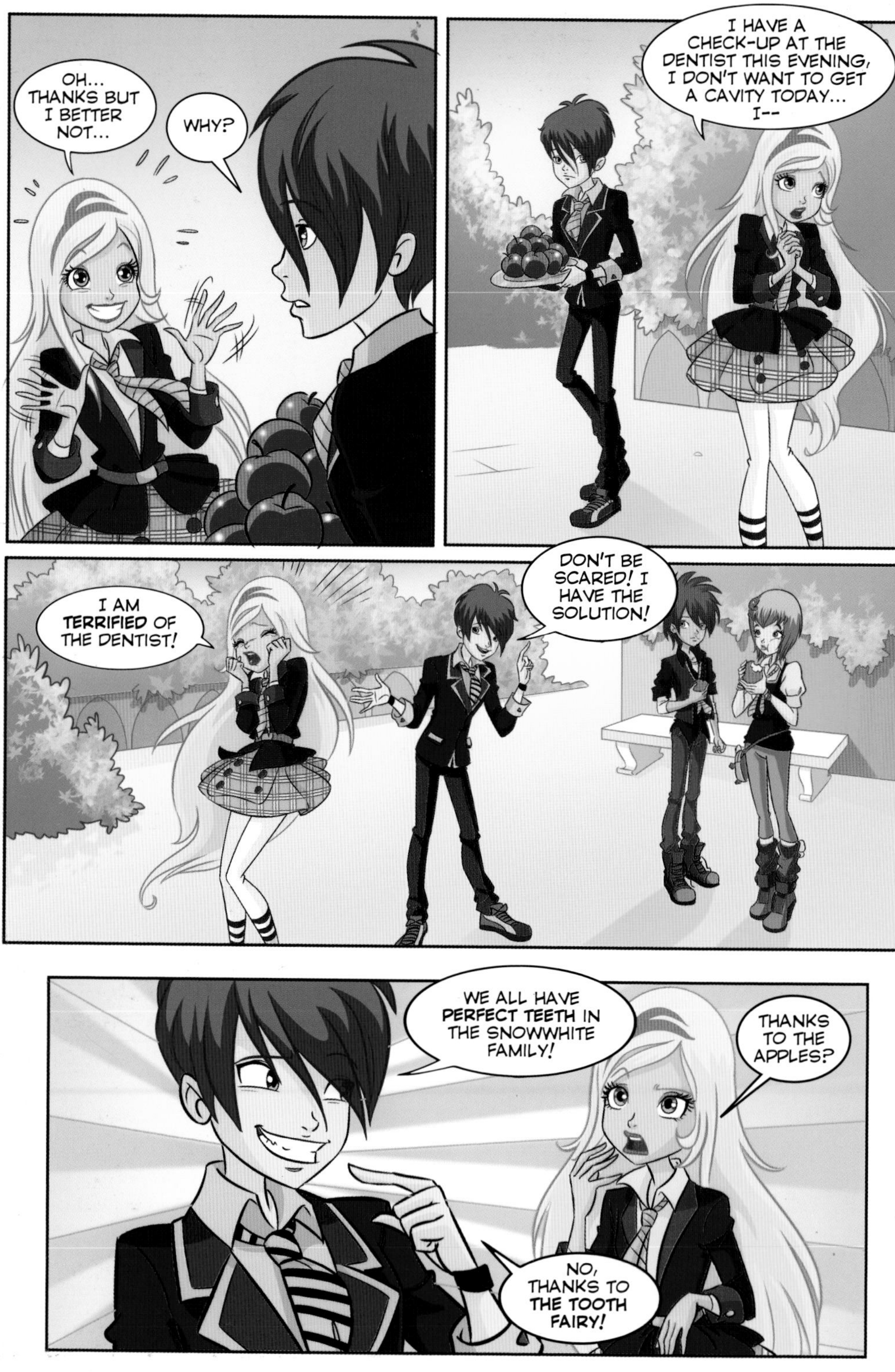
OH... THANKS BUT I BETTER NOT...
WHY?
I HAVE A CHECK-UP AT THE DENTIST THIS EVENING, I DON'T WANT TO GET A CAVITY TODAY... I--
I AM TERRIFIED OF THE DENTIST!
DON'T BE SCARED! I HAVE THE SOLUTION!
WE ALL HAVE PERFECT TEETH IN THE SNOWWHITE FAMILY!
THANKS TO THE APPLES?
NO, THANKS TO THE TOOTH FAIRY!

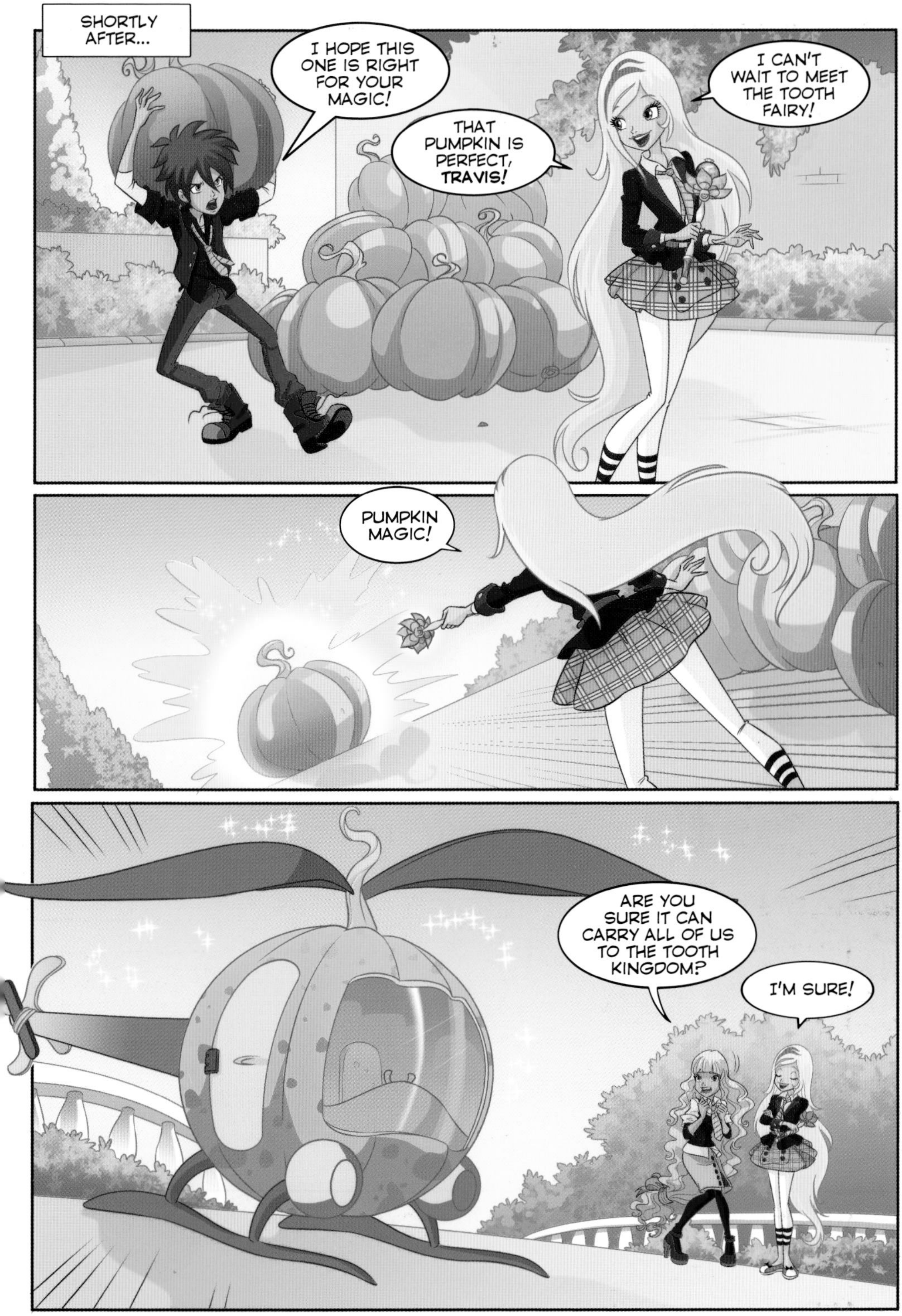
SHORTLY AFTER...
I HOPE THIS ONE IS RIGHT FOR YOUR MAGIC!
THAT PUMPKIN IS PERFECT, **TRAVIS!**
I CAN'T WAIT TO MEET THE TOOTH FAIRY!
PUMPKIN MAGIC!
ARE YOU SURE IT CAN CARRY ALL OF US TO THE TOOTH KINGDOM?
I'M SURE!

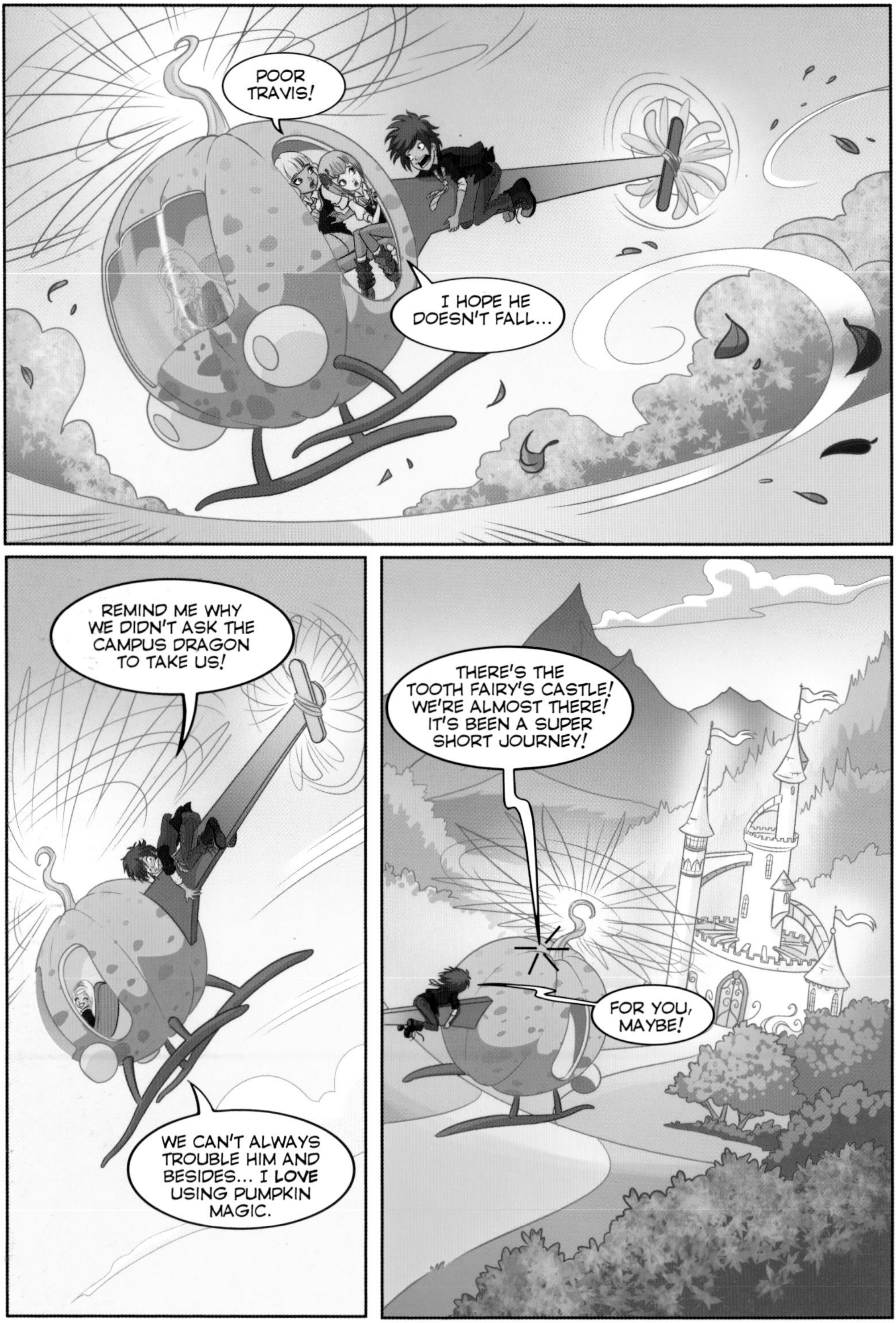
POOR TRAVIS!
I HOPE HE DOESN'T FALL...
REMIND ME WHY WE DIDN'T ASK THE CAMPUS DRAGON TO TAKE US!
WE CAN'T ALWAYS TROUBLE HIM AND BESIDES... I **LOVE** USING PUMPKIN MAGIC.
THERE'S THE TOOTH FAIRY'S CASTLE! WE'RE ALMOST THERE! IT'S BEEN A SUPER SHORT JOURNEY!
FOR YOU, MAYBE!

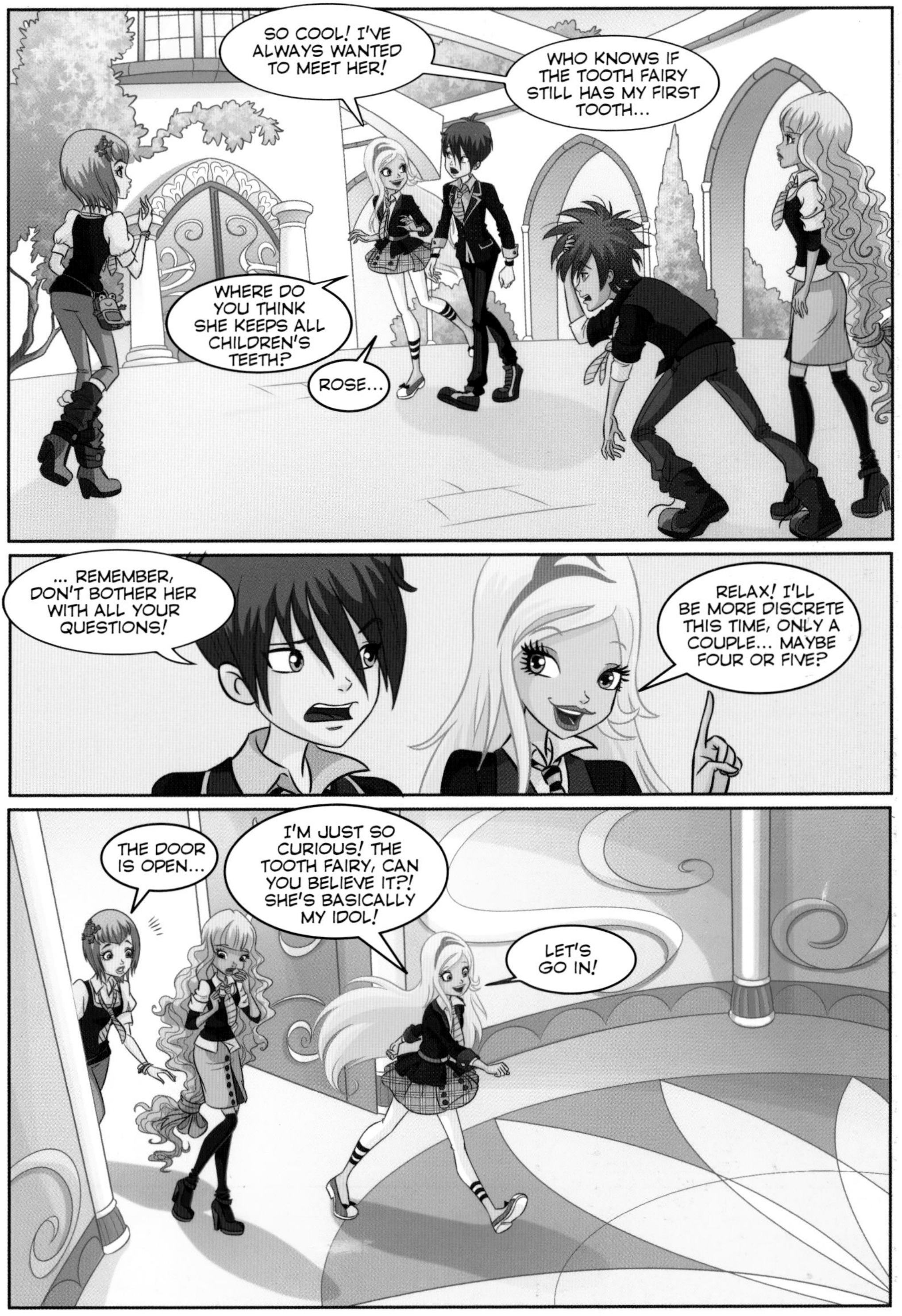

SO COOL! I'VE ALWAYS WANTED TO MEET HER!
WHO KNOWS IF THE TOOTH FAIRY STILL HAS MY FIRST TOOTH...
WHERE DO YOU THINK SHE KEEPS ALL CHILDREN'S TEETH?
ROSE...
... REMEMBER, DON'T BOTHER HER WITH ALL YOUR QUESTIONS!
RELAX! I'LL BE MORE DISCRETE THIS TIME, ONLY A COUPLE... MAYBE FOUR OR FIVE?
THE DOOR IS OPEN...
I'M JUST SO CURIOUS! THE TOOTH FAIRY, CAN YOU BELIEVE IT?! SHE'S BASICALLY MY IDOL!
LET'S GO IN!

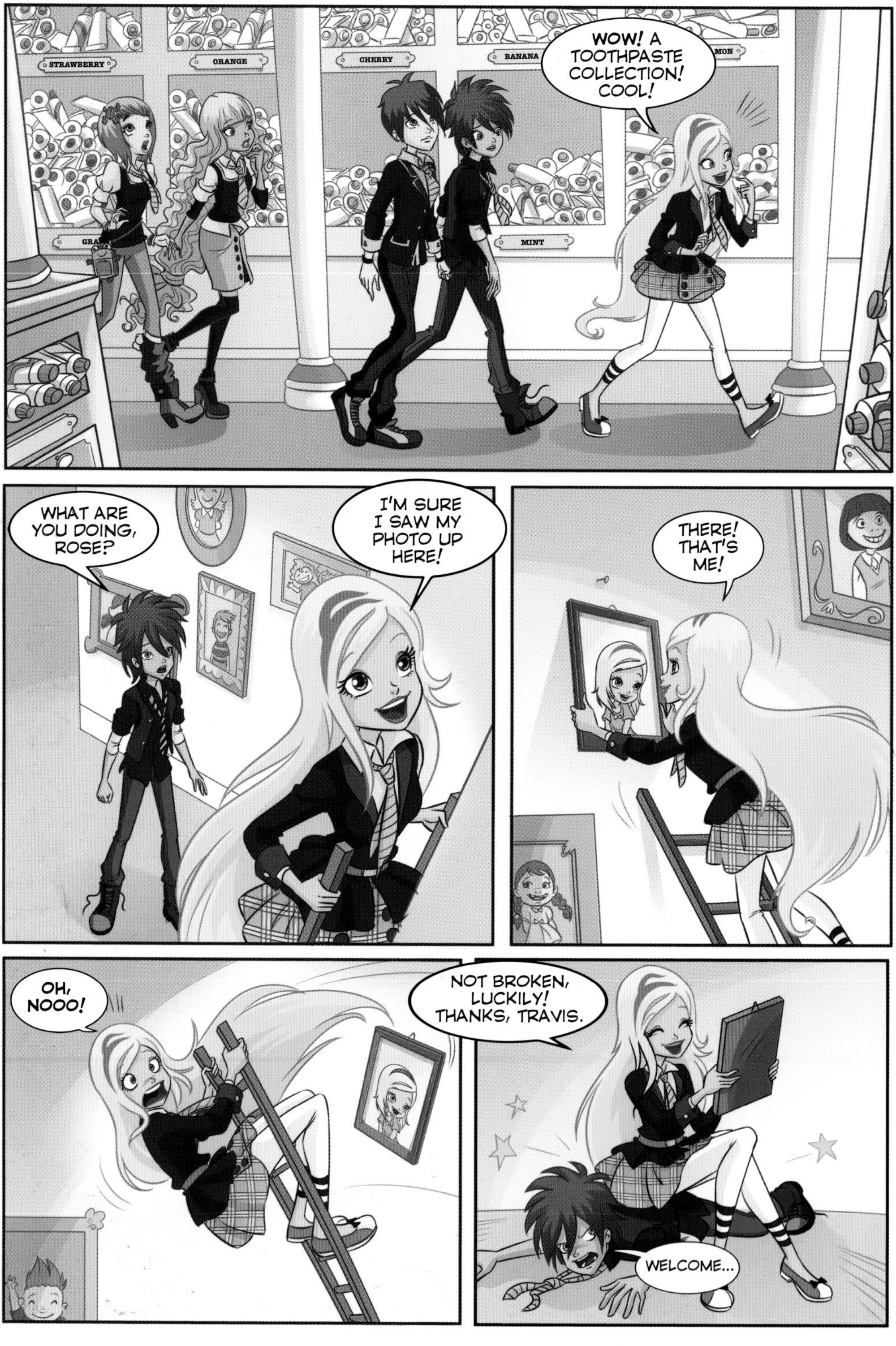
STRAWBERRY
ORANGE
CHERRY
BANANA
MINT
WOW! A TOOTHPASTE COLLECTION! COOL!
WHAT ARE YOU DOING, ROSE?
I'M SURE I SAW MY PHOTO UP HERE!
THERE! THAT'S ME!
OH, NOOO!
NOT BROKEN, LUCKILY! THANKS, TRAVIS.
WELCOME...

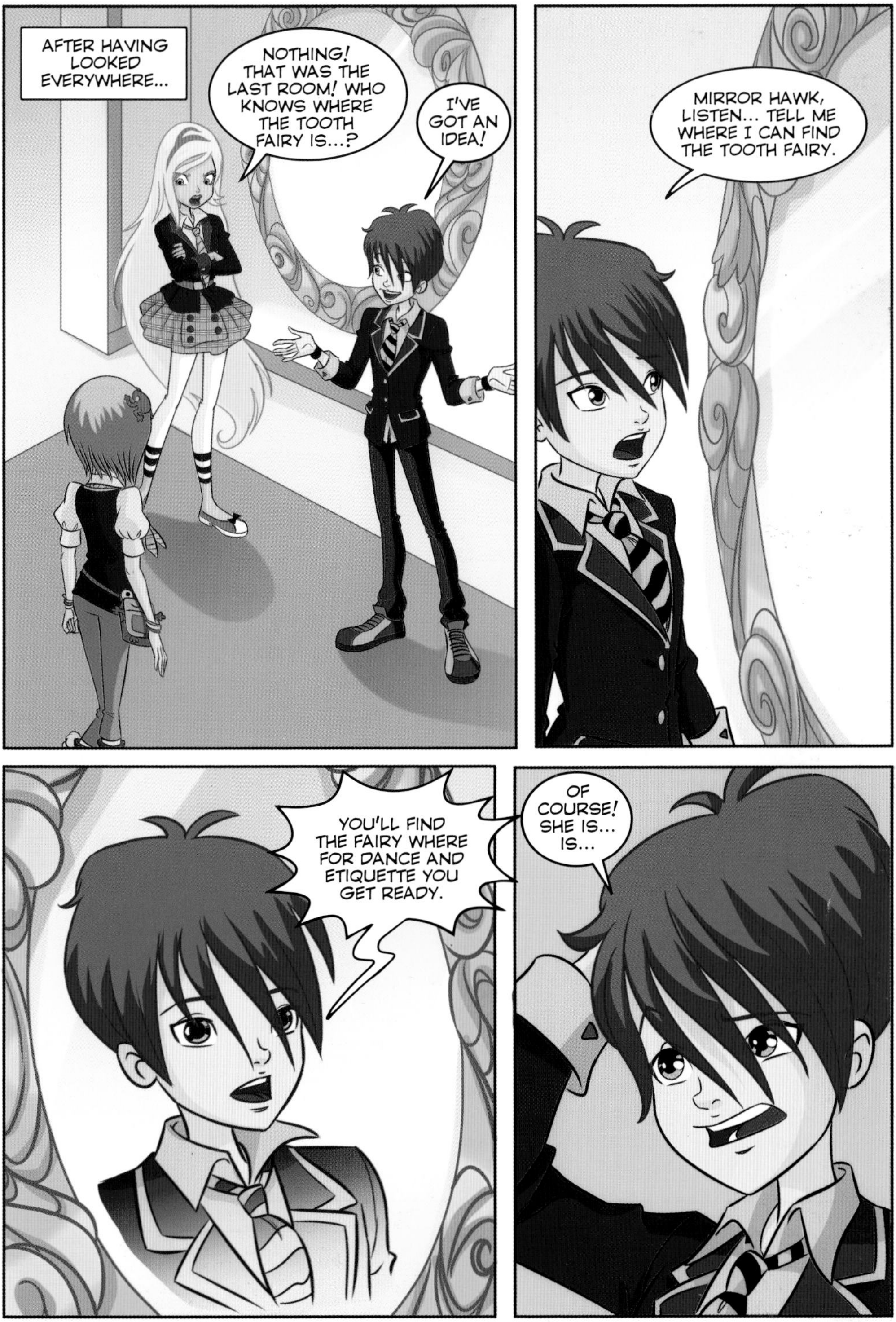
AFTER HAVING LOOKED EVERYWHERE...
NOTHING! THAT WAS THE LAST ROOM! WHO KNOWS WHERE THE TOOTH FAIRY IS...?
I'VE GOT AN IDEA!
MIRROR HAWK, LISTEN... TELL ME WHERE I CAN FIND THE TOOTH FAIRY.
YOU'LL FIND THE FAIRY WHERE FOR DANCE AND ETIQUETTE YOU GET READY.
OF COURSE! SHE IS... IS...

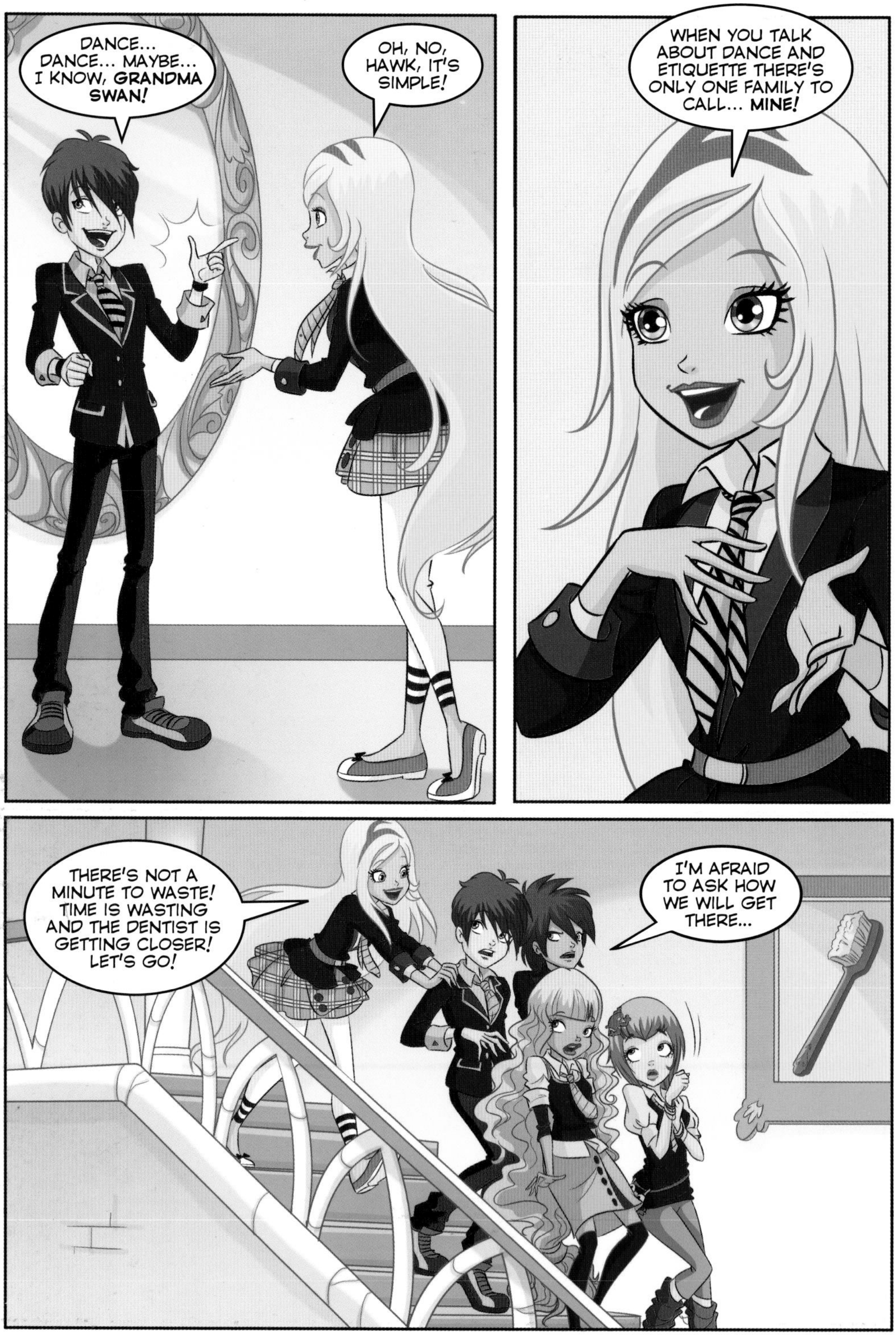
DANCE... DANCE... MAYBE... I KNOW, **GRANDMA SWAN!**
OH, NO, HAWK, IT'S SIMPLE!
WHEN YOU TALK ABOUT DANCE AND ETIQUETTE THERE'S ONLY ONE FAMILY TO CALL... **MINE!**
THERE'S NOT A MINUTE TO WASTE! TIME IS WASTING AND THE DENTIST IS GETTING CLOSER! LET'S GO!
I'M AFRAID TO ASK HOW WE WILL GET THERE...

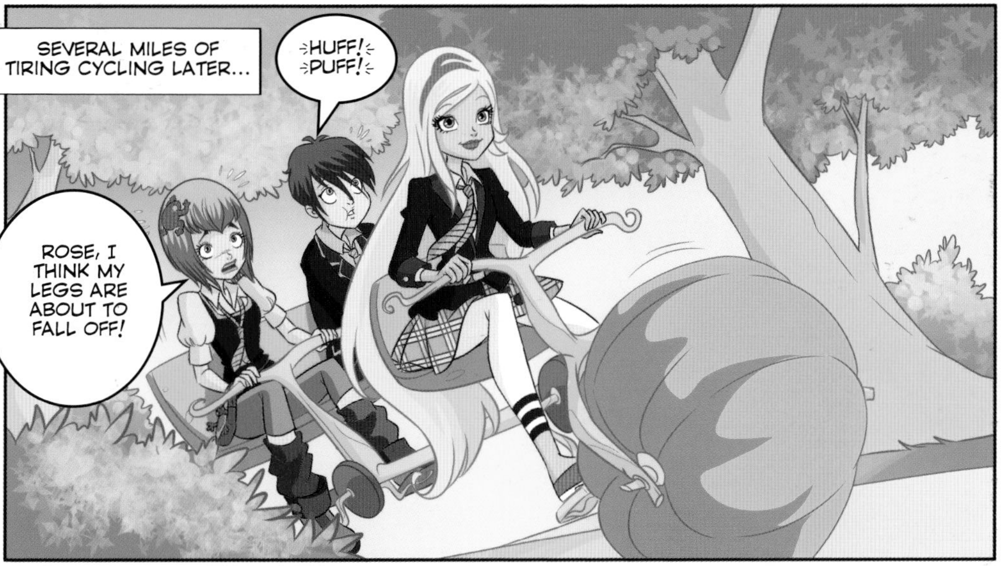
SEVERAL MILES OF TIRING CYCLING LATER...
HUFF! PUFF!
ROSE, I THINK MY LEGS ARE ABOUT TO FALL OFF!

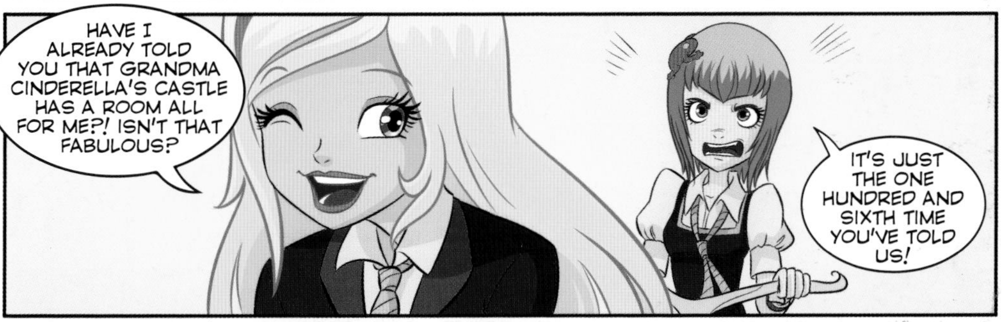
HAVE I ALREADY TOLD YOU THAT GRANDMA CINDERELLA'S CASTLE HAS A ROOM ALL FOR ME?! ISN'T THAT FABULOUS?
IT'S JUST THE ONE HUNDRED AND SIXTH TIME YOU'VE TOLD US!

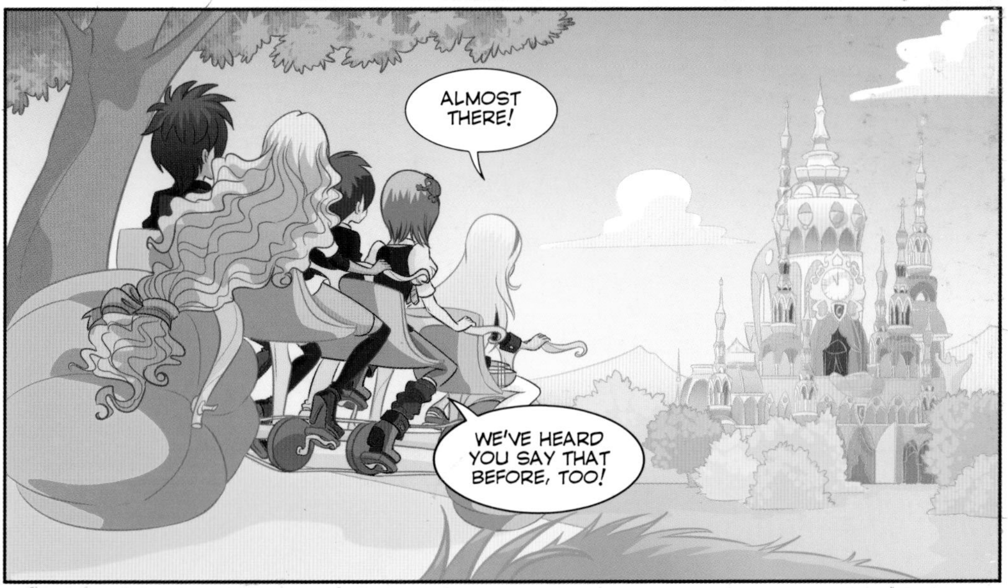
ALMOST THERE!
WE'VE HEARD YOU SAY THAT BEFORE, TOO!

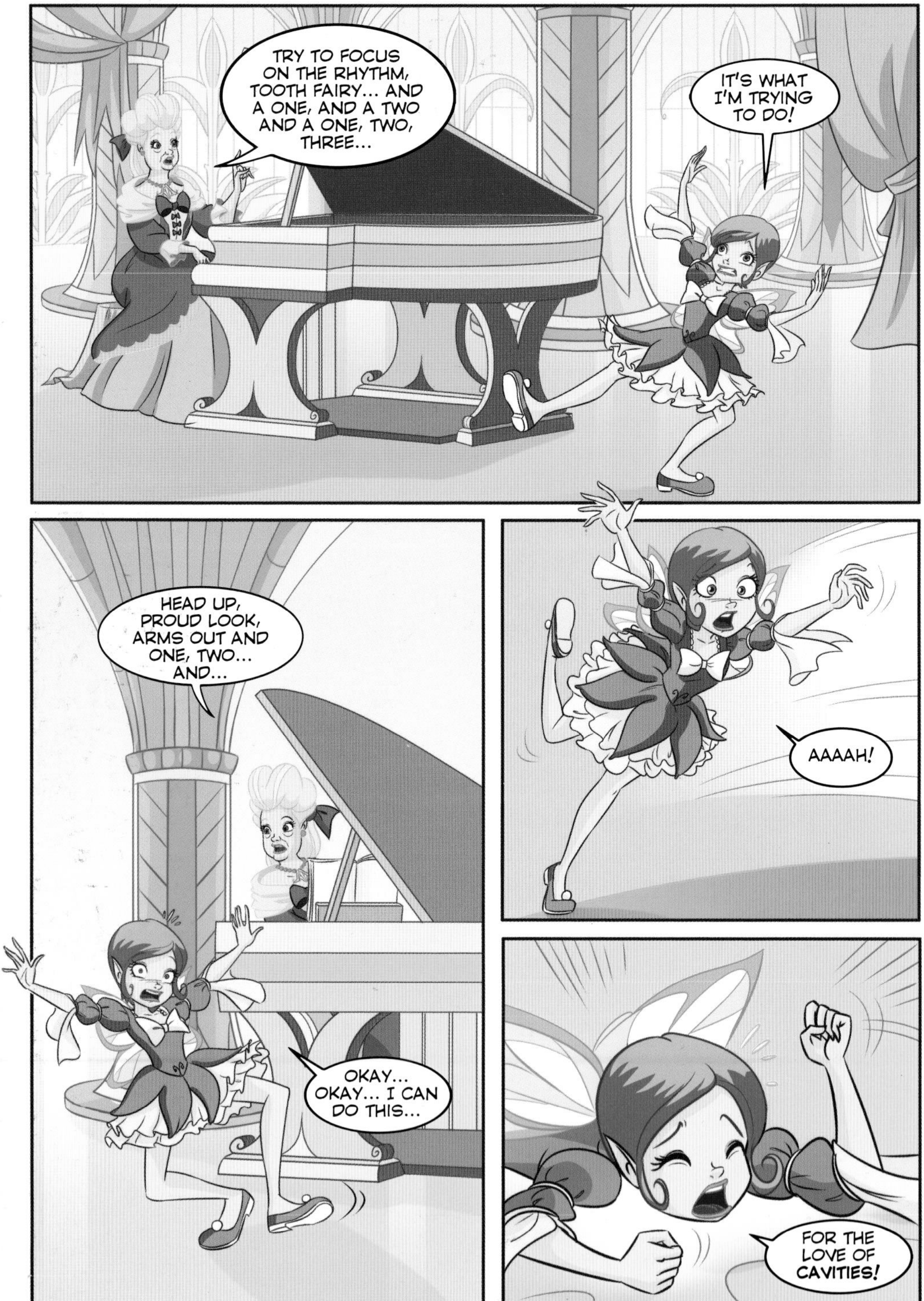

TRY TO FOCUS ON THE RHYTHM, TOOTH FAIRY... AND A ONE, AND A TWO AND A ONE, TWO, THREE...
IT'S WHAT I'M TRYING TO DO!
HEAD UP, PROUD LOOK, ARMS OUT AND ONE, TWO... AND...
OKAY... OKAY... I CAN DO THIS...
AAAAH!
FOR THE LOVE OF CAVITIES!

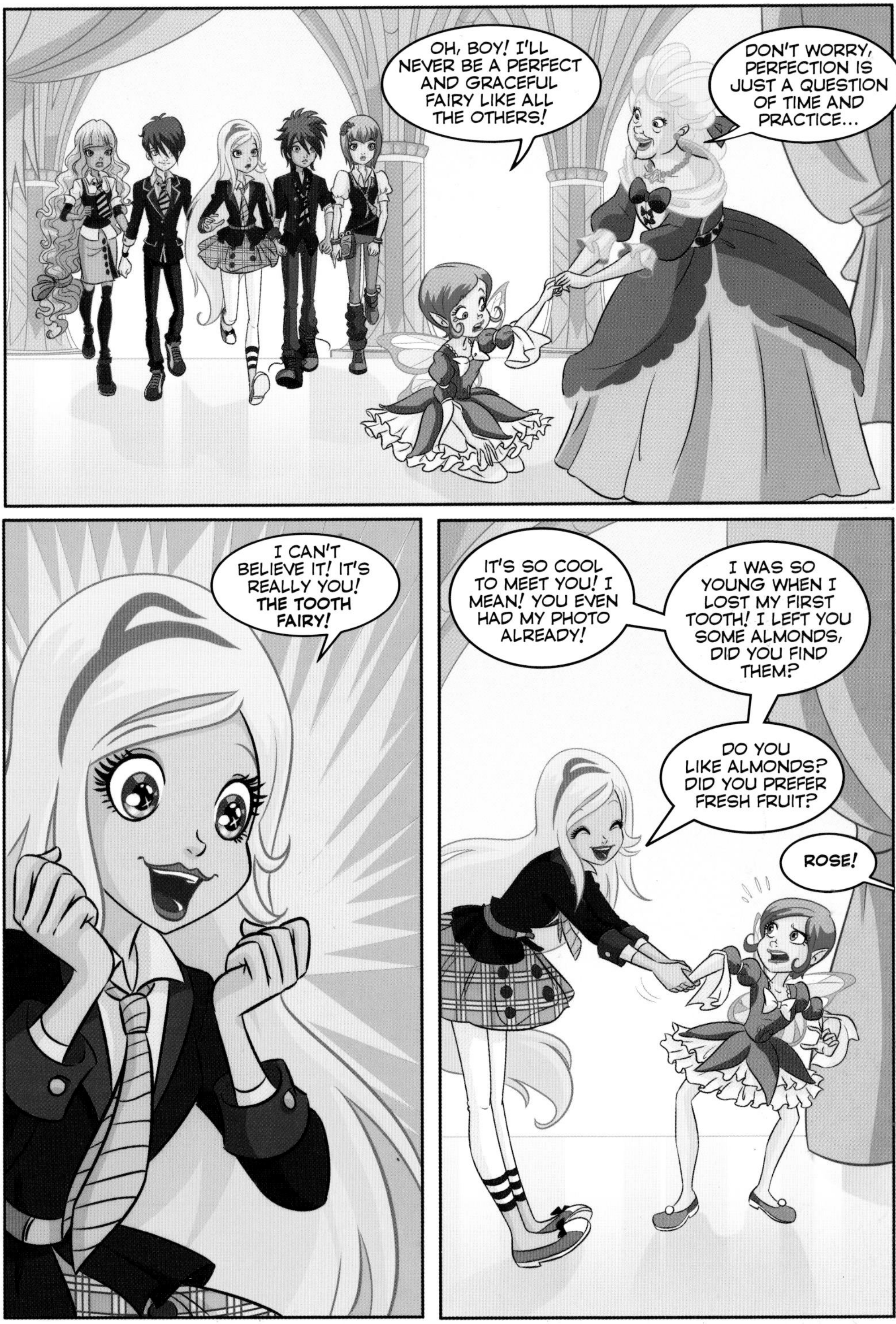

OH, BOY! I'LL NEVER BE A PERFECT AND GRACEFUL FAIRY LIKE ALL THE OTHERS!
DON'T WORRY, PERFECTION IS JUST A QUESTION OF TIME AND PRACTICE...
I CAN'T BELIEVE IT! IT'S REALLY YOU! THE TOOTH FAIRY!
IT'S SO COOL TO MEET YOU! I MEAN! YOU EVEN HAD MY PHOTO ALREADY!
I WAS SO YOUNG WHEN I LOST MY FIRST TOOTH! I LEFT YOU SOME ALMONDS, DID YOU FIND THEM?
DO YOU LIKE ALMONDS? DID YOU PREFER FRESH FRUIT?
ROSE!

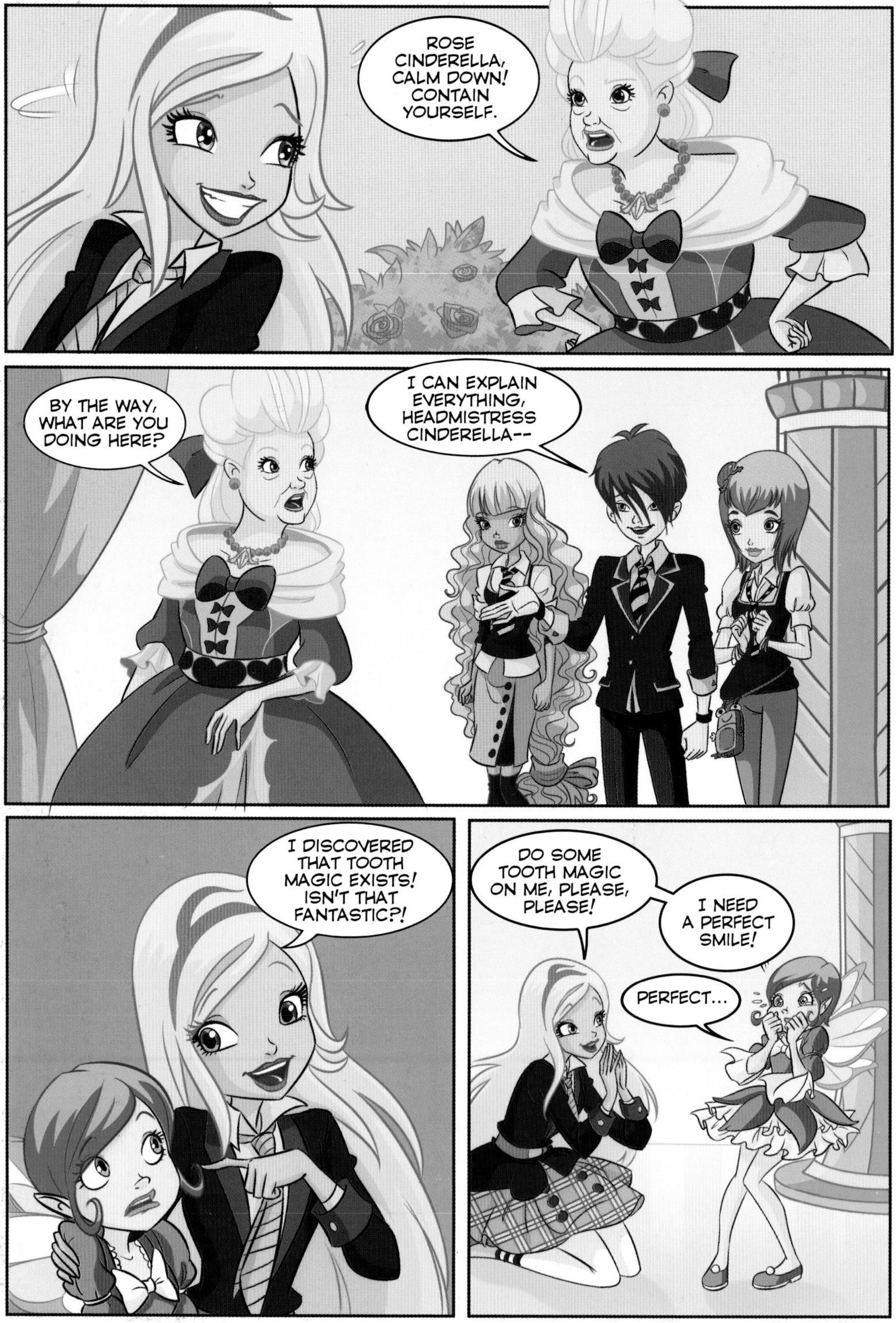
ROSE CINDERELLA, CALM DOWN! CONTAIN YOURSELF.
BY THE WAY, WHAT ARE YOU DOING HERE?
I CAN EXPLAIN EVERYTHING, HEADMISTRESS CINDERELLA--
I DISCOVERED THAT TOOTH MAGIC EXISTS! ISN'T THAT FANTASTIC?!
DO SOME TOOTH MAGIC ON ME, PLEASE, PLEASE!
I NEED A PERFECT SMILE!
PERFECT...

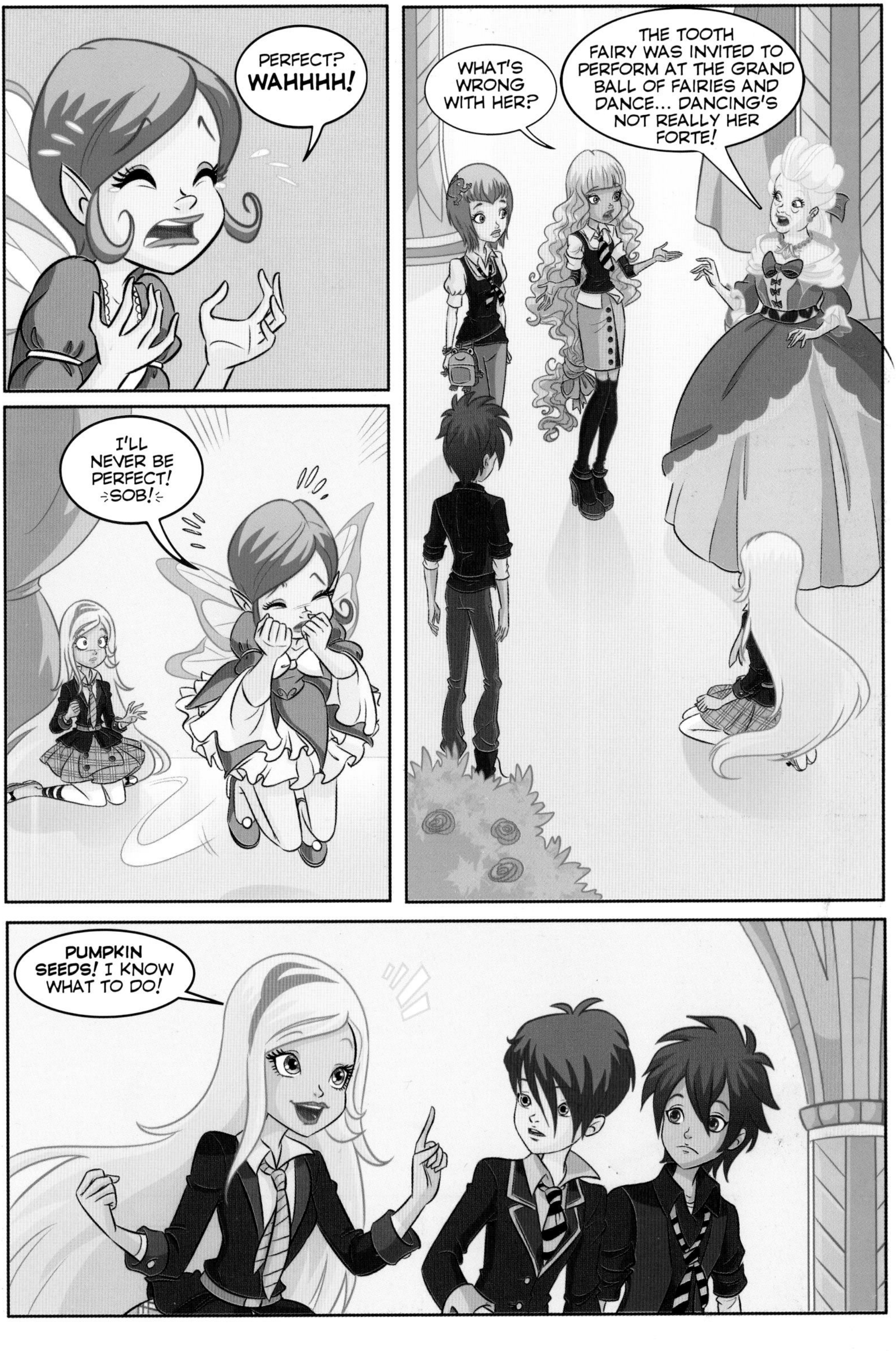
PERFECT? **WAHHHH!**
WHAT'S WRONG WITH HER?
THE TOOTH FAIRY WAS INVITED TO PERFORM AT THE GRAND BALL OF FAIRIES AND DANCE... DANCING'S NOT REALLY HER FORTE!
I'LL NEVER BE PERFECT! SOB!
PUMPKIN SEEDS! I KNOW WHAT TO DO!

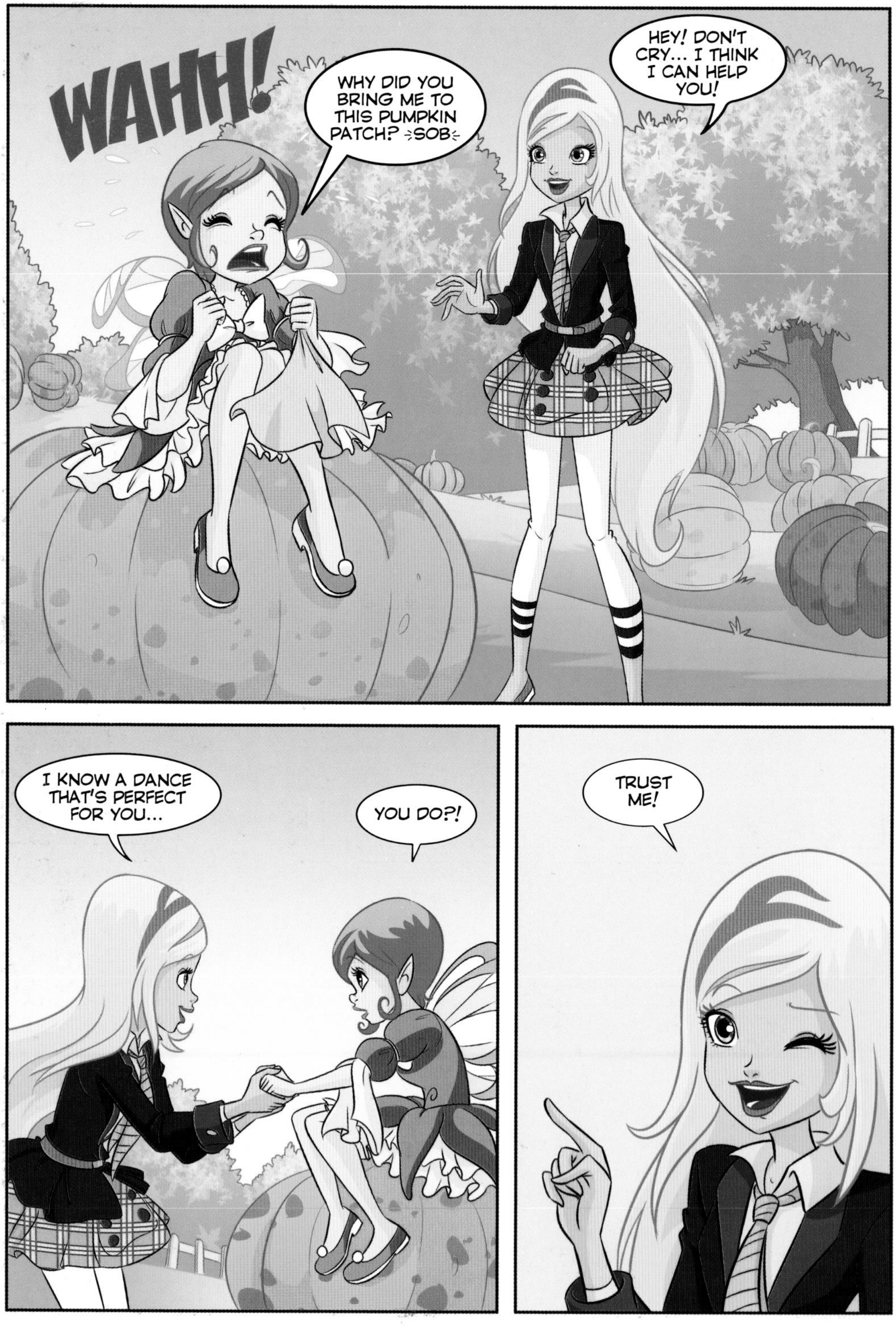
WAHH!
WHY DID YOU BRING ME TO THIS PUMPKIN PATCH? ≑SOB≑
HEY! DON'T CRY... I THINK I CAN HELP YOU!
I KNOW A DANCE THAT'S PERFECT FOR YOU...
YOU DO?!
TRUST ME!

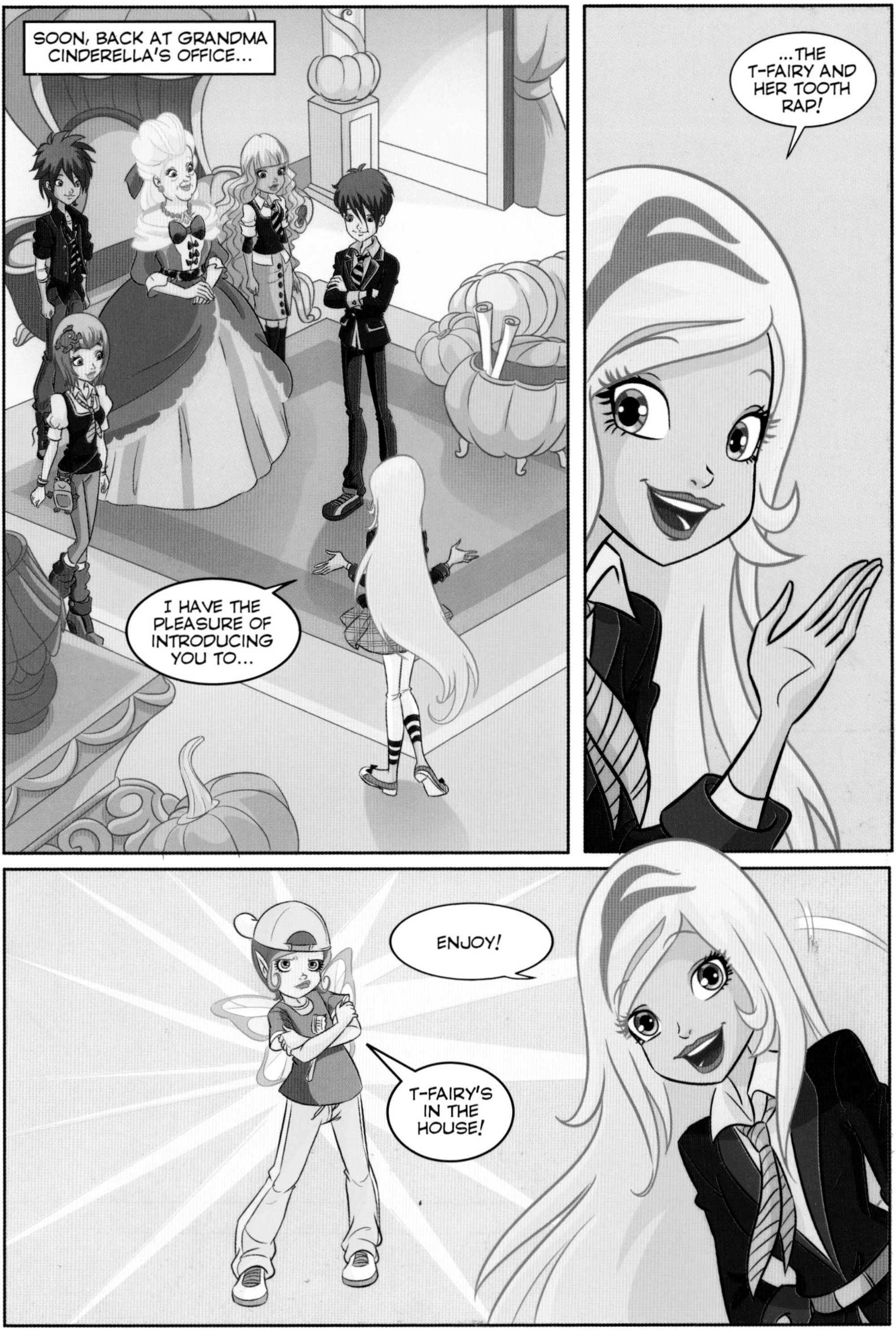
SOON, BACK AT GRANDMA CINDERELLA'S OFFICE...
I HAVE THE PLEASURE OF INTRODUCING YOU TO...
...THE T-FAIRY AND HER TOOTH RAP!
ENJOY!
T-FAIRY'S IN THE HOUSE!

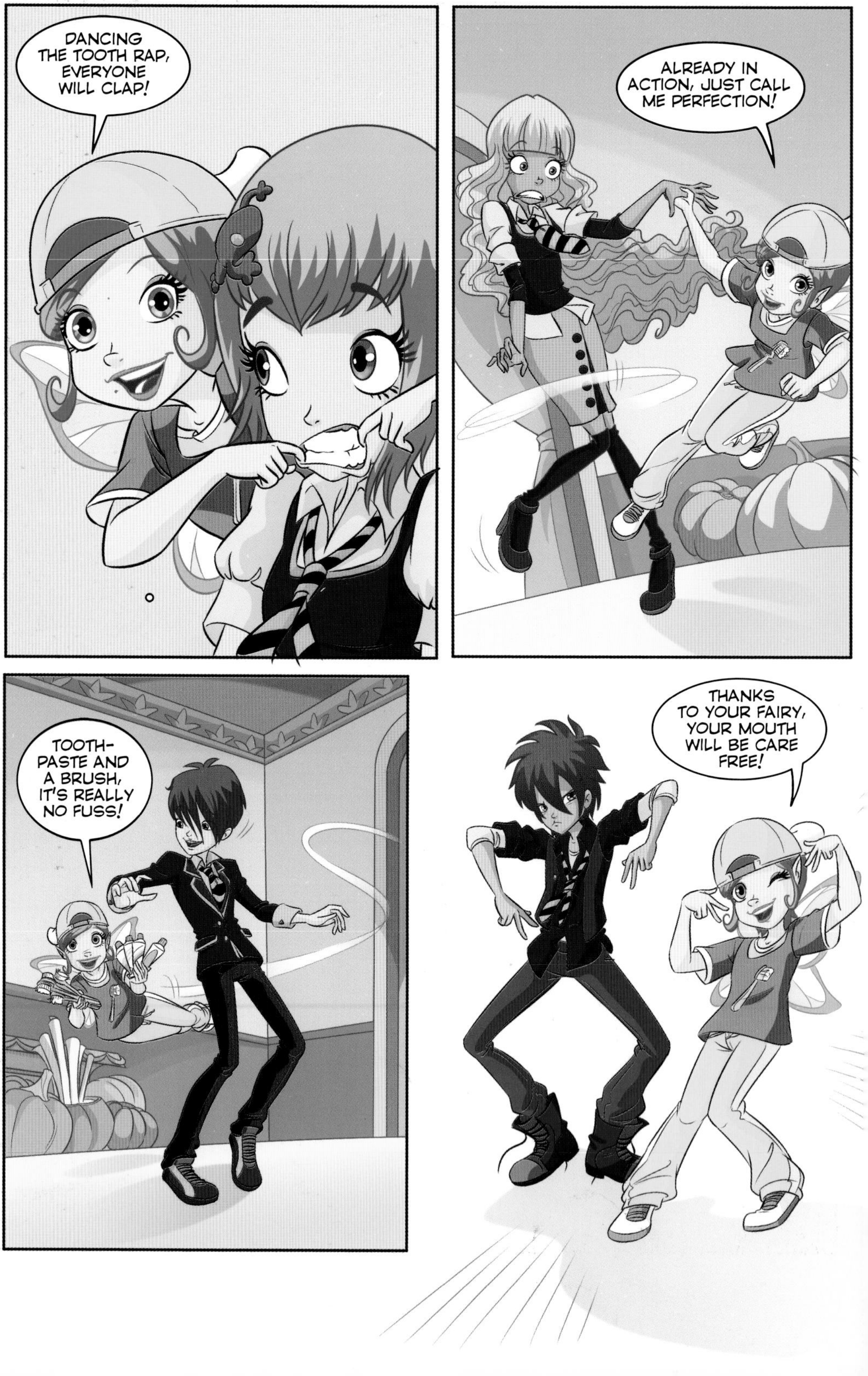
DANCING THE TOOTH RAP, EVERYONE WILL CLAP!
ALREADY IN ACTION, JUST CALL ME PERFECTION!
TOOTH-PASTE AND A BRUSH, IT'S REALLY NO FUSS!
THANKS TO YOUR FAIRY, YOUR MOUTH WILL BE CARE FREE!

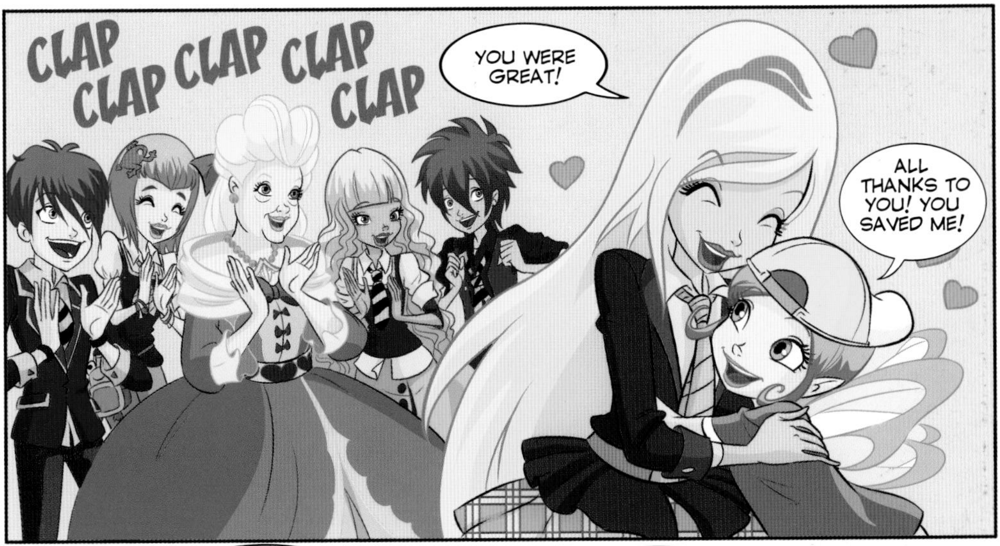
CLAP
CLAP CLAP CLAP
CLAP
YOU WERE GREAT!
ALL THANKS TO YOU! YOU SAVED ME!

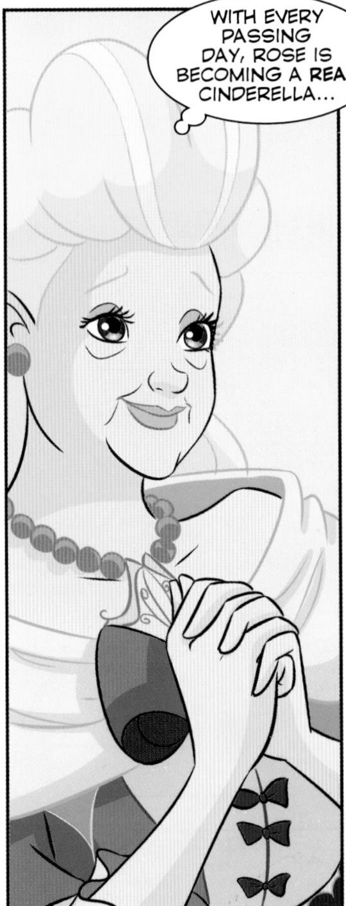
WITH EVERY PASSING DAY, ROSE IS BECOMING A **REAL** CINDERELLA...

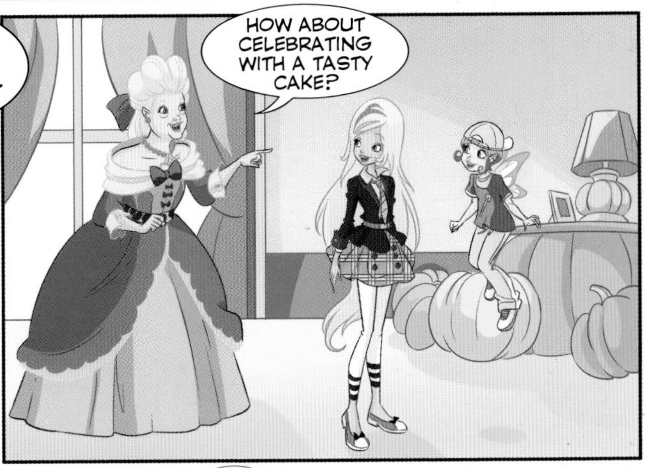
HOW ABOUT CELEBRATING WITH A TASTY CAKE?

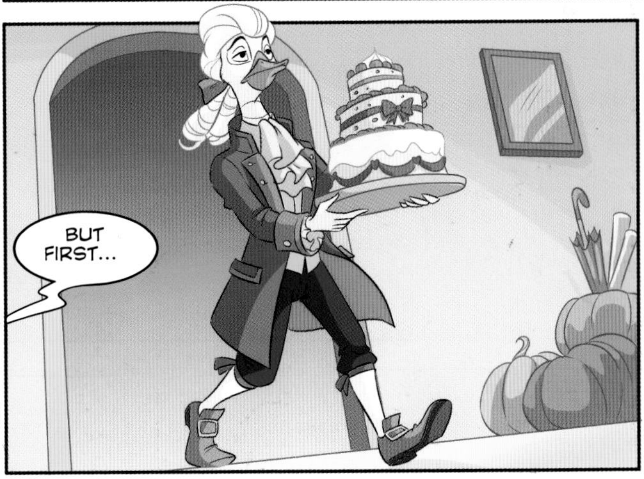
BUT FIRST...

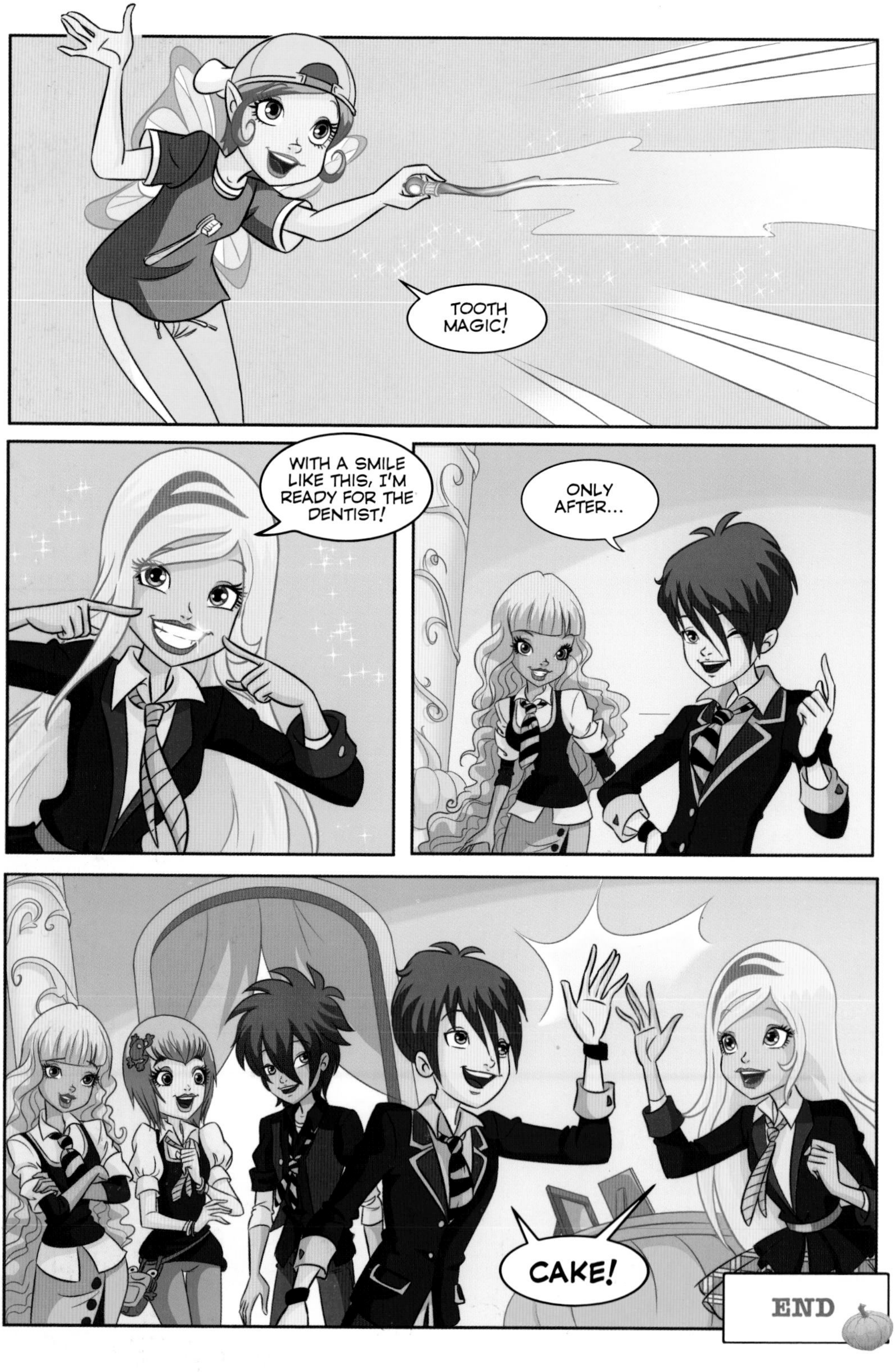
TOOTH MAGIC!
WITH A SMILE LIKE THIS, I'M READY FOR THE DENTIST!
ONLY AFTER...
CAKE!
END

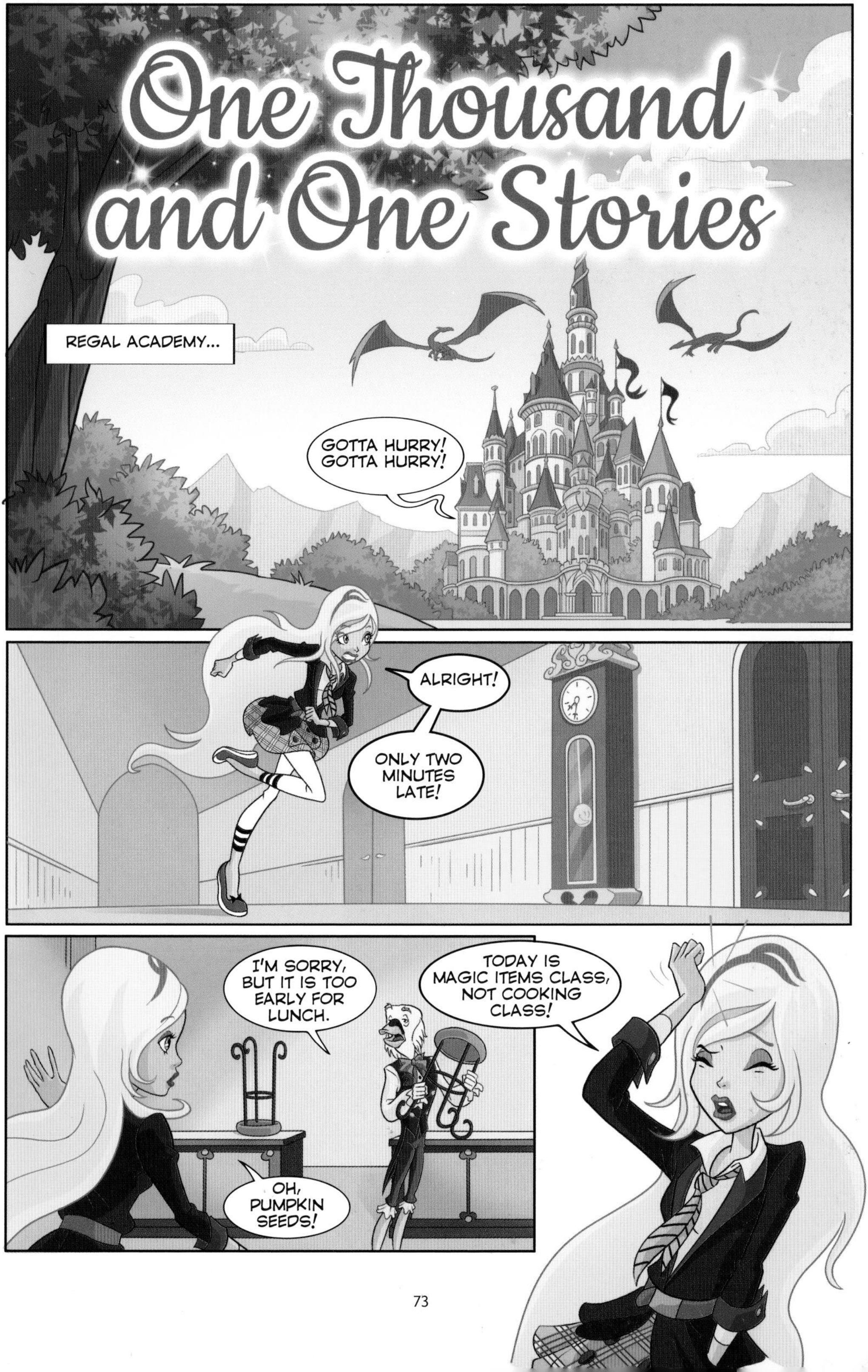
One Thousand and One Stories
REGAL ACADEMY...
GOTTA HURRY! GOTTA HURRY!
ALRIGHT!
ONLY TWO MINUTES LATE!
I'M SORRY, BUT IT IS TOO EARLY FOR LUNCH.
OH, PUMPKIN SEEDS!
TODAY IS MAGIC ITEMS CLASS, NOT COOKING CLASS!

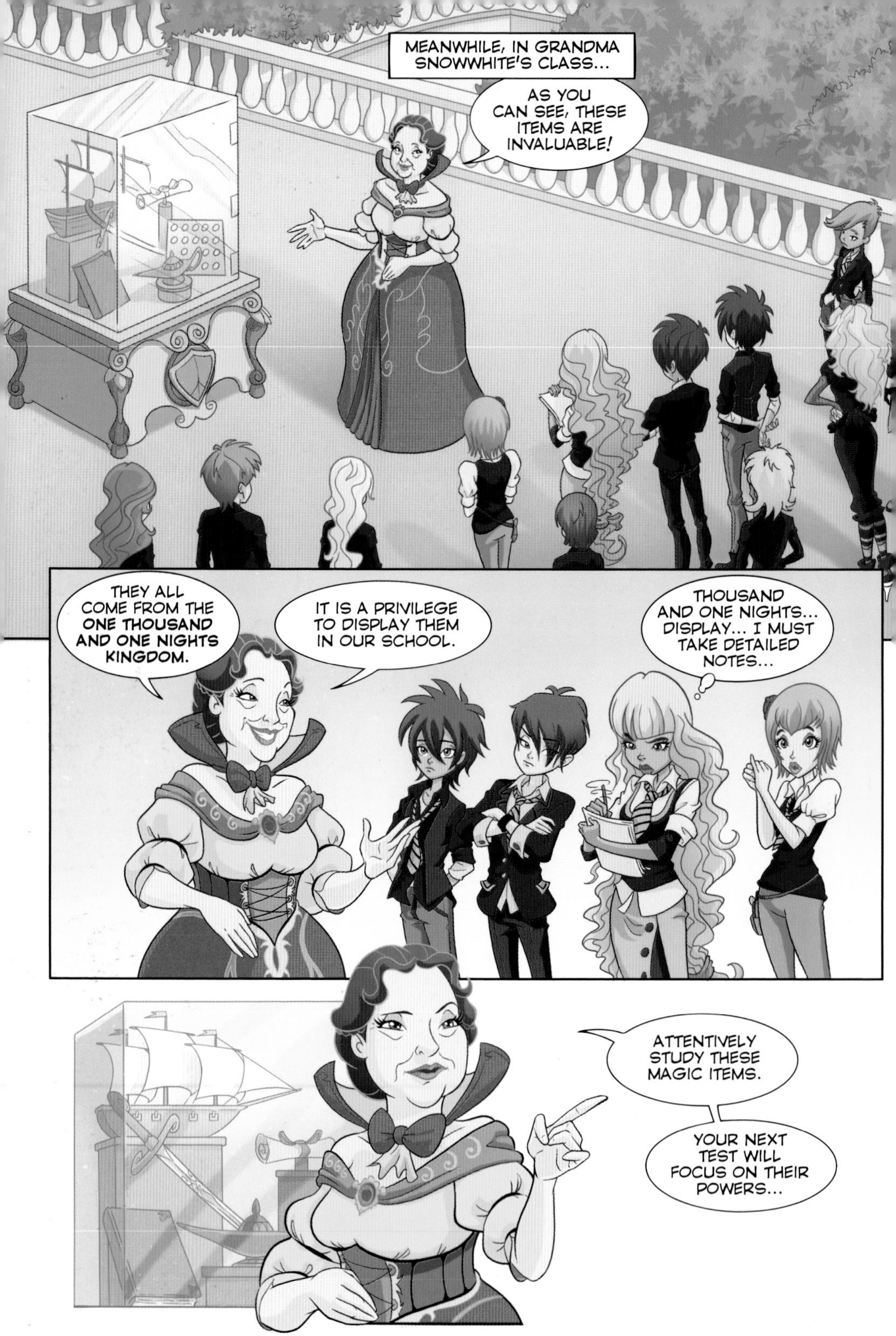
MEANWHILE, IN GRANDMA SNOWWHITE'S CLASS...
AS YOU CAN SEE, THESE ITEMS ARE INVALUABLE!
THEY ALL COME FROM THE ONE THOUSAND AND ONE NIGHTS KINGDOM.
IT IS A PRIVILEGE TO DISPLAY THEM IN OUR SCHOOL.
THOUSAND AND ONE NIGHTS... DISPLAY... I MUST TAKE DETAILED NOTES...
ATTENTIVELY STUDY THESE MAGIC ITEMS.
YOUR NEXT TEST WILL FOCUS ON THEIR POWERS...

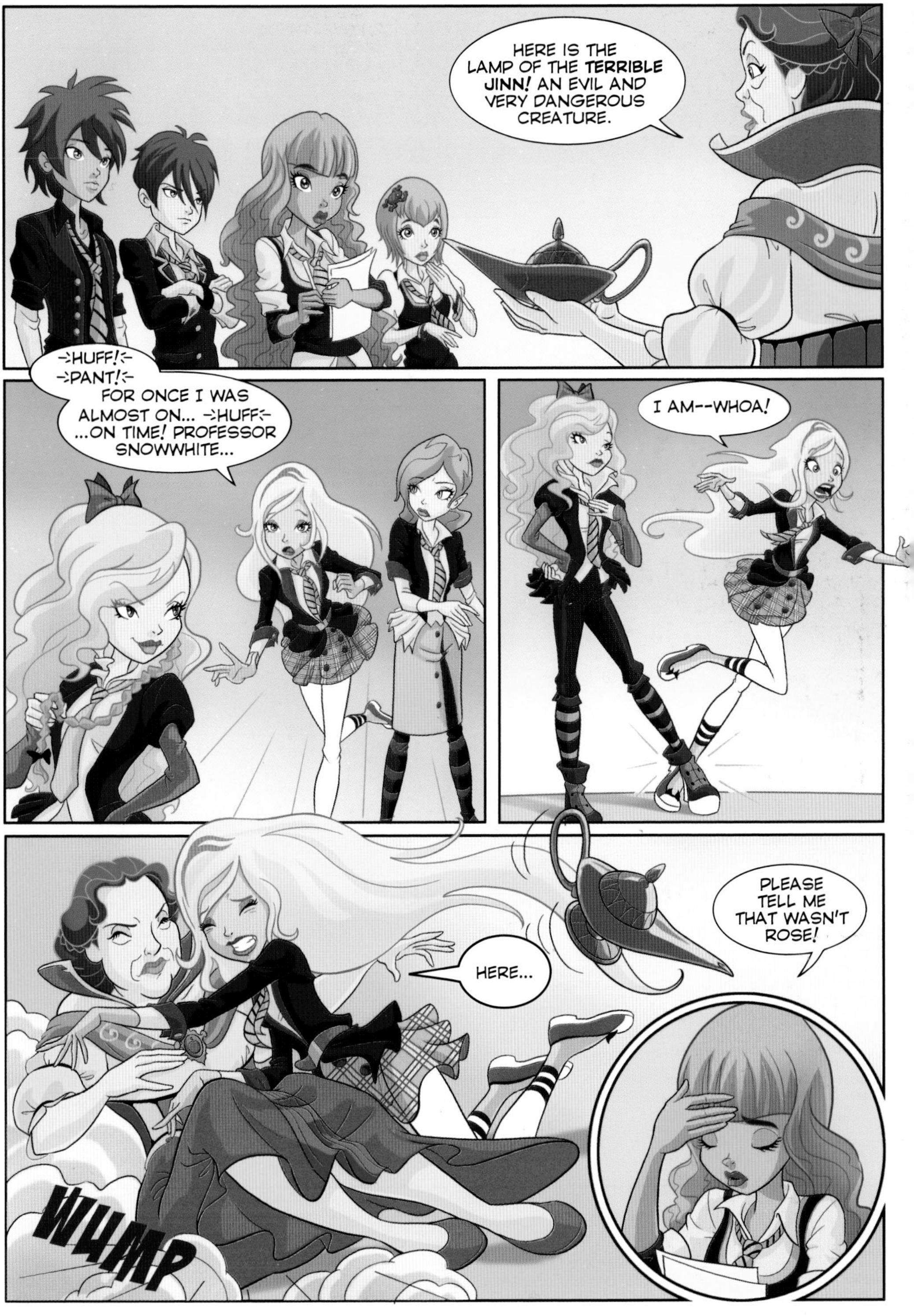
HERE IS THE LAMP OF THE **TERRIBLE JINN!** AN EVIL AND VERY DANGEROUS CREATURE.
~HUFF!~ ~PANT!~ FOR ONCE I WAS ALMOST ON... ~HUFF~ ...ON TIME! PROFESSOR SNOWWHITE...
I AM--WHOA!
HERE...
PLEASE TELL ME THAT WASN'T ROSE!
WUMP

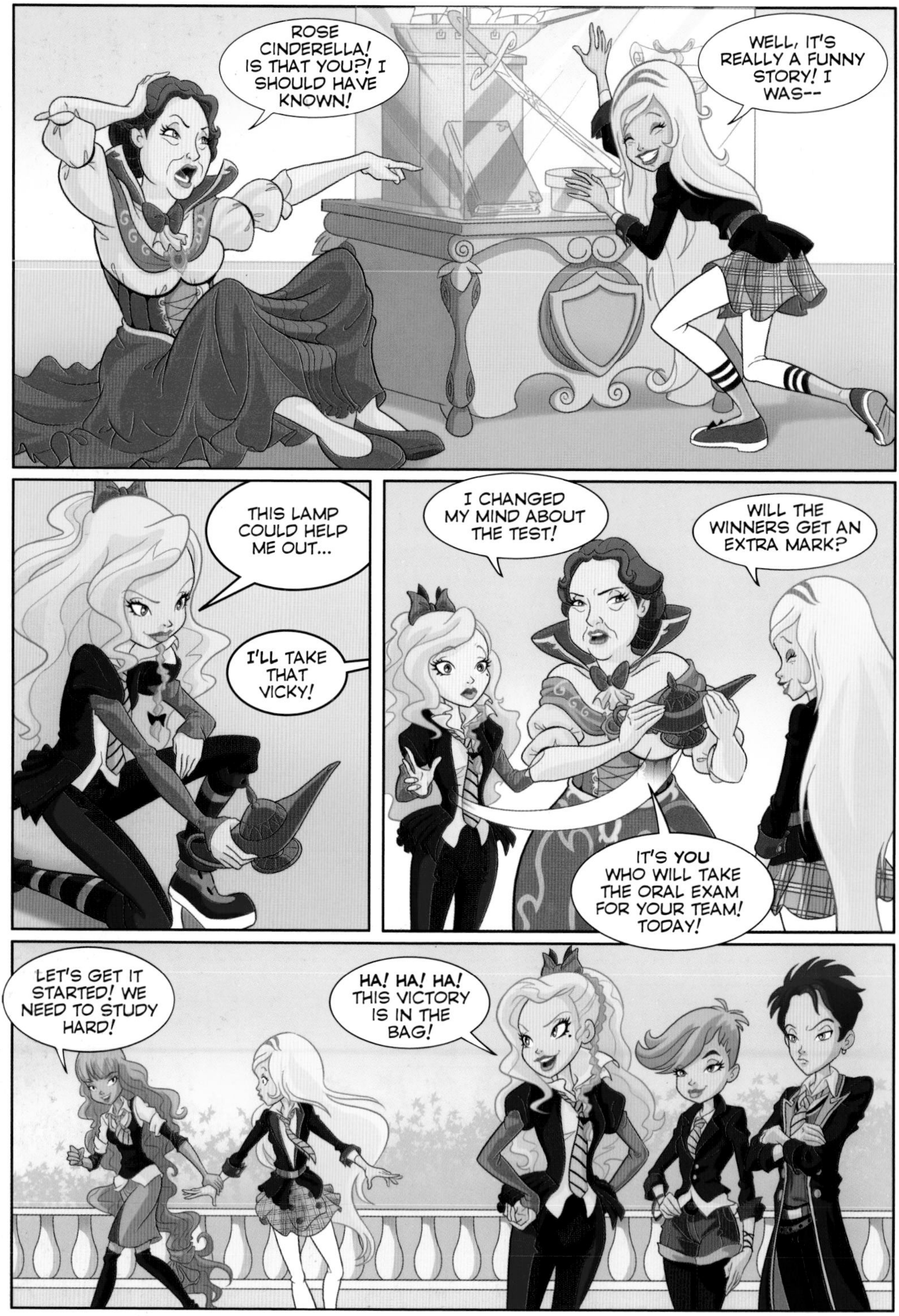
ROSE CINDERELLA! IS THAT YOU?! I SHOULD HAVE KNOWN!
WELL, IT'S REALLY A FUNNY STORY! I WAS--
THIS LAMP COULD HELP ME OUT...
I'LL TAKE THAT VICKY!
I CHANGED MY MIND ABOUT THE TEST!
WILL THE WINNERS GET AN EXTRA MARK?
IT'S YOU WHO WILL TAKE THE ORAL EXAM FOR YOUR TEAM! TODAY!
LET'S GET IT STARTED! WE NEED TO STUDY HARD!
HA! HA! HA! THIS VICTORY IS IN THE BAG!

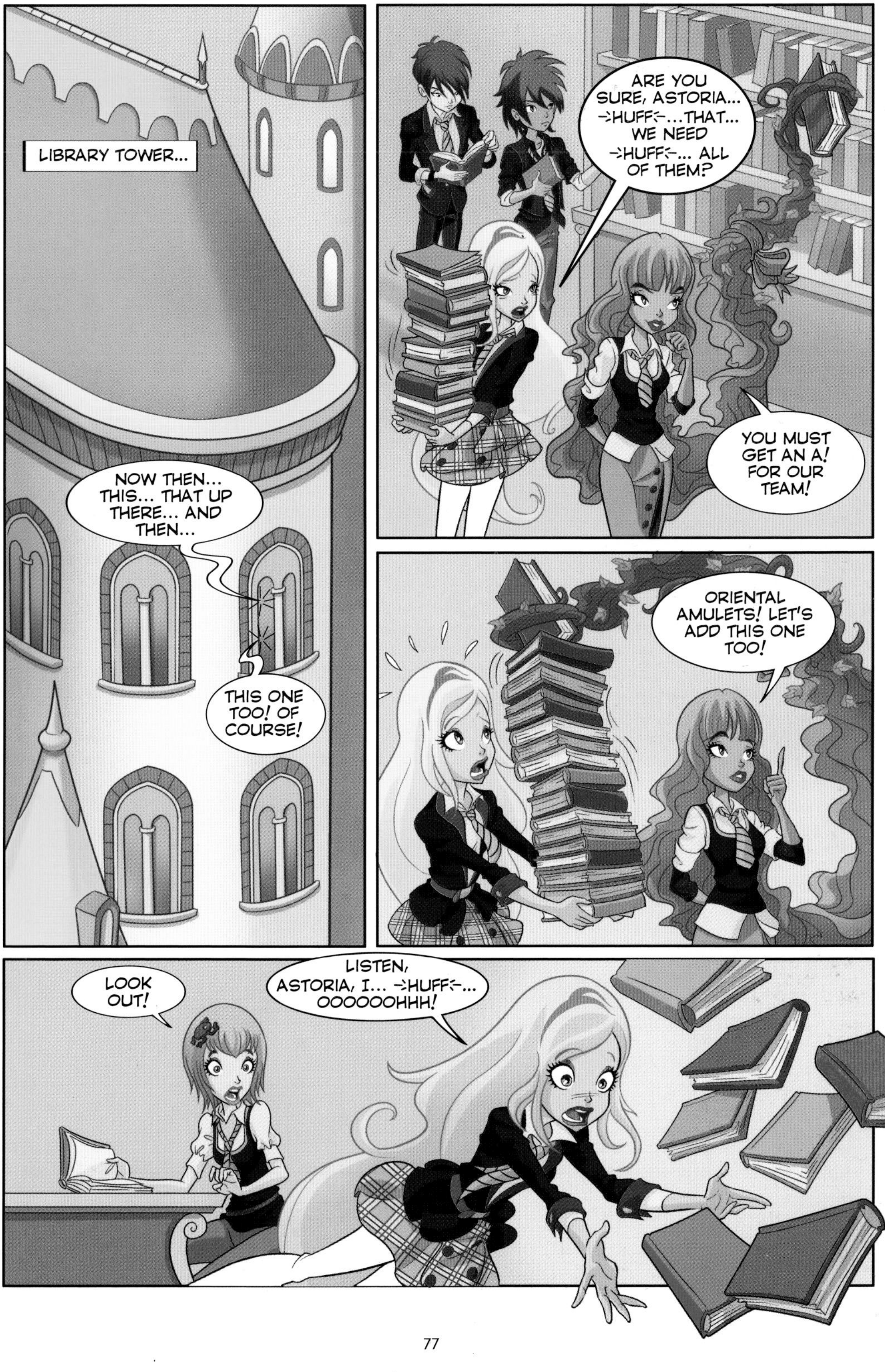

LIBRARY TOWER...
NOW THEN... THIS... THAT UP THERE... AND THEN...
THIS ONE TOO! OF COURSE!
ARE YOU SURE, ASTORIA... -HUFF-... THAT... WE NEED -HUFF-... ALL OF THEM?
YOU MUST GET AN A! FOR OUR TEAM!
ORIENTAL AMULETS! LET'S ADD THIS ONE TOO!
LOOK OUT!
LISTEN, ASTORIA, I... -HUFF-... OOOOOOHHH!

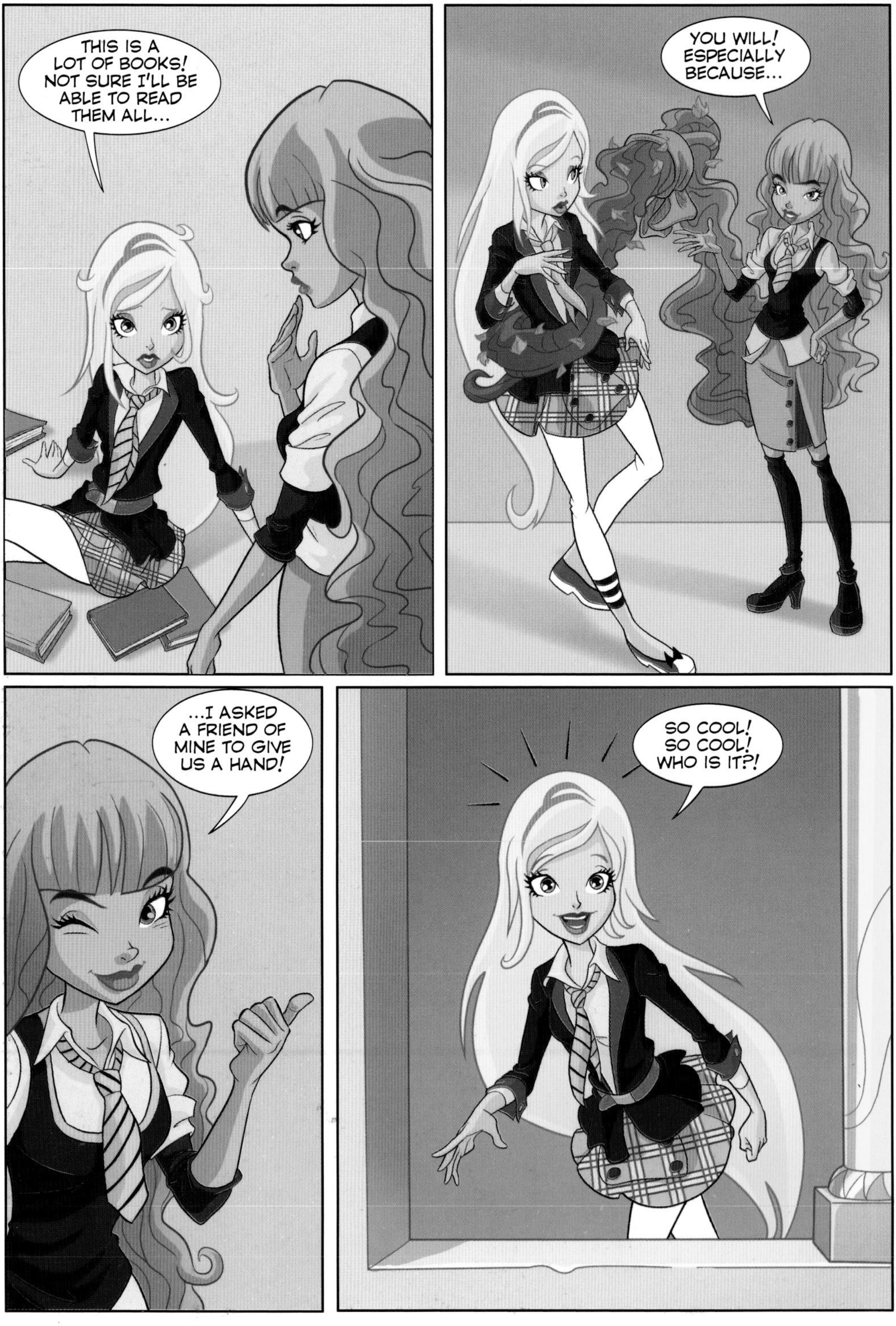
THIS IS A LOT OF BOOKS! NOT SURE I'LL BE ABLE TO READ THEM ALL...
YOU WILL! ESPECIALLY BECAUSE...
...I ASKED A FRIEND OF MINE TO GIVE US A HAND!
SO COOL! SO COOL! WHO IS IT?!

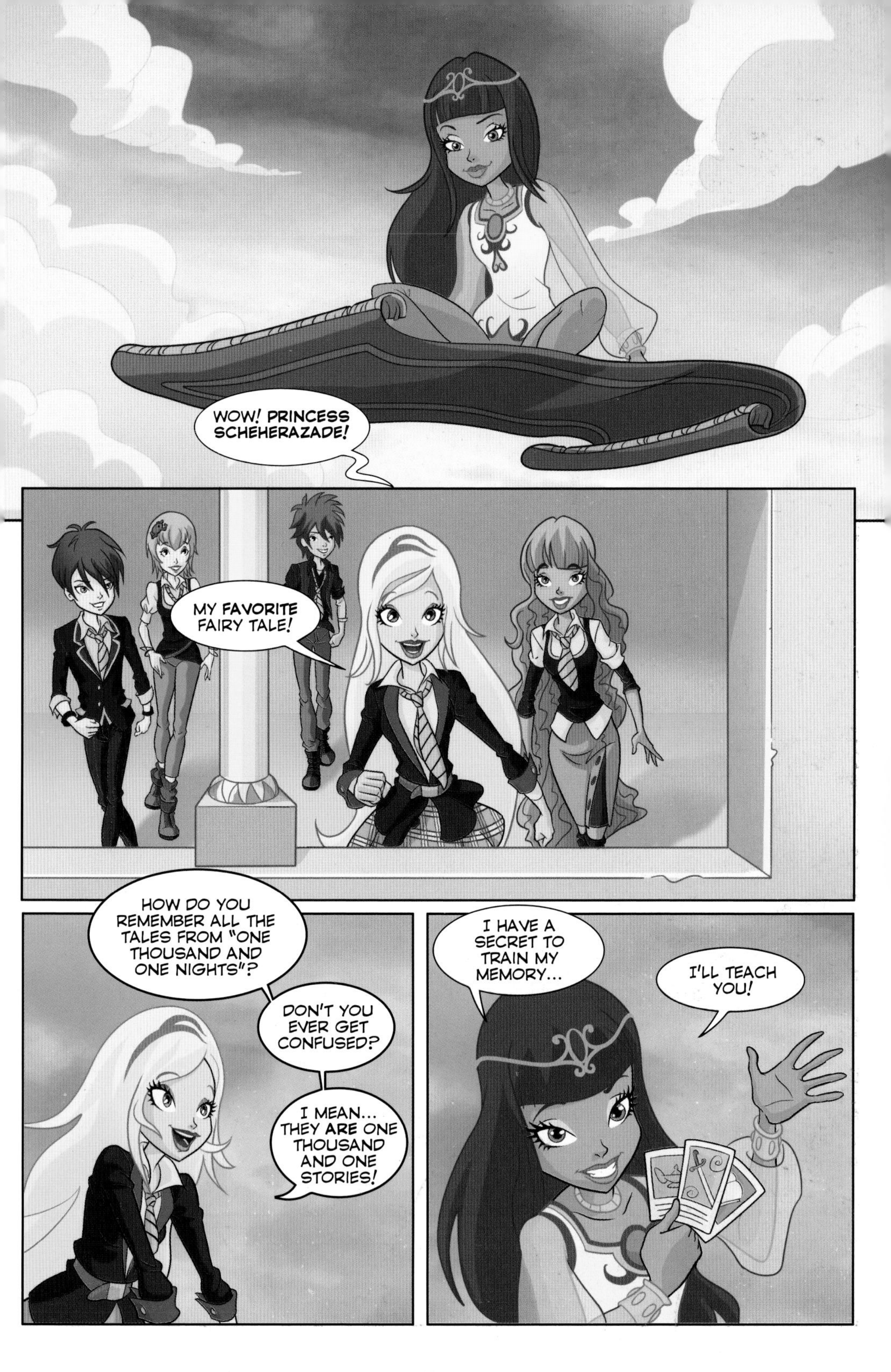
WOW! PRINCESS SCHEHERAZADE!
MY FAVORITE FAIRY TALE!
HOW DO YOU REMEMBER ALL THE TALES FROM "ONE THOUSAND AND ONE NIGHTS"?
DON'T YOU EVER GET CONFUSED?
I MEAN... THEY ARE ONE THOUSAND AND ONE STORIES!
I HAVE A SECRET TO TRAIN MY MEMORY...
I'LL TEACH YOU!

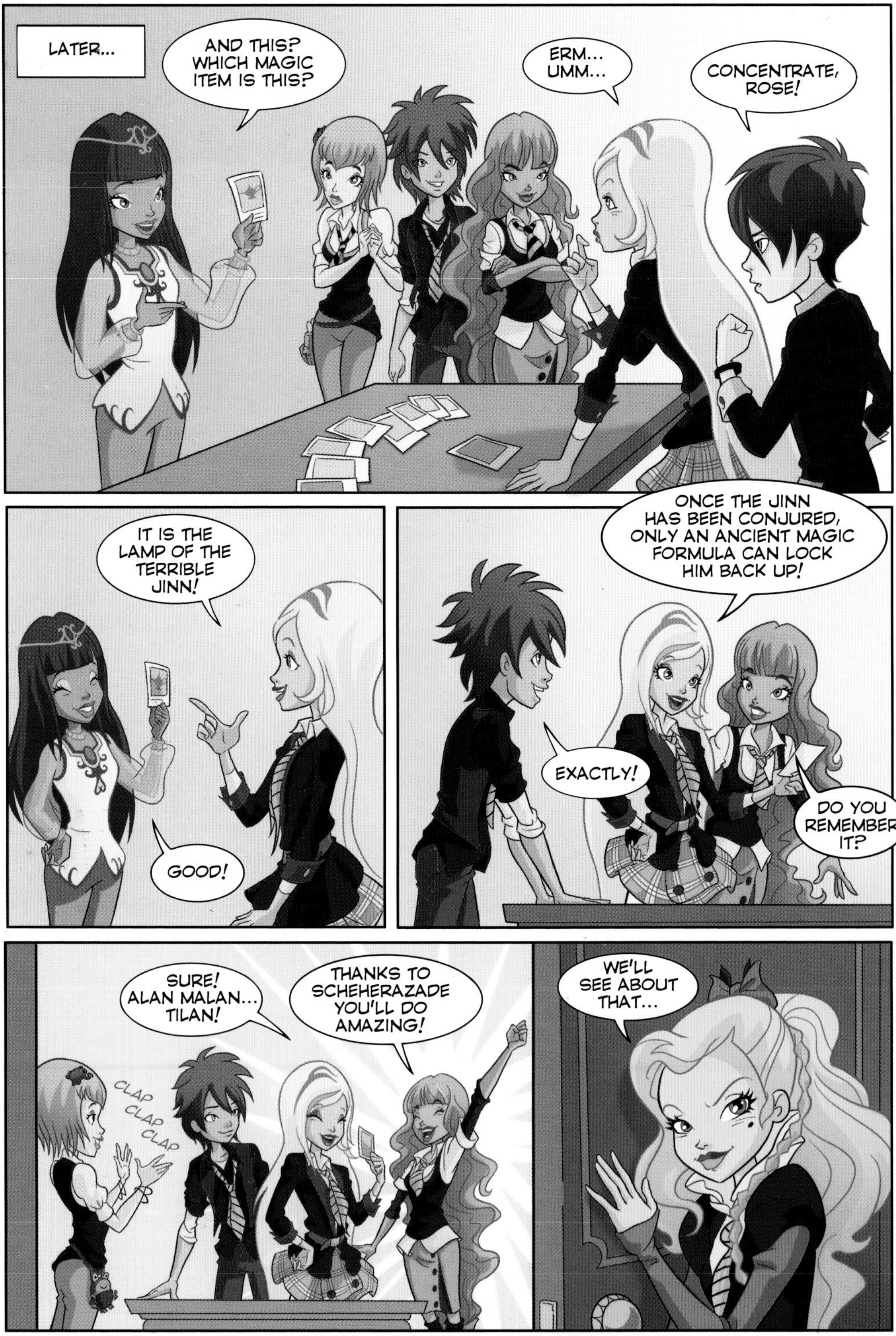
LATER...
AND THIS? WHICH MAGIC ITEM IS THIS?
ERM... UMM...
CONCENTRATE, ROSE!
IT IS THE LAMP OF THE TERRIBLE JINN!
GOOD!
ONCE THE JINN HAS BEEN CONJURED, ONLY AN ANCIENT MAGIC FORMULA CAN LOCK HIM BACK UP!
EXACTLY!
DO YOU REMEMBER IT?
SURE! ALAN MALAN... TILAN!
THANKS TO SCHEHERAZADE YOU'LL DO AMAZING!
CLAP CLAP CLAP
WE'LL SEE ABOUT THAT...

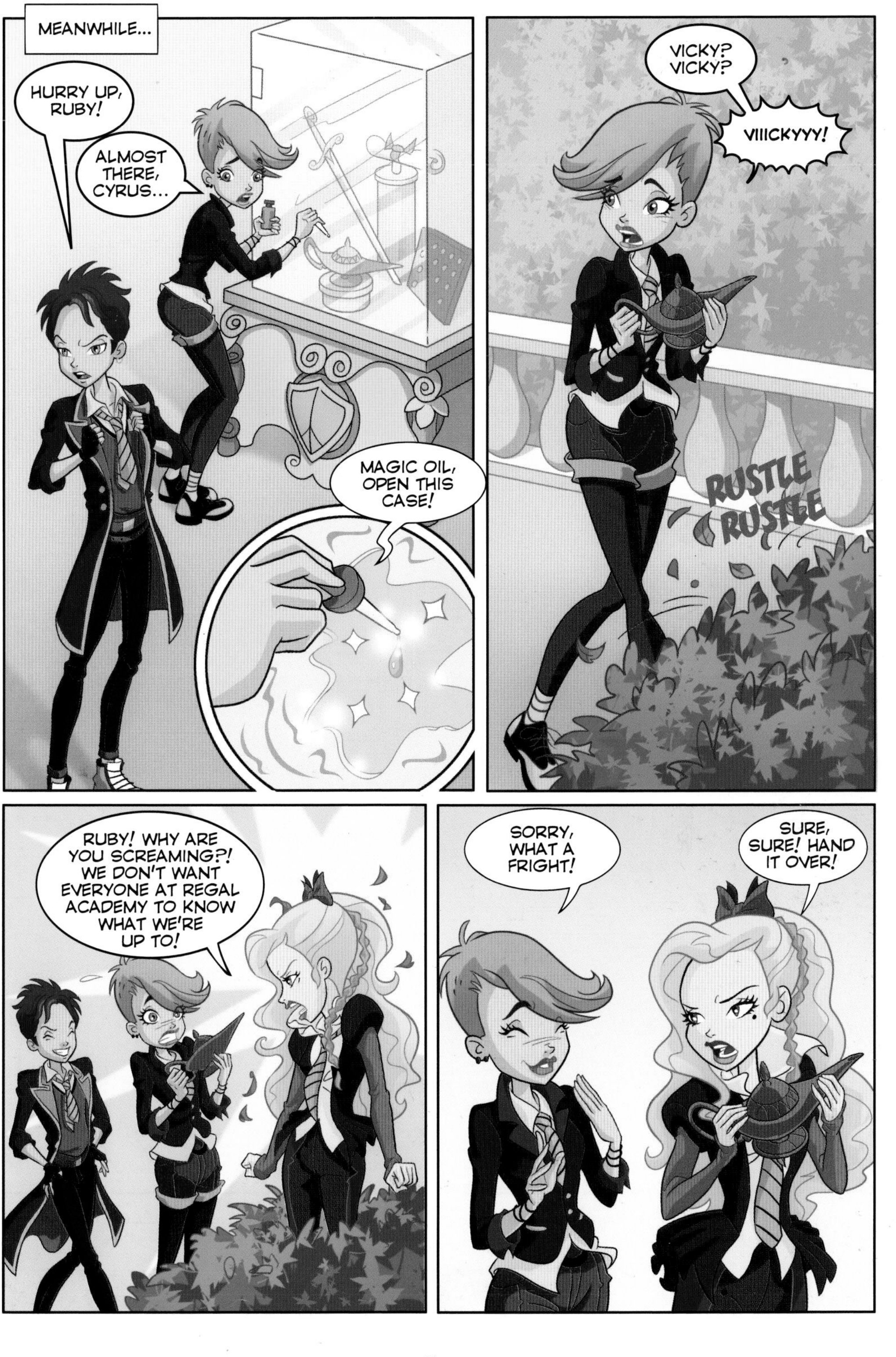
MEANWHILE...
HURRY UP, RUBY!
ALMOST THERE, CYRUS...
MAGIC OIL, OPEN THIS CASE!
VICKY? VICKY?
VIIICKYYY!
RUSTLE RUSTLE
RUBY! WHY ARE YOU SCREAMING?! WE DON'T WANT EVERYONE AT REGAL ACADEMY TO KNOW WHAT WE'RE UP TO!
SORRY, WHAT A FRIGHT!
SURE, SURE! HAND IT OVER!

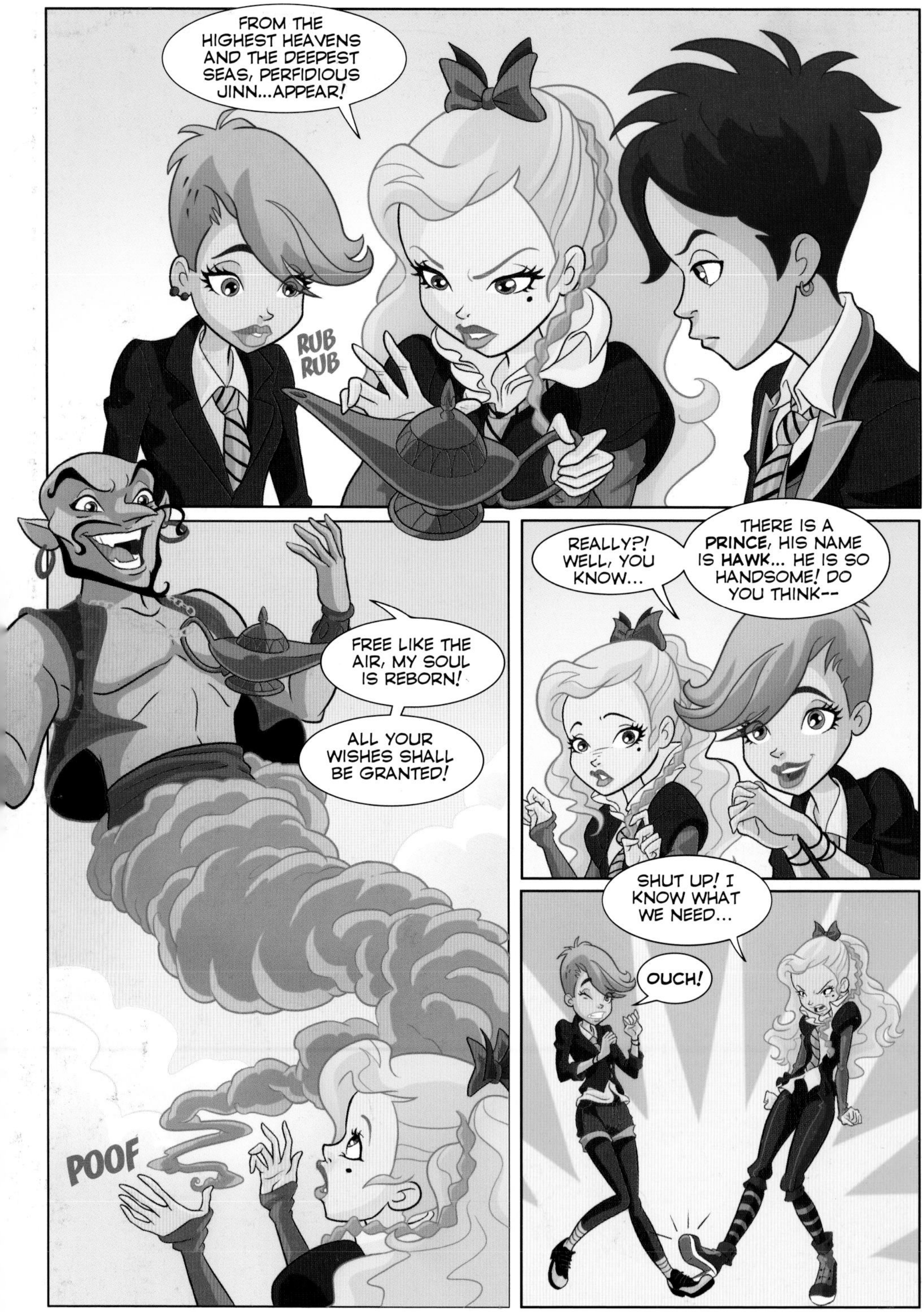
FROM THE HIGHEST HEAVENS AND THE DEEPEST SEAS, PERFIDIOUS JINN...APPEAR!
RUB RUB
FREE LIKE THE AIR, MY SOUL IS REBORN!
ALL YOUR WISHES SHALL BE GRANTED!
POOF
REALLY?! WELL, YOU KNOW...
THERE IS A PRINCE, HIS NAME IS HAWK... HE IS SO HANDSOME! DO YOU THINK--
SHUT UP! I KNOW WHAT WE NEED...
OUCH!

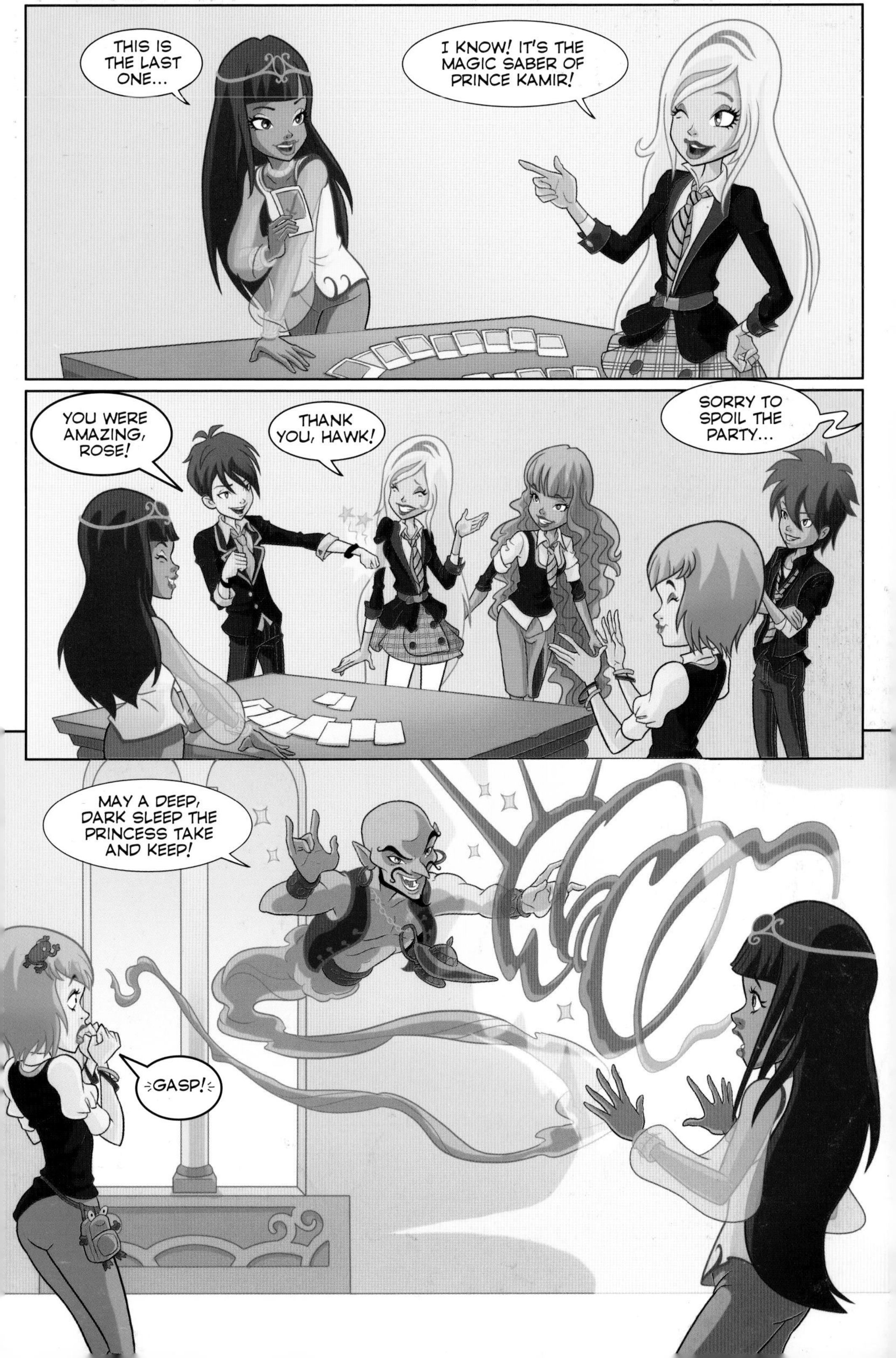
THIS IS THE LAST ONE...
I KNOW! IT'S THE MAGIC SABER OF PRINCE KAMIR!
YOU WERE AMAZING, ROSE!
THANK YOU, HAWK!
SORRY TO SPOIL THE PARTY...
MAY A DEEP, DARK SLEEP THE PRINCESS TAKE AND KEEP!
GASP!

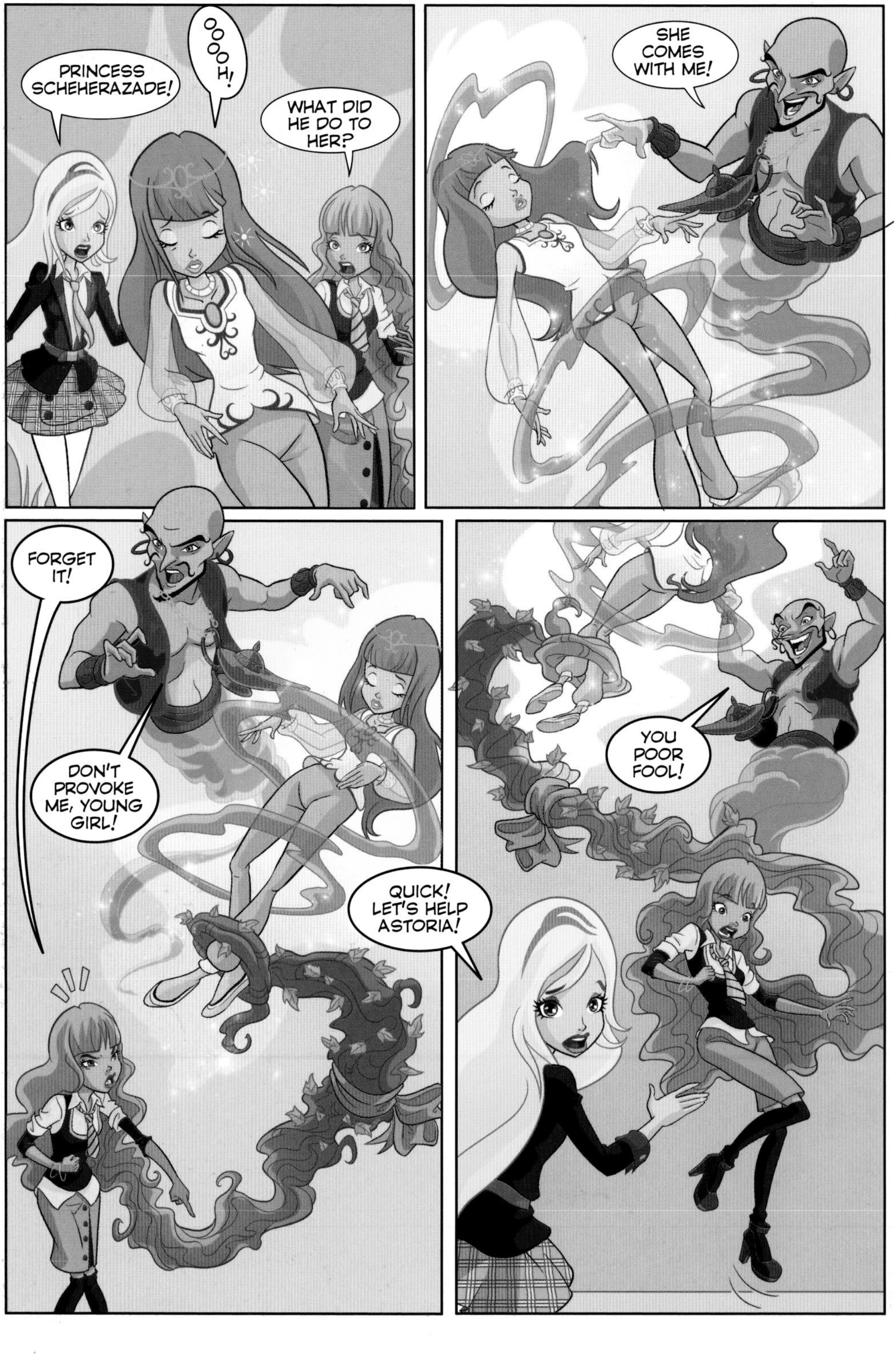
PRINCESS SCHEHERAZADE!
OOOOH!
WHAT DID HE DO TO HER?
SHE COMES WITH ME!
FORGET IT!
DON'T PROVOKE ME, YOUNG GIRL!
QUICK! LET'S HELP ASTORIA!
YOU POOR FOOL!

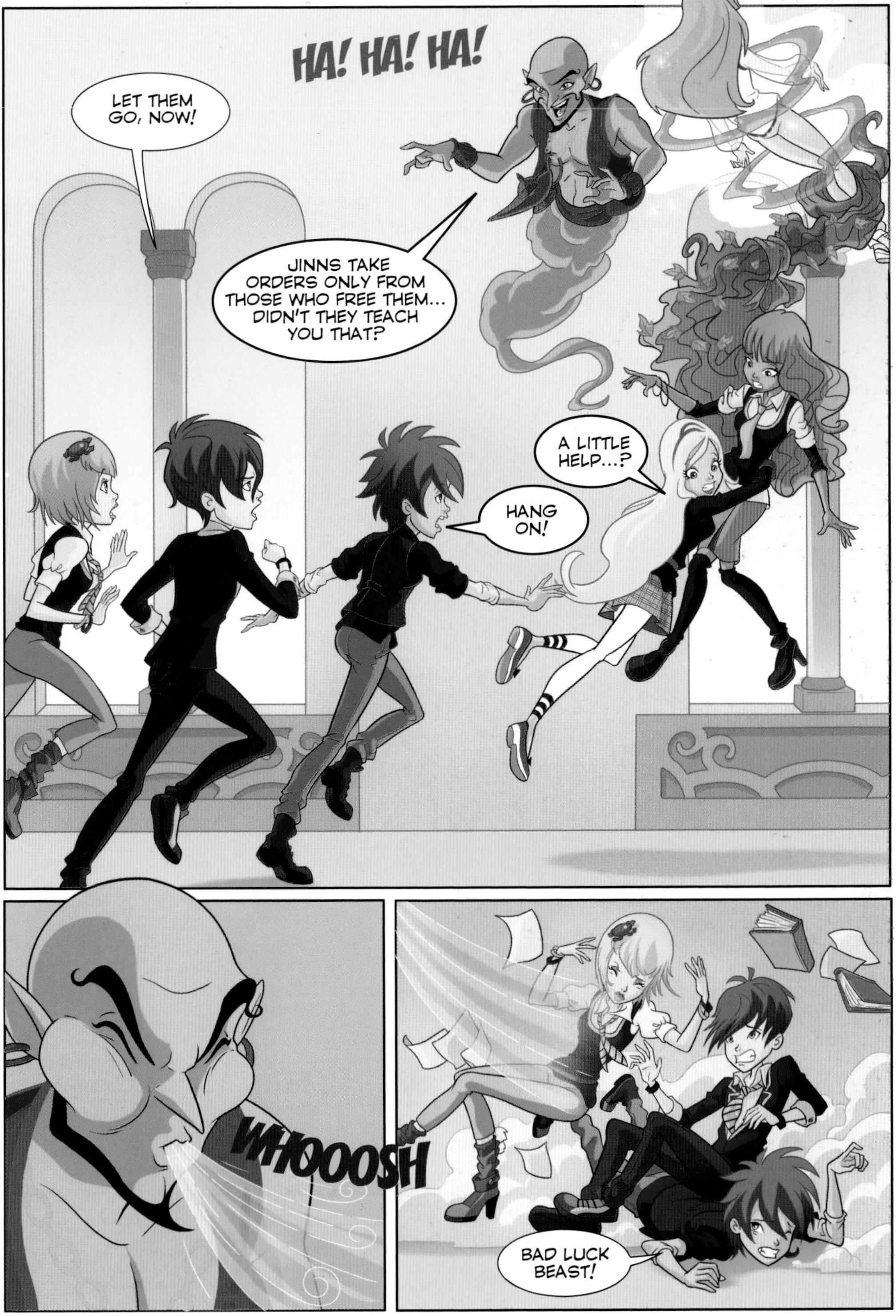
HA! HA! HA!
LET THEM GO, NOW!
JINNS TAKE ORDERS ONLY FROM THOSE WHO FREE THEM... DIDN'T THEY TEACH YOU THAT?
A LITTLE HELP...?
HANG ON!
WHOOOSH
BAD LUCK BEAST!

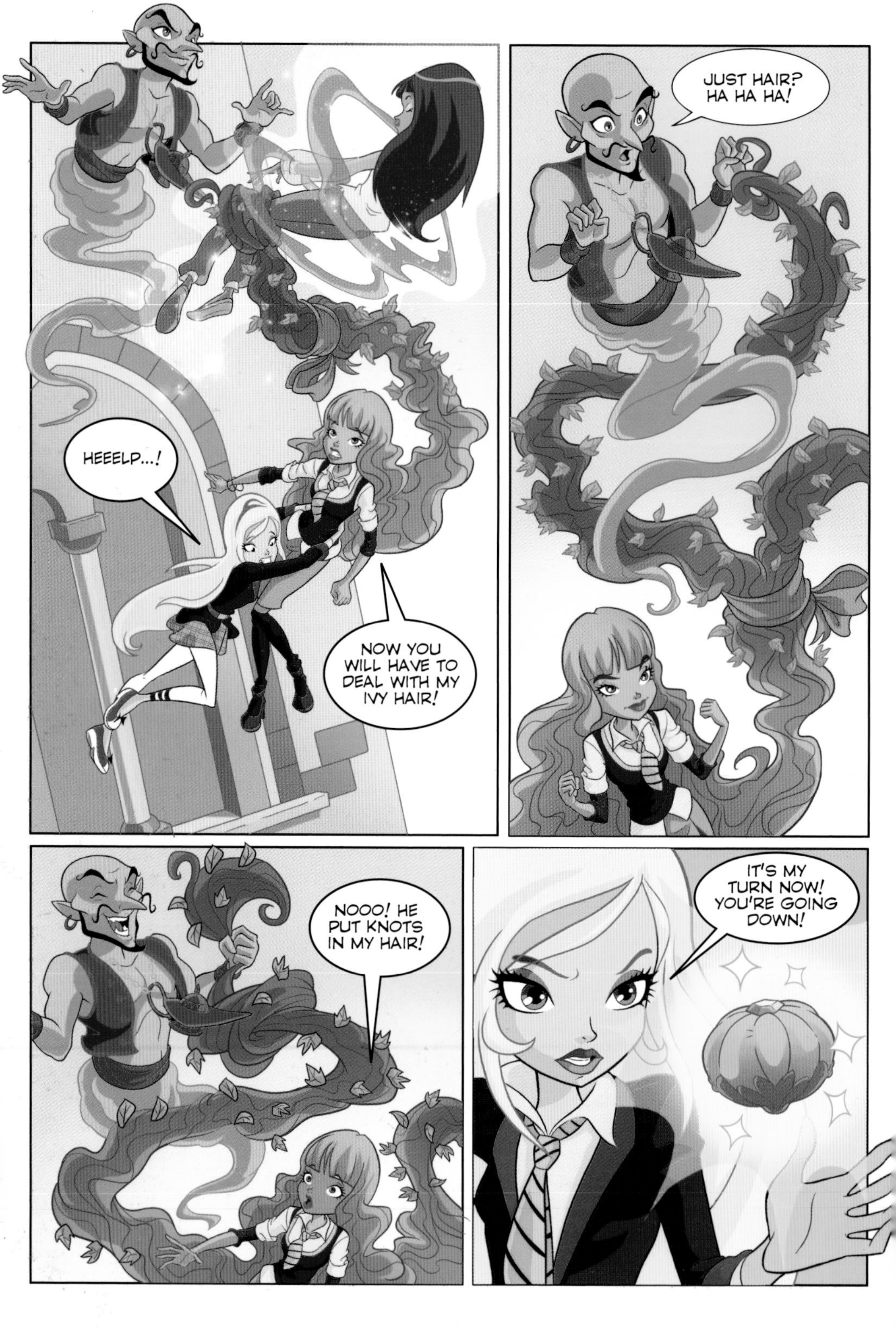
HEEELP...!
NOW YOU WILL HAVE TO DEAL WITH MY IVY HAIR!
JUST HAIR? HA HA HA!
NOOO! HE PUT KNOTS IN MY HAIR!
IT'S MY TURN NOW! YOU'RE GOING DOWN!

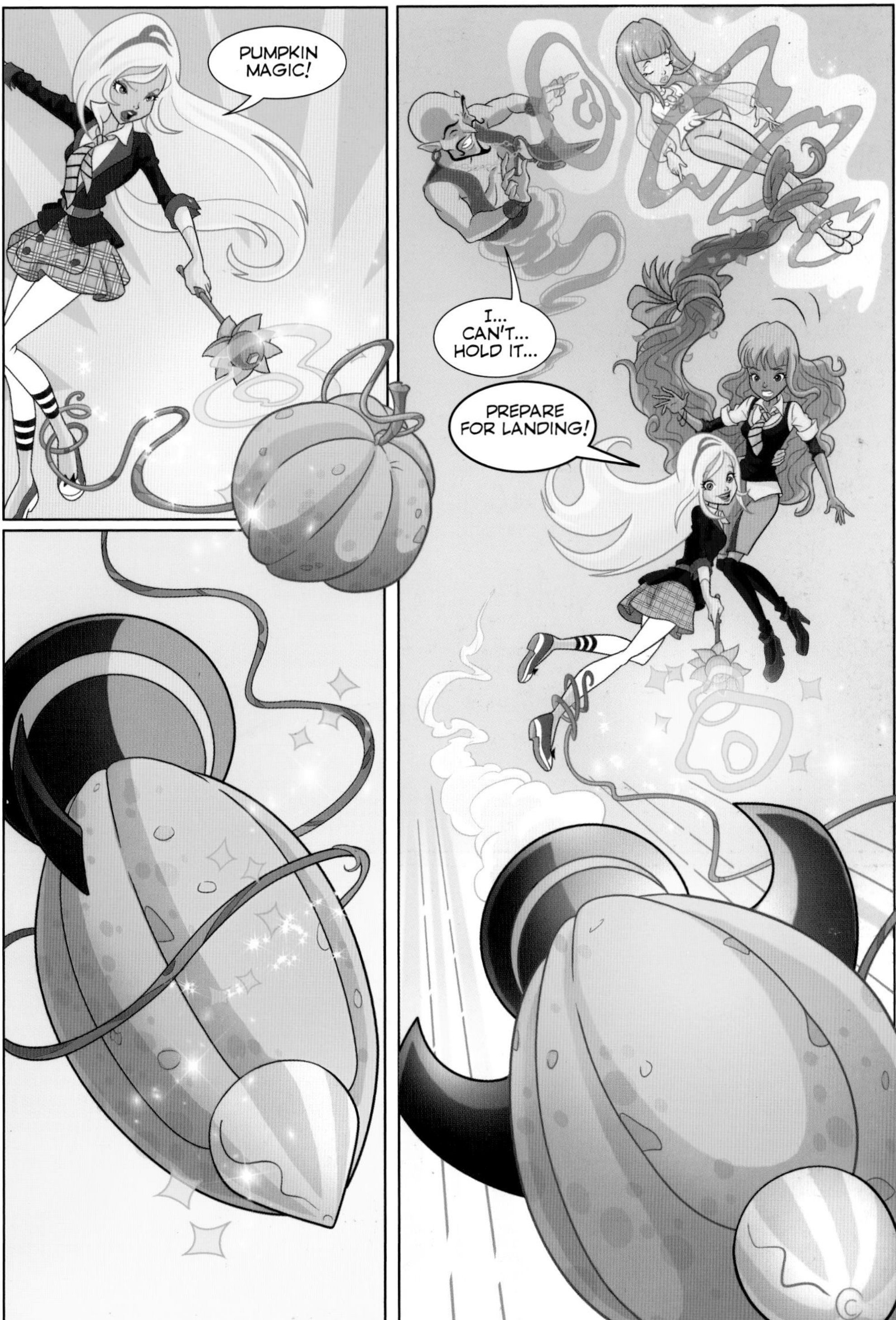
PUMPKIN MAGIC!
I... CAN'T... HOLD IT...
PREPARE FOR LANDING!

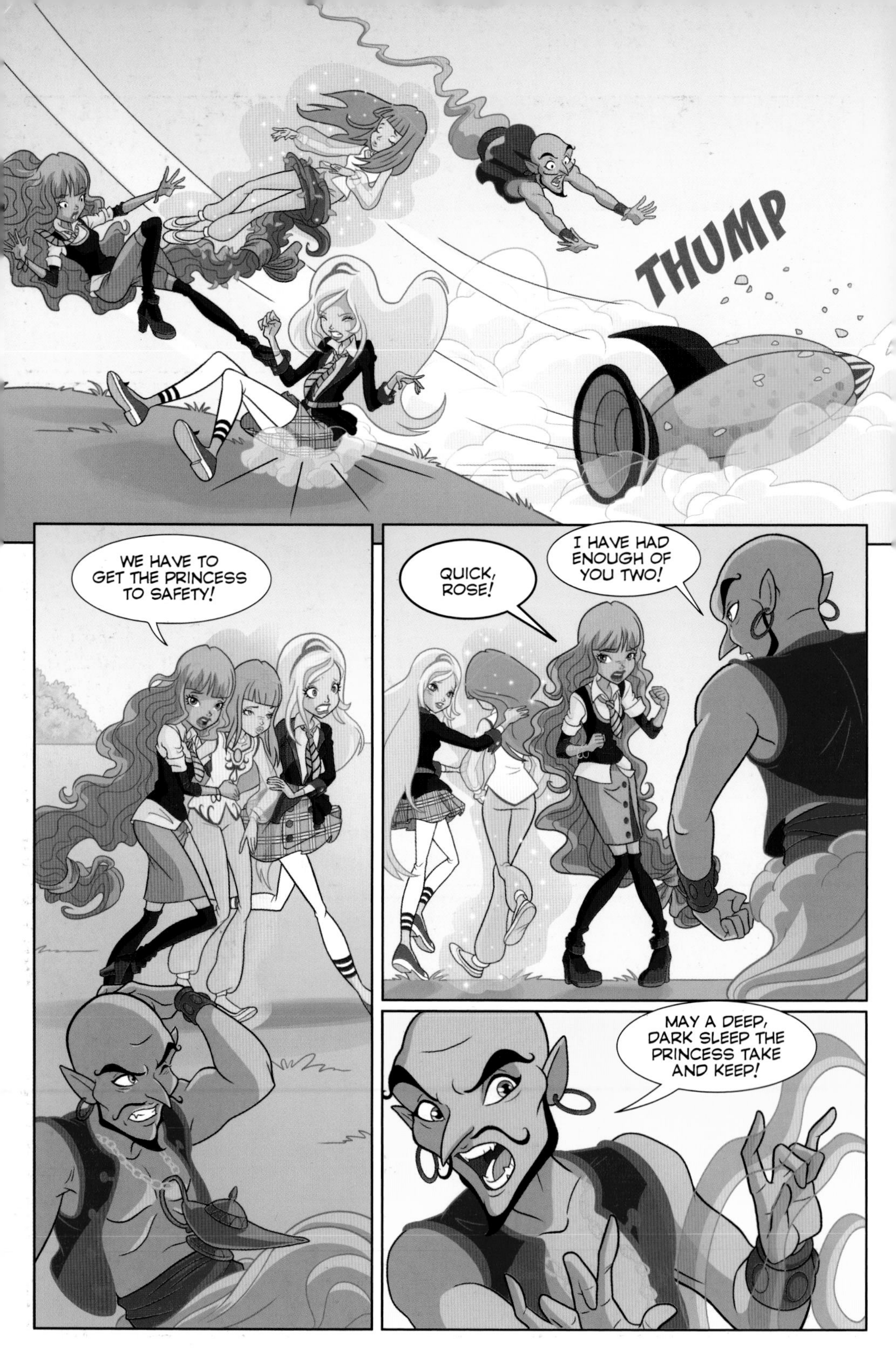
THUMP
WE HAVE TO GET THE PRINCESS TO SAFETY!
QUICK, ROSE!
I HAVE HAD ENOUGH OF YOU TWO!
MAY A DEEP, DARK SLEEP THE PRINCESS TAKE AND KEEP!

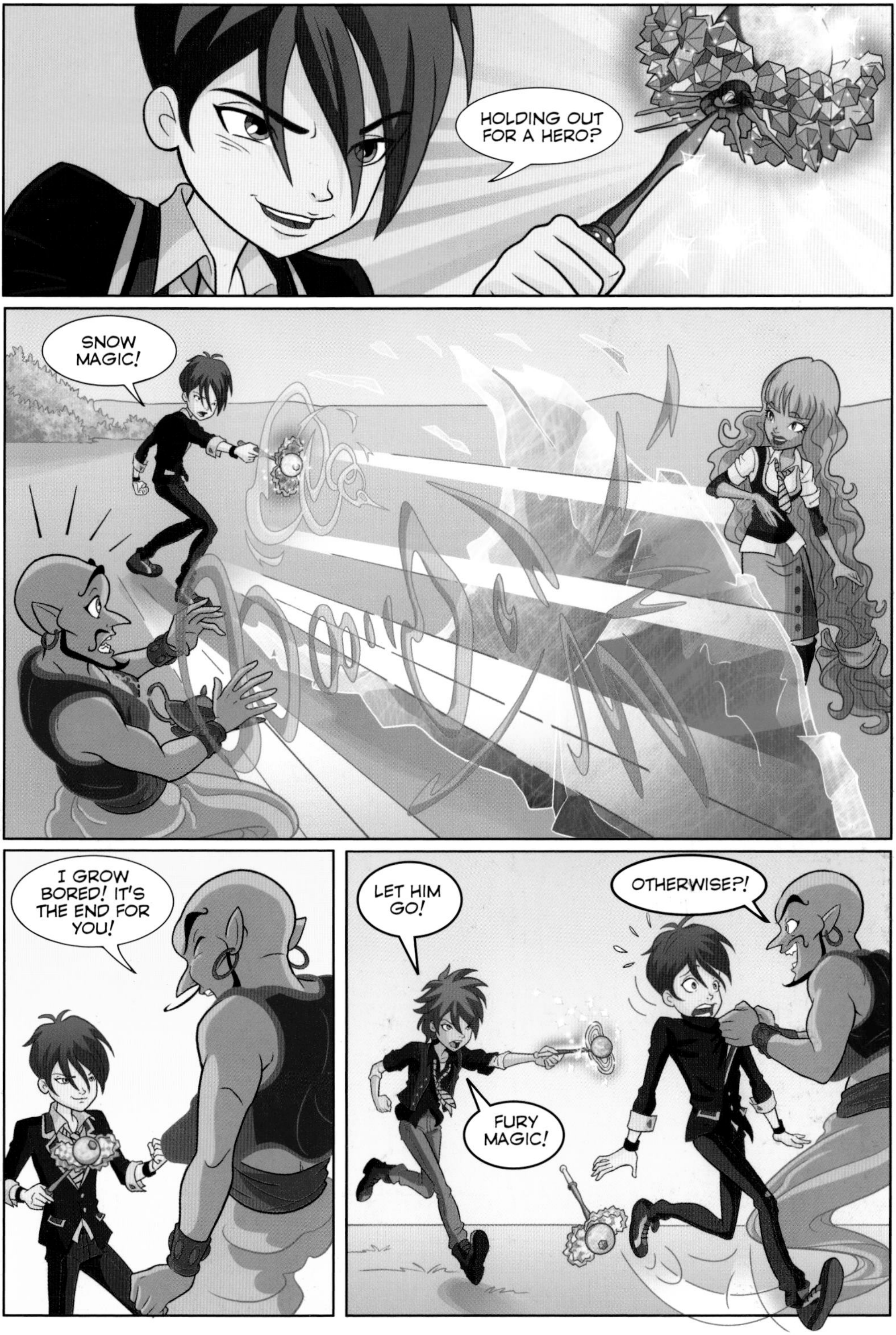
HOLDING OUT FOR A HERO?
SNOW MAGIC!
I GROW BORED! IT'S THE END FOR YOU!
LET HIM GO!
OTHERWISE?!
FURY MAGIC!

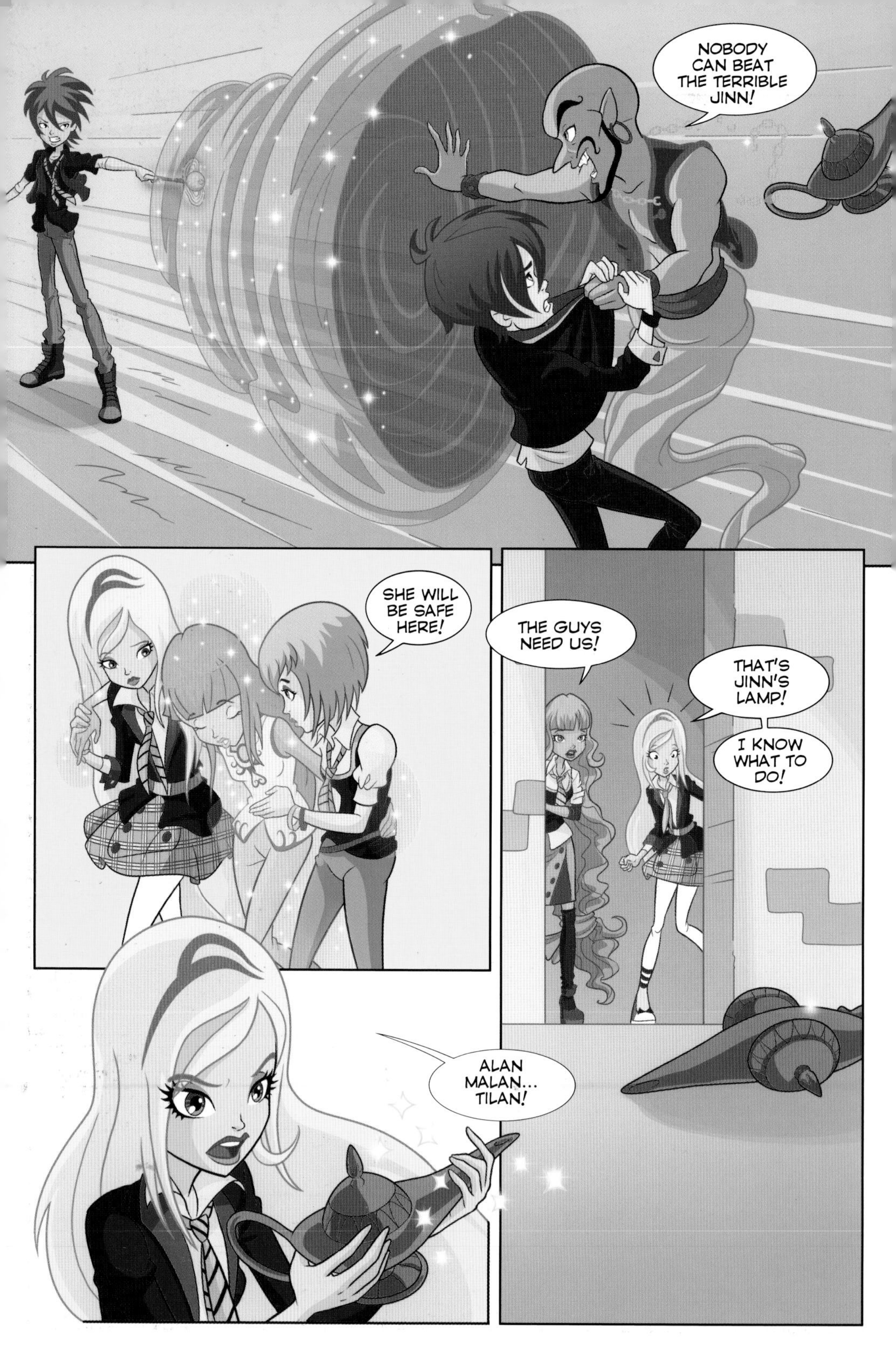
NOBODY CAN BEAT THE TERRIBLE JINN!
SHE WILL BE SAFE HERE!
THE GUYS NEED US!
THAT'S JINN'S LAMP!
I KNOW WHAT TO DO!
ALAN MALAN... TILAN!

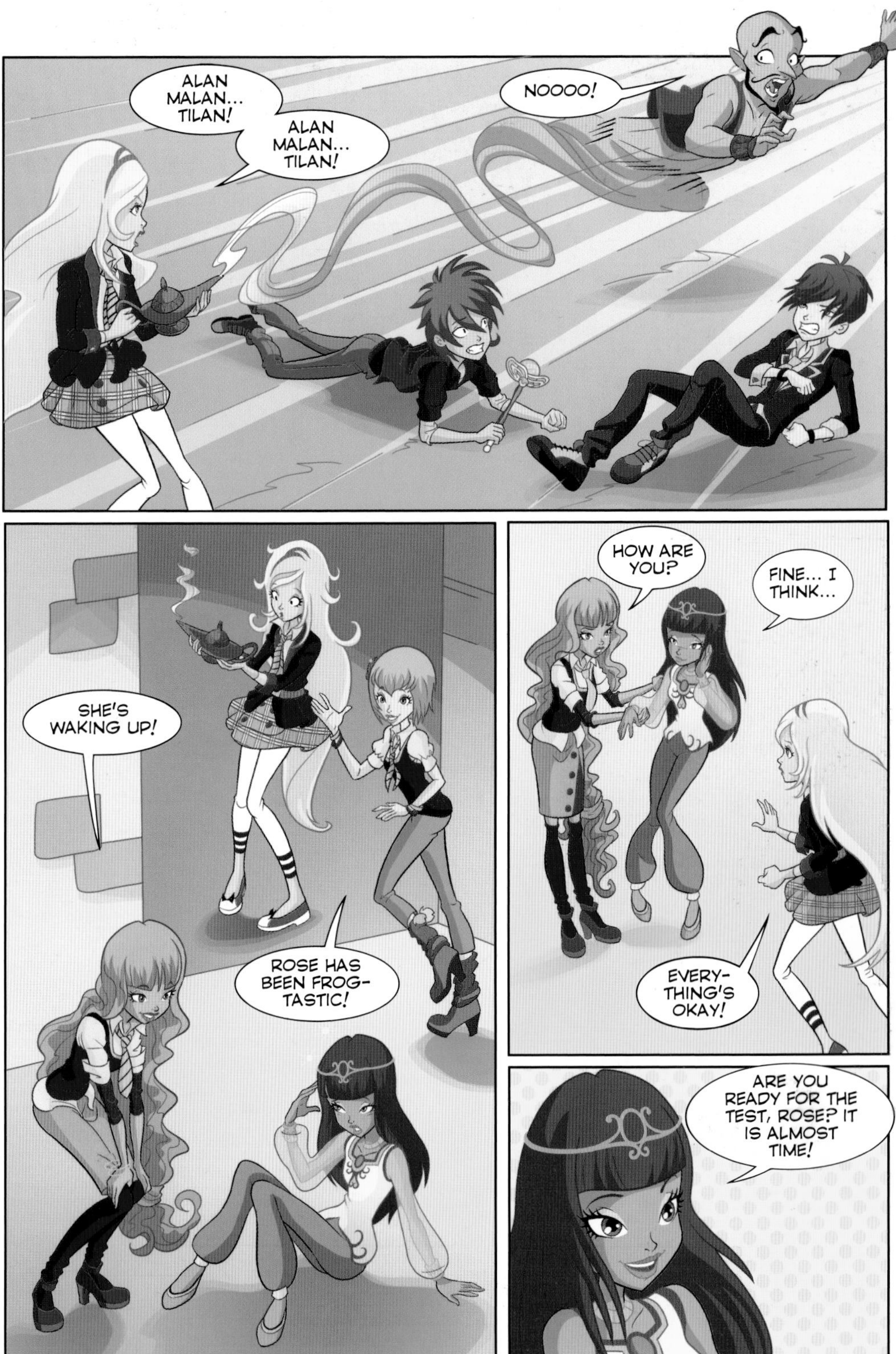
ALAN MALAN... TILAN!
ALAN MALAN... TILAN!
NOOOO!
SHE'S WAKING UP!
ROSE HAS BEEN FROG-TASTIC!
HOW ARE YOU?
FINE... I THINK...
EVERY-THING'S OKAY!
ARE YOU READY FOR THE TEST, ROSE? IT IS ALMOST TIME!

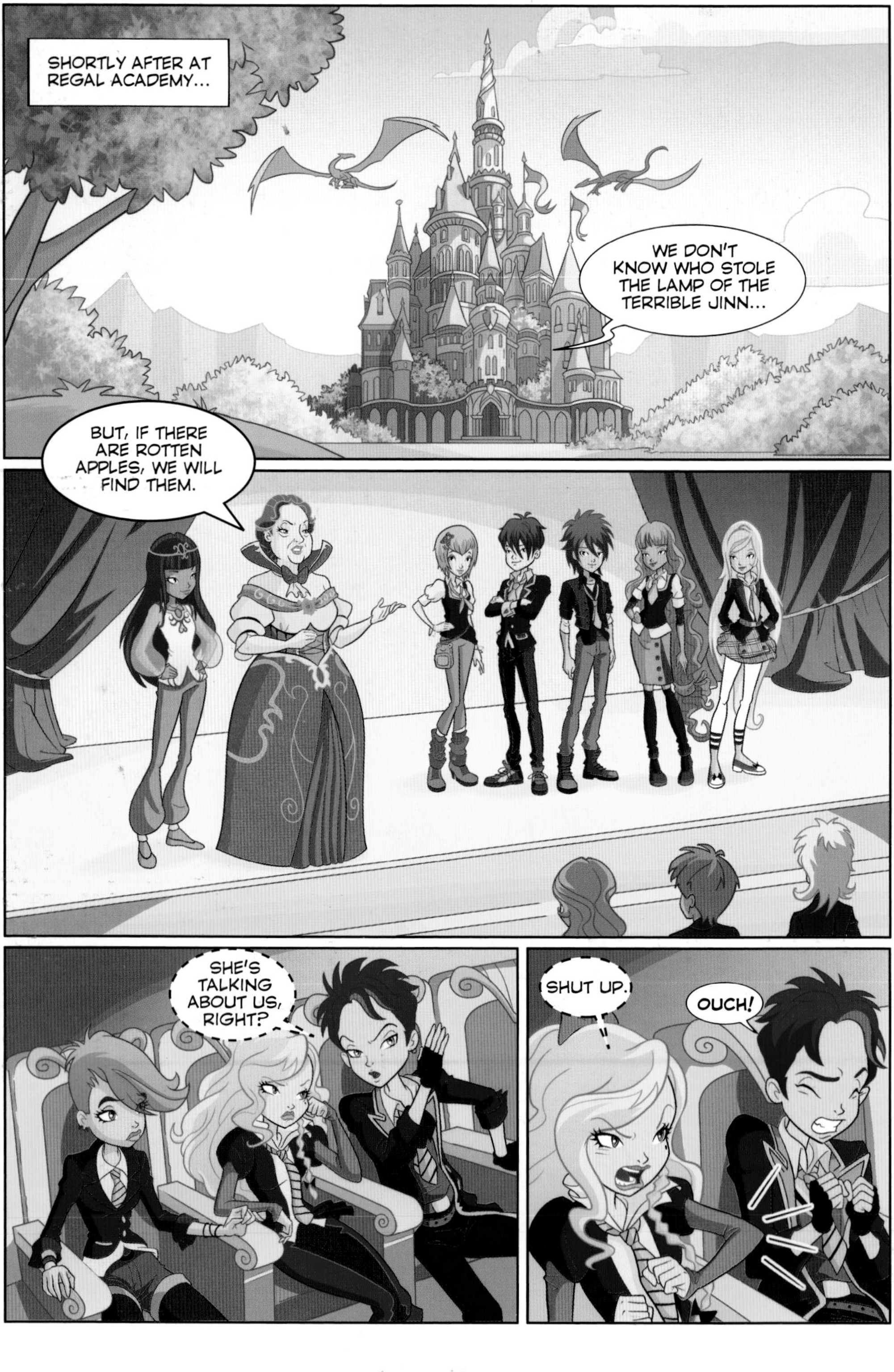
SHORTLY AFTER AT REGAL ACADEMY...
WE DON'T KNOW WHO STOLE THE LAMP OF THE TERRIBLE JINN...
BUT, IF THERE ARE ROTTEN APPLES, WE WILL FIND THEM.
SHE'S TALKING ABOUT US, RIGHT?
SHUT UP.
OUCH!

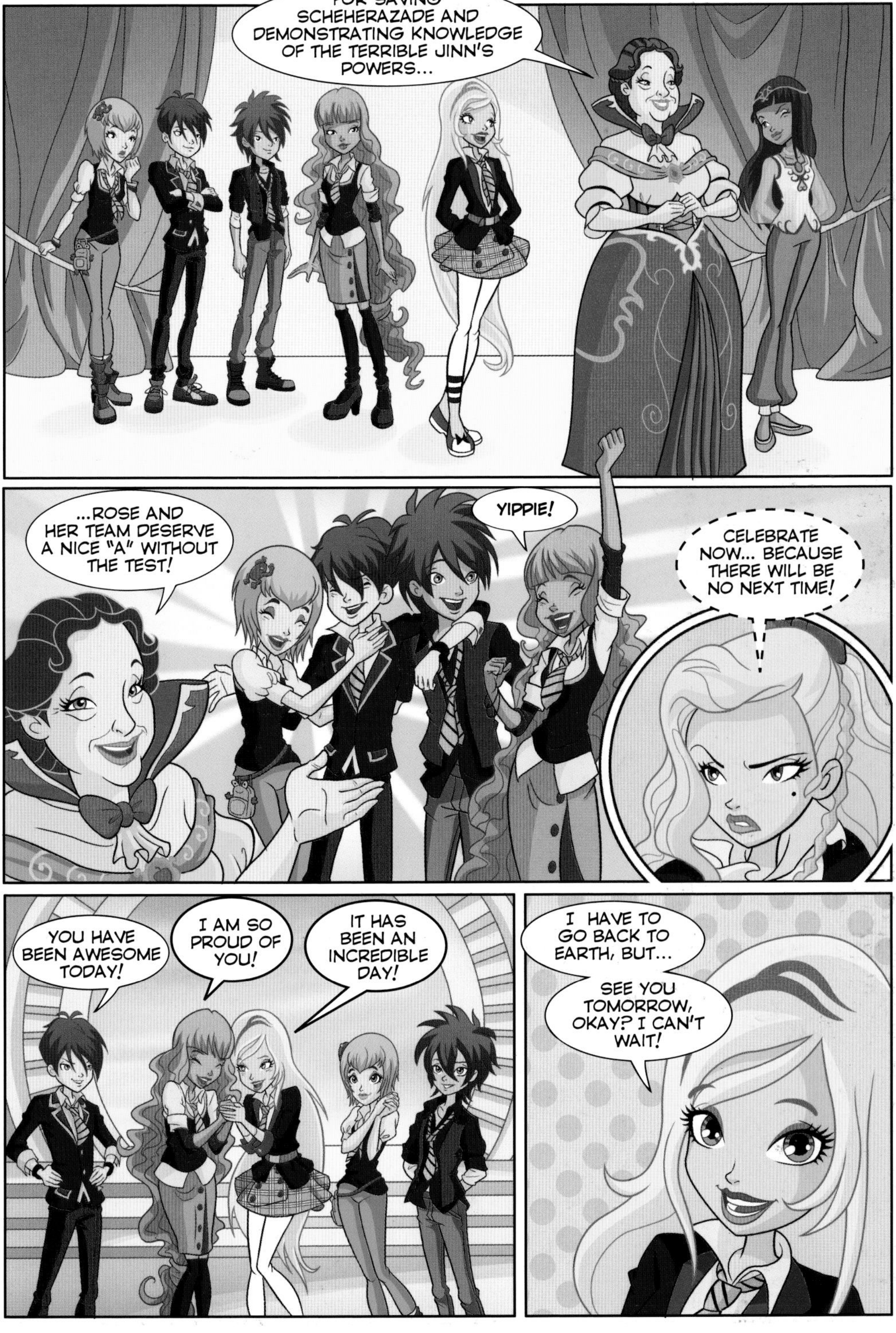
FOR SAVING SCHEHERAZADE AND DEMONSTRATING KNOWLEDGE OF THE TERRIBLE JINN'S POWERS...
...ROSE AND HER TEAM DESERVE A NICE "A" WITHOUT THE TEST!
YIPPIE!
CELEBRATE NOW... BECAUSE THERE WILL BE NO NEXT TIME!
YOU HAVE BEEN AWESOME TODAY!
I AM SO PROUD OF YOU!
IT HAS BEEN AN INCREDIBLE DAY!
I HAVE TO GO BACK TO EARTH, BUT...
SEE YOU TOMORROW, OKAY? I CAN'T WAIT!

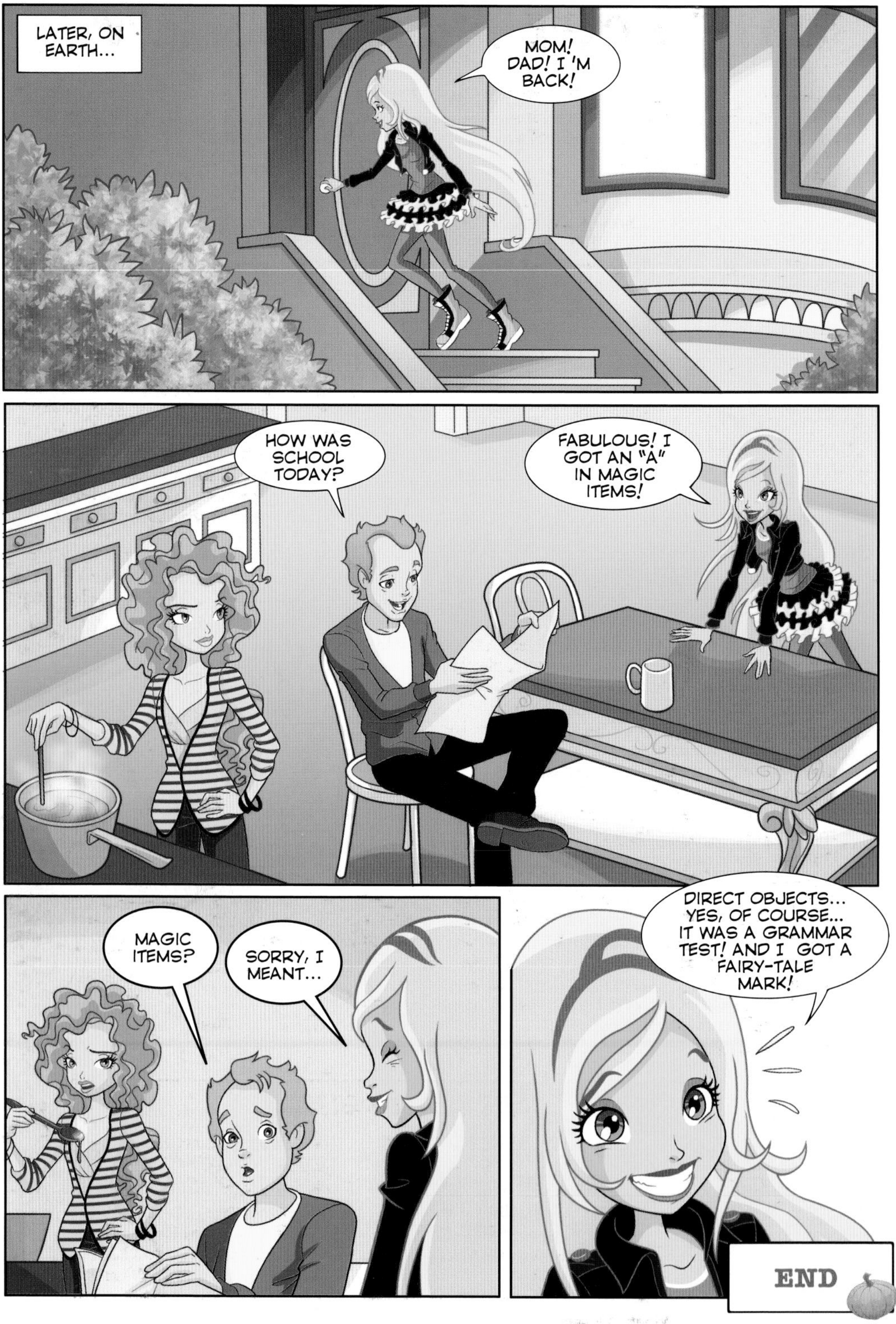
LATER, ON EARTH...
MOM! DAD! I 'M BACK!
HOW WAS SCHOOL TODAY?
FABULOUS! I GOT AN "A" IN MAGIC ITEMS!
MAGIC ITEMS?
SORRY, I MEANT...
DIRECT OBJECTS... YES, OF COURSE... IT WAS A GRAMMAR TEST! AND I GOT A FAIRY-TALE MARK!
END

WATCH OUT FOR PAPERCUTZ

Welcome to the magic-filled first REGAL ACADEMY graphic novel, by Rainbow Srl, from Papercutz, those enchanted souls dedicated to publishing great graphic novels for all ages. I'm Jim Salicrup, the Editor-in-Chief and part-time Regal Academy Truant Officer, and I'm here to tell you a little Fairy Tale.

Once upon a time, a man named Terry had dreamed of publishing beautifully illustrated and brilliantly written comics for adults, which would be available in bookstores and libraries. Terry had seen on his journeys that such books existed in other lands, but there were none to found in the land where Terry lived. Comics, no matter the subject matter or the talents creating them, were considered only for children, and Terry had to struggle for years to convince the adults in his land to try these "grown-up" comics.

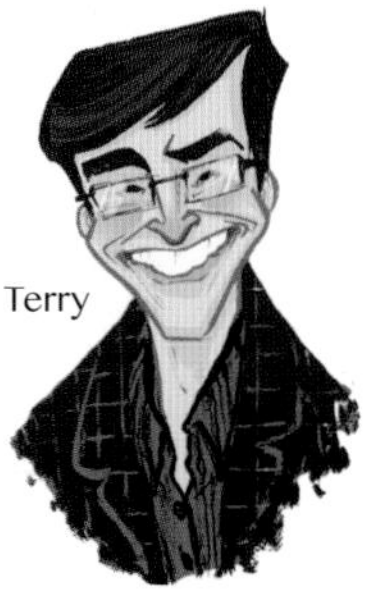
Terry

Turned out Terry wasn't alone, others were also trying to convince folks that comics weren't just for kids. As the years went by, more and more adults began to see that they too could enjoy comics.

Then one day, Terry saw that something magical had happened. His dream had come true! Bookstores and libraries were now stocked with these books, now called "graphic novels," that he and other publishers were now publishing. He couldn't believe it—his dream had come true!

Terry couldn't be happier. Finally grown-ups could enjoy and appreciate comics without anyone thinking they were being childish. But then Terry noticed something, while more and more publishers were publishing graphic novels for grown-ups, less and less publishers were publishing graphic novels for children! This wasn't something Terry wanted at all. Yes, he wanted there to be comics for adults, but he never wanted the comics for kids to go away.

Thinking the whole situation over very carefully, which is something Terry is very good at doing, he realized there was only one solution—he would have to start a new company to publish graphic novels for all ages. But how could he start another publishing company when he was already busy as can be publishing comics for grown-ups? Terry thought about that very carefully too, and decided he'd find someone to help run this new company. He chose a comicbook editor named Jim, who also believed that there should be comics for all ages. Together they created this new company called Papercutz!

Papercutz—it's like a magic word. If you see the name on a graphic novel you know it's filled with wonderful comics that everyone can enjoy. The moral of this particular fairy tale is that dreams can come true! It happened for Terry Nantier and Jim Salicrup, and it can happen for you too! Just keep attending REGAL ACADEMY! (Look for REGAL ACADEMY #2 "The First Ball," available now at booksellers everywhere.)

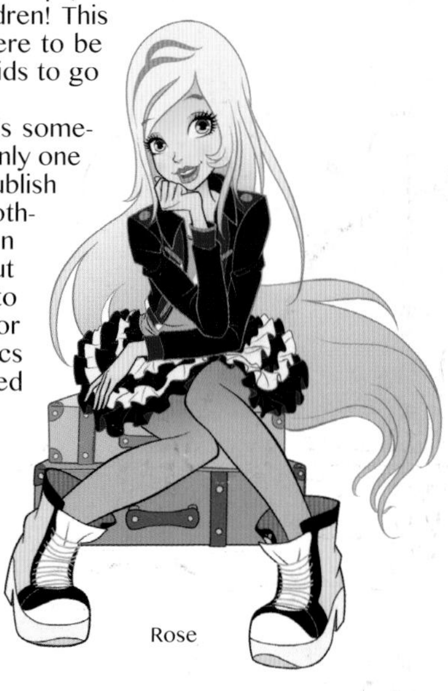
Rose

Class dismissed!

Thanks,

Jim

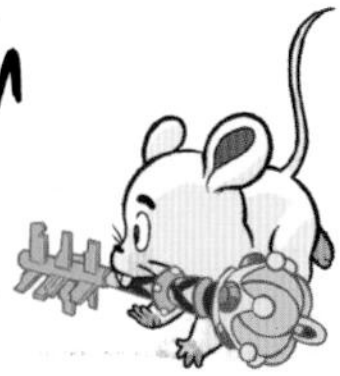
Gigi the Mouse

STAY IN TOUCH!

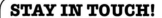

EMAIL:	salicrup@papercutz.com
WEB:	papercutz.com
TWITTER:	@papercutzgn
INSTAGRAM:	@papercutzgn
FACEBOOK:	PAPERCUTZGRAPHICNOVELS
FAN MAIL:	Papercutz, 160 Broadway, Suite 700, East Wing, New York, NY 10038

MORE GREAT GRAPHIC NOVEL SERIES AVAILABLE FROM PAPERCUTZ

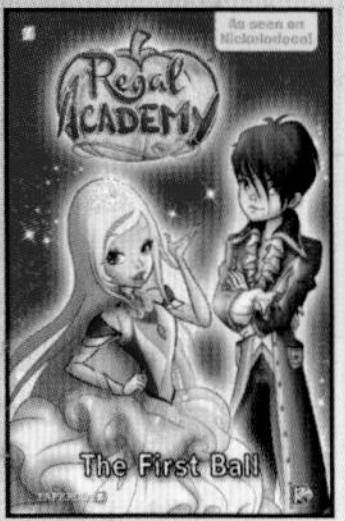
As seen on Nickelodeon!
Regal Academy
The First Ball
PAPERCUTZ

REGAL ACADEMY #2

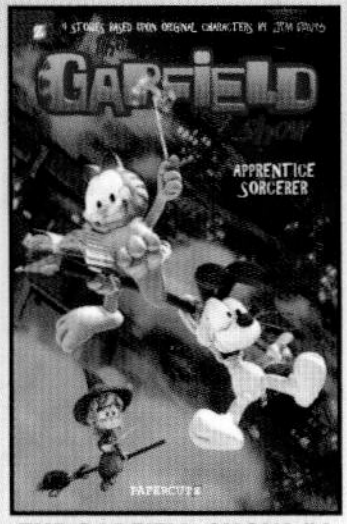
Garfield Show
APPRENTICE SORCERER
PAPERCUTZ

THE GARFIELD SHOW #6

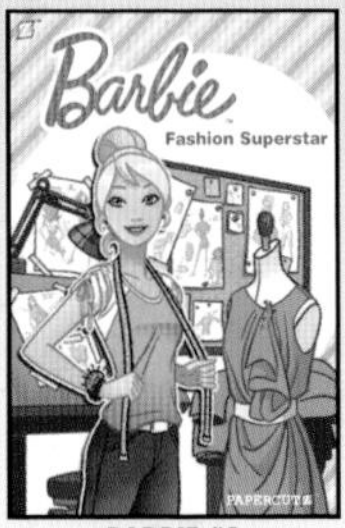
Barbie
Fashion Superstar
PAPERCUTZ

BARBIE #1

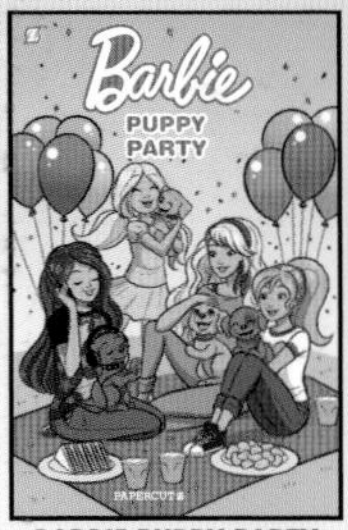
Barbie
PUPPY PARTY
PAPERCUTZ

BARBIE PUPPY PARTY

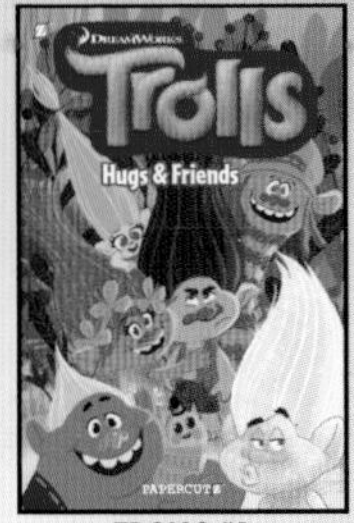
Trolls
Hugs & Friends
PAPERCUTZ

TROLLS #1

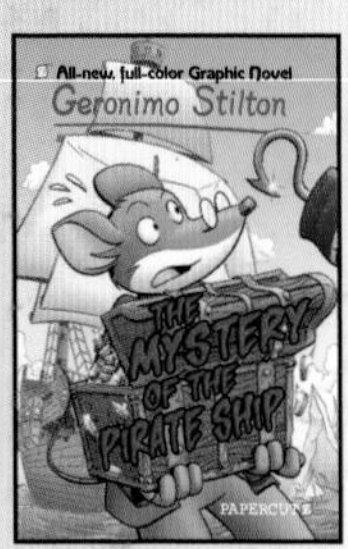
All-new, full-color Graphic Novel
Geronimo Stilton
THE MYSTERY OF THE PIRATE SHIP
PAPERCUTZ

GERONIMO STILTON #17

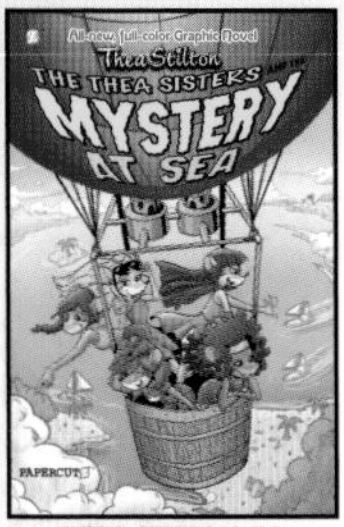
All-new, full-color Graphic Novel
Thea Stilton
THE THEA SISTERS
MYSTERY AT SEA
PAPERCUTZ

THEA STILTON #6

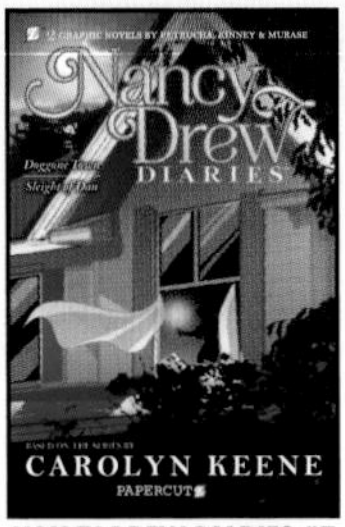
Nancy Drew
DIARIES
CAROLYN KEENE
PAPERCUTZ

NANCY DREW DIARIES #7

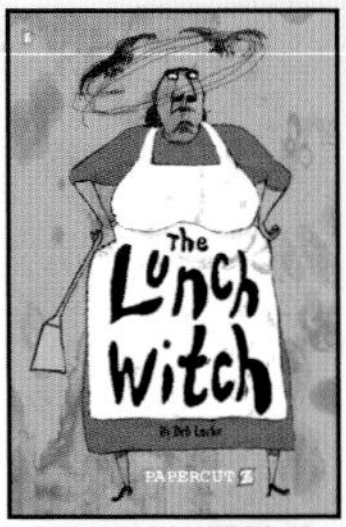
The Lunch Witch
PAPERCUTZ

THE LUNCH WITCH #1

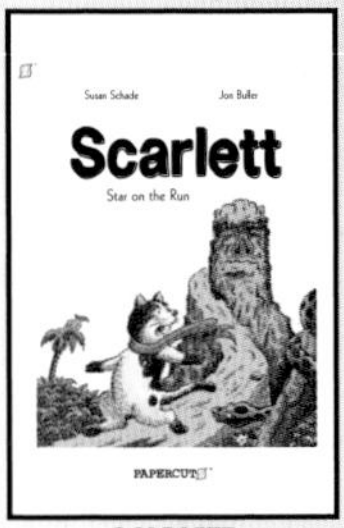
Susan Schade
Jon Buller
Scarlett
Star on the Run
PAPERCUTZ

SCARLETT

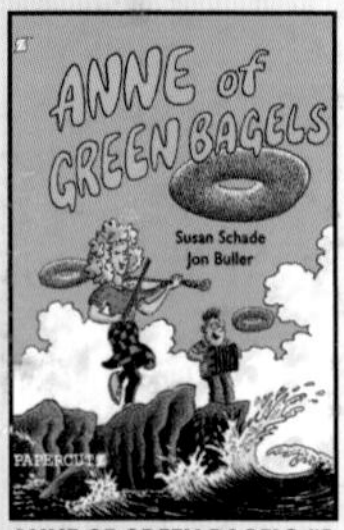
ANNE of GREEN BAGELS
Susan Schade
Jon Buller
PAPERCUTZ

ANNE OF GREEN BAGELS #1

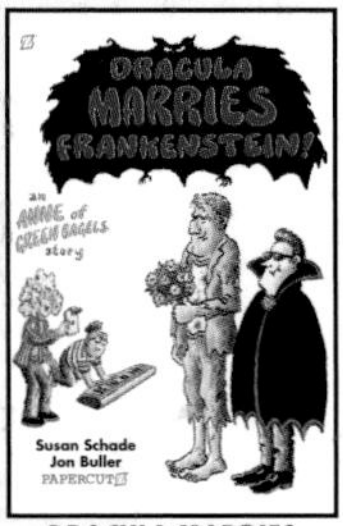
DRACULA MARRIES FRANKENSTEIN!
an ANNE of GREEN BAGELS story
Susan Schade
Jon Buller
PAPERCUTZ

DRACULA MARRIES FRANKENSTEIN!

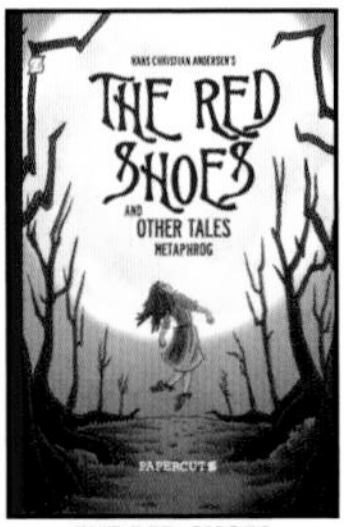
HANS CHRISTIAN ANDERSEN'S
THE RED SHOES
AND OTHER TALES
METAPHROG
PAPERCUTZ

THE RED SHOES

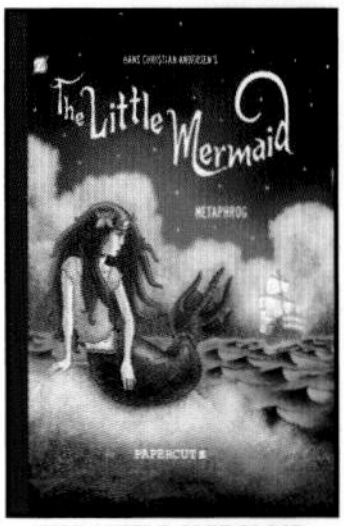
HANS CHRISTIAN ANDERSEN'S
The Little Mermaid
METAPHROG
PAPERCUTZ

THE LITTLE MERMAID

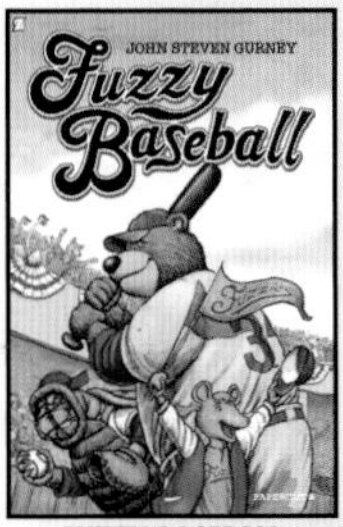
JOHN STEVEN GURNEY
Fuzzy Baseball

FUZZY BASEBALL

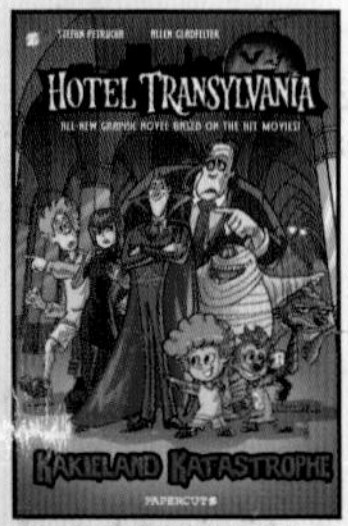
HOTEL TRANSYLVANIA
KAKIELAND KATASTROPHE
PAPERCUTZ

HOTEL TRANSYLVANIA #1

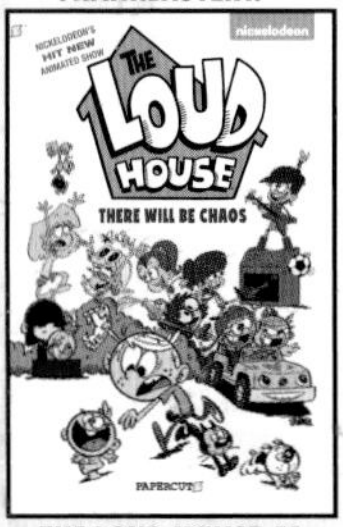
nickelodeon
The LOUD HOUSE
THERE WILL BE CHAOS
PAPERCUTZ

THE LOUD HOUSE #1

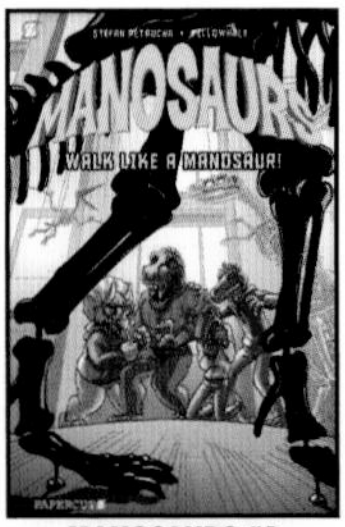
MANOSAURS
WALK LIKE A MANOSAUR!
PAPERCUTZ

MANOSAURS #1

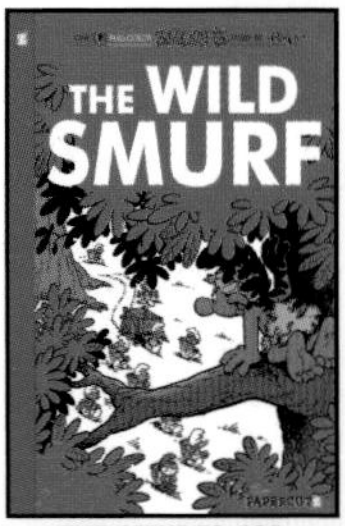
THE WILD SMURF
PAPERCUTZ

THE SMURFS #21

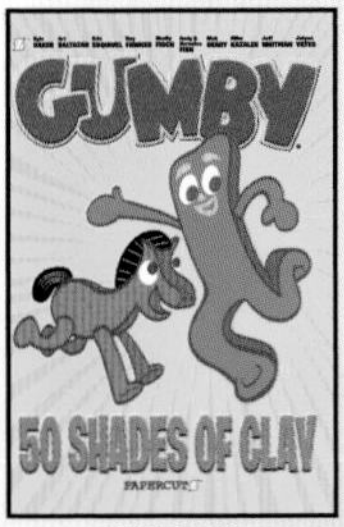
GUMBY
50 SHADES OF CLAY
PAPERCUTZ

GUMBY #1

THE SMURFS, THE GARFIELD SHOW, BARBIE, HOTEL TRANSYLVANIA, MANOSAURS, THE LOUD HOUSE and TROLLS graphic novels are available for $7.99 in paperback, and $12.99 in hardcover. THE ONLY LIVING BOY and GUMBY graphic novels are available for $8.99 in paperback, and $13.99 in hardcover. GERONIMO STILTON and THEA STILTON graphic novels are available for $9.99 in hardcover only. FUZZY BASEBALL graphic novels are available for $9.99 in paperback only. THE LUNCH WITCH, SCARLETT, and ANNE OF GREEN BAGELS graphic novels are available for $14.99 in paperback only. THE RED SHOES and THE LITTLE MERMAID graphic novels are available for $12.99 in hardcover only. DRACULA MARRIES FRANKENSTEIN graphic novels are available for $12.99 in paperback only.

Available from booksellers everywhere. You can also order online from www.papercutz.com. Or call 1-800-886-1223, Monday through Friday, 9–5 EST. MC, Visa, and AmEx accepted. To order by mail, please add $5.00 for postage and handling for first book ordered, $1.00 for each additional book and make check payable to NBM Publishing. Send to: Papercutz, 160 Broadway, Suite 700, East Wing, New York, NY 10038.

THE SMURFS, GUMBY, THE GARFIELD SHOW, THE LOUD HOUSE, THE ONLY LIVING BOY, BARBIE, TROLLS, GERONIMO STILTON, THEA STILTON, FUZZY BASEBALL, THE LUNCH WITCH, THE LITTLE MERMAID, HOTEL TRANSYLVANIA, MANOSAURS, THE RED SHOES, ANNE OF GREEN BAGELS, and SCARLETT graphic novels are also available wherever e-books are sold.